AF448130

TURN YOUR TELESCOPE AROUND

YOU CAN HEAL YOURSELF

SCRIPTOR HOUSE
The Epitome of Greatness

SAMEER ZAHR

Scriptor House LLC

2810 N Church St Wilmington, Delaware, 19802

www.scriptorhouse.com

Phone: +1302-205-2043

© 2024 Sameer Zahr. All rights reserved.

No part of this book may be reproduced, stored in a retrieval system, or transmitted by any means without the written permission of the author.

Published by Scriptor House LLC

Paperback ISBN: 979-8-88692-227-1

eBook ISBN: 979-8-88692-228-8

Hardback ISBN: 979-8-88692-286-8

Because of the dynamic nature of the Internet, any web addresses or links contained in this book may have changed since publication and may no longer be valid. The opinions expressed in this manuscript are solely the opinions of the author and do not represent the opinions or thoughts of the publisher and the publisher hereby disclaims any responsibility for them. The author has represented and warranted full ownership and/or legal right to publish all the materials in this book.

TURN YOUR TELESCOPE AROUND

YOU CAN HEAL YOURSELF

SAMEER ZAHR

Introduction

I write fiction novels and poetry with positive spiritual messages embedded within the book stories.

Lately, a friend of mine who is familiar with my work, and a good writer/editor himself, asked me to consider writing self-help books. He thought that the combination of my vast international business experience and my keen interest in spiritual teaching could present a unique hybrid form to the genre of self-help books .

My friend suggested I could still build a story with the self-help message I want to convey. It might even be more attractive to readers to learn a spiritual lesson from a story.

I followed my friend's advice, and this is my first attempt at a hybrid self-help book built around a story. This would be the 11th book I write and hope it receives the approval of my readers.

The story in this book is about an intelligent and well-educated man who achieved great success in the business world. Nevertheless, he was not aware of the damage his success could cause in his personal life. He became oblivious to live a balanced life between his work and his family. He chose to separate from his family and ran after worldly pleasures. His egoic mind convinced him that he deserved a better life away from home.

He experienced serious inner sufferings instead. His guilt and regrets led him to the process of inner awakening to discover his true self.

The healing process is common to many of us. We go through traumas and down periods before we taste the sweeter flavors of internal success. It goes beyond the short-lived worldly temptations and welcomes the pursuit of finding a true life-purpose that reveals what really matters to enjoy a meaningful life journey.

Chapter 1

Flying High in Worldly Skies

A slow and stressful week in Beijing, China? This was too long for Jim Mayden to spare. His trip was not for leisure, or the study of the ancient Chinese culture, but to finalize a bid deal with a government agency that imports substantial volumes of soft commodities. Jim, well-known as an international commodities trader, valued the use of his precious time and was patient to wait this time. His success and shrewd trading skills preceded him. He spent five grueling meetings with his hosts during that week. His goal was to conclude a substantial sale worth about $30 million.

On his flight to Beijing Jim recalled his early motivation to succeed in business. His dark childhood was engrossed with upbringing limitations, and his parents had lean financial resources. Those hardships awakened young Jim to promise himself a successful career to conquer such limitations. He was determined not to live a life of lack and scarcity. He missed out on what a child would normally enjoy and, he also lacked the warmth of love from his parents growing up.

He realized his dreams of success by studying and working hard. His climbed he ladder of his trade early in his career, and his competitive spirit, brought him many sunny periods with clients who respected him, but not without spurs of challenge from his competitors. Among his host of clients, he developed excellent relations with the two biggest. They were government procurement agencies in China and India, buying huge volumes of the commodities Jim handled well.

In addition, he dealt with twenty-five other clients in different countries around the world and achieved a substantial sales volume year after year.

The company he founded grew rapidly with a staff of forty-five employees, and a vast network of representatives/agents in all the countries he dealt with. Above all else, his business became his main pre-occupation. He knew by going to China it would take a week of his time, but it was worth it. The big client demanded the quarterly contract negotiations be done directly with him and not another of his executives.

On the fifth day of relentless negotiations with the Chinese delegation of six, the conference room door was suddenly pushed open, and an astute-looking woman appeared, walking swiftly, and followed by two gentlemen. It resembled a scene from the movies when a commander-in-chief walks into a room unexpectedly. Everyone in the room stopped talking and stood up silently. The lady took her seat at the head of the table and signaled them to sit.

Jim knew who she was, but Mr. Chen, the team leader, had to formally introduce her, Madam Xu, the president of the agency. She nodded her head in recognition of Jim's presence, and asked Mr. Chen to continue. Jim had told Mr. Chen that he could not drop the price any further, and that was his final offer. He stated that it would be okay if they did not agree, as his Indian clients were waiting to see him the next day.

Madam Xu had been advised about the gridlock in the negotiations and knew that Jim was not bluffing. She knew that the Indian government was also badly in need of the same commodity. She spoke briefly with Mr. Chen in Chinese, then she looked at Jim with a courteous smile and said:

"Mr. Mayden, my colleagues, tell me that you cannot give us a lower price, and that you are prepared to leave tomorrow without a contract. Is that your final position? Our country has been a friend and a loyal client of yours for several years. We always honored our contracts, and we value our friendship. Why don't you consider an additional discount and we sign the contract this afternoon?"

"Thank you, Madam Xu, but you should have seen how hard Mr. Chen had squeezed me already, and I truly don't have much room to drop the price further." Jim remarked and paused before he continued: "Nevertheless, and as a friend, I would give you a final reduction of $0.50 per metric ton, as a sign of goodwill. That is an additional $100,000 cut in the total value. It is also fine with me if you do not accept. My Indian clients are eagerly waiting for me to give them the same supply, but I wanted to honor my word to Mr. Chen, that I would come here and give you the right of first refusal."

Another discussion took place in Chinese, and a few minutes later, Madam Xu looked at Jim again, with a capricious smile across her face, and said:

"Fine, we agree. We will have the contract ready for you to sign within one hour, and we invite you to dinner tonight to celebrate our deal. Thank you!"

Everyone stood up, including Jim this time, and Madam Xu came around to shake his hand before she left the room. Jim took a deep breath and was pleased that this relentless marathon had finally come to an end.

As a courtesy to his Indian clients, Jim proceeded to visit them as planned. He notified them that he had signed a contract with the Chinese, and he could give them a similar contract if they agreed to extend the shipment period by another month. It took only two days of amicable negotiations, and Jim signed the deal at a slightly higher price than the one agreed upon with the Chinese.

Jim Mayden was the founder and president of a mid-sized international trading company headquartered in New York City. He started out from scratch eighteen years ago. Jim quickly developed a reputation as a smart and honorable trader specialized in soft commodities and his business grew rapidly around the world.

He was tall and handsome, sharp looking and known for his savvy demeanor. He married a beautiful woman, Janet, fifteen years ago, and had two children. The two had met in the graduate school of Business Administration. They lived in a beautiful house in Rye, in the suburbs of New York city,

◆

As soon as he finalized these two big contracts, Jim flew back directly, with a short connection in Dubai. As soon as he settled down on board, relaxing in his comfortable seat, he reflected on his current business situation and the latest developments in his personal life. His thoughts carried him far beyond the success of his company during the past fifteen years. His stream of memories also included the gradual impact of his success on his normal life.

He recalled how he naively allowed his business success to boost his ego, which brewed to develop an arrogant attitude towards his family, and his wife in particular. He unintentionally made her feel inferior and insecure.

While bathing in the ocean of his self-glorified thoughts, fiddling with his fingers about his past, he recalled how he had paid much more attention to his work, and spent much less time at home. His family life which was initially cherished with love and affection deteriorated proportionally with his increasing success in later years. He had admired his wife and adored his two children. Nevertheless, and as his business grew, his time with them diminished gradually. He did not realize how deeply he hurt them by his frequent absence from home. It reached a point where he couldn't nurture the tree of love that was planted long time ago.

Jim used his hard work and absence as an excuse for providing the family with a secure and luxurious life. The sweet unconditional love he had enjoyed before, shifted increasingly to outer temptations during the last couple of years. His excessive travel exacerbated the increasing tension between him and his wife, Janet, and impacted the relationship with his two children, Laura and Todd.

While still stretched in his first-class seat Jim remembering how he eventually succumbed to the tactics of ego that creeped to take control of his mind. It boosted his 'me' perceptions and tricked him into believing he was invincible. He started believing that he deserved a better life, commensurate with his worldly success.

The humble and conscientious young man he used to be, had his eyes covered with a thick veil of egotistical unconsciousness. His ego ruled and shifted his mind to a negative assessment of his 'life' at home. He lacked vital spiritual awareness and was falsely convinced that he was not doing anything wrong. He thus surrendered to the egoic games that poisoned his mind with thoughts imprisoning him in its dark chambers.

Without further ado, his friend Joe, a recently divorced man, was at his beck and call to introduce him to the pleasures of the night. Joe's wildlife opened new doors to late-night parties with unattached younger women.

That deviation went on for more than two months, and Janet, his wife, noticed the increasing frequency of his delays and was getting angry sensing how this could potentially endanger the smoothness of their marriage heretofore. She occasionally confronted him with questions, but Jim was always quick to deny the truth, pretending he was out on business. His answers, however, did not eradicate Janet's suspicions, and the tension between them was noticeably increased.

Within six months, the warmth of their love started to get colder and the original fire was extinguishing. With desolate and sad faces exchanged between them, Janet was alerted by sharp warning signals shooting rapidly in her mind. She suggested counseling, but Jim arrogantly refused. She loved him and begged him to confess the truth, but to no avail.

Jim, in his mid-forties, did not even realize that he could be experiencing a problematic mid-life shift of his consciousness. He became oblivious to his wife's feelings and even dared to threaten to leave her if she could not understand or accept his situation.

Janet, a well-shaped beautiful lady with light brown hair and piercing green eyes that enhanced her smooth white skin and her dainty nose and luscious lips, was feeling helpless and deceived with Jim's denial of the truth. She would stand in front of the mirror, to check her facial features for any wrinkles, her height, and the shape of her body. Her sudden feelings of insecurity made her wonder if it was her outer looks that's causing Jim's fading interest in her.

Jim, on the other hand was oblivious to his wife's concern and bragged about his six-foot height, his dark-blond hair and his masculine features, with blue eyes and full lips holding his sharp nose. He used his smart looks to attract women. His well- built body and his charismatic aura played a decisive role in boosting his ego which he used in his business as well.

Stretched down on his sleeper-seat, Jim was still floating with his egoic thoughts. He vividly remembered one night after dinner, when he rudely accused his wife,

"I believe you are jealous of my success. Look at you! you have done nothing to show for yourself, as I've done."

That remark infuriated Janet. She controlled her temper, not to wake up the kids, who took all her attention growing up, and Jim didn't appreciate that. With a depressed, low voice, he recalled her saying something like:

"Jim, I don't believe what I just heard, you can't be serious! What in God's name prompts you to say that? I've been proud of you and your success since we got married. I appreciated your hard work and your providing us a better life. Your success is not the reason behind the tension brewing between us. It's the late nights you've been frequenting, and the increasing travels that never slow down. Above all, it is your attitude that has changed negatively from your good old loving behavior at home. In the name of truth, please tell me what is going on?"

"Nothing! I am just too busy." Jim replied with a malicious voice.

"Come on, Jim! I know you… Please give me a better answer! Did you stop loving me lately? Are you bored with me and the children? If so, tell me, and I'll do my best to change and make you happy, because I love you, you idiot!"

"I don't know! Perhaps I'm going through a soul-searching period in my life, to kick some old demons out of my mind."

"Okay! That's a start… can you elaborate on what demons are creeping in your mind? Perhaps I can help!"

"Listen, Janet, you know the story about my impoverished and sad upbringing, and about how humble and naïve I used to be before we met in graduate school. Perhaps the success which I dreamt about for so long, is now inviting me to explore new avenues how to live my life, I don't know?"

"What new avenues? A younger woman? A bigger house? A better wardrobe or a fast sports car? Or a better romance… what? Say it!" Janet expressed her anger keeping her voice down.

"I told you, Janet, I need time to work things out, don't push me, please, be patient."

Janet was dumbfounded by his refusal to elaborate. She remained silent for a while, then said:

"Fine, don't take forever to spit it out. I'm suffering now. Please be mindful and remember the love that brought us together, the songs we used to sing, and the dances we used to have. Remember the wonderful children we're blessed with, and this beautiful home we live in. I hope you'll be able to let me know very soon, as I cannot guarantee I have enough strength to cope with this haunted and scary situation for too long."

The ghost of silence invaded the room and chilled the air with horrible thoughts. The scent of flowers in the vase ran away, and their petals bent down from fear. The silence was loud, though, could not be heard. No fire was sufficient to keep the warmth enjoyed in the good old times. Such a frozen atmosphere became a first in their togetherness, and fear of separation magnified its icy condition. They were both holding tight to racing thoughts in their minds, like prisoners holding tight to the iron bars of their cells.

Jim sat in his armchair, fixated with an aimless gaze at the ceiling. Janet sat across on the sofa that felt like a seat of thorns. She looked at him with sad and tearful eyes, manifesting her agony with tears cascading down her cheeks. Jim remained frozen in his seat, lifeless like a statue of stone, tightly holding his hands in his lap and staring aimlessly at the ceiling. His cold poker face showed no affection toward his agonizing wife, not even to sit close to her to lighten her load with a loving hug.

The dense air in the room was too heavy to breathe and Janet could not tolerate sitting there any longer. It was past midnight, she stood up and went to her bedroom. Jim continued to lament with thoughts in his entranced state of mind, swimming in an ocean of despair and wondering the next unknown. He neither moved nor uttered a single word, even to himself. He stayed alone, digging deep into his archaic and troubled thoughts for another hour in the dark chambers of his mind. He then stood and helped himself with a drink on ice, hoping to get the edge off his unresolved turmoil before stretching out on the sofa to try and get some sleep.

Two weeks had passed since that scary night, and Jim remembered how the communication became minimal between him and his unhappy wife. The two teenage children sensed the electrifying mood between their parents and Laura, the oldest, approached her mother and asked what was going on. She said she and her brother, Todd, were feeling new waves of a chilling atmosphere between her and their father, whom they also adored.

Janet responded with a wicked smile and said their father was going through a rough period and needed some quiet time to think things through. In fact, Janet was covering her boiling vibrations of fear and anxiety from her two children, hoping to hear some positive remarks from Jim soon, before the lid over the pot of her anger explodes high and hits the ceiling aloud.

◆

Jim took a break from his stream of troubled memories and shut his eyes for a long nap on his twelve-hour flight from Dubai to JFK airport in New York.

He woke up two hours later when a meal was being served. He felt hungry and adjusted his seat up to eat. He watched a comedy movie while eating, and then went back to a reclined position to continue replaying the film of his own life drama.

Janet's patience could not last more than two months, during which time Jim explored new adventures. He tried to hide his escapades from Janet, but his load of pretense and false self became too heavy to carry. Denying the truth further confused his mind and burdened his heart with guilt and shame. He needed to shoot the truth out to the surface to lighten his inner suffering and living a harmful lie. With agonizing courage, he asked Janet for dinner out in a restaurant away from home. Janet agreed, sensing that he was going to finally be forthright, she prepared herself to stay calm while absorbing the expected horror of his words.

After some general but tense chitchat about the children and his work, and after the main course was served, Jim looked at Janet with a sympathetic but cold smile, and said:

"Listen, Janet, I know you've been quite upset with me lately, and you've been quite patient giving me some time to sort out the mess I've been going through. First, I want to say that I was wrong when I accused you of being jealous of my business success. The truth is I was projecting on you the indiscrete damage that success had caused to my mind, and its evil influence, thus crumbling the feelings of my heart.

"I'm truly grateful to the life we had together during the last fifteen years, and to the joy of having two children, we both love so much. What I'm about to say now may hurt your feelings, and I'm sorry, but it is my mess, not yours. You've been a wonderful and loyal wife and a great mother."

"Jim, can you please stop with your poetic remarks "it's me, not you stuff" and tell me what you decided to do with your life?" Janet asked impatiently.

Jim drank some water from his glass trying to shake out his reluctance to speak, then he nervously said:

"I broke our marriage vows… and I've been seeing another woman. I don't know if I'm in love with her, and I ask you to let me move out of the house and live in a hotel in the city for a while, to figure out my next move. That is the truth in a nutshell."

Jim sat back and drank a big gulp of wine, waiting for Janet's reaction. There was a deafening silence despite the chatting noise in the room for about two minutes. The big well-lit room shrank to a dark small cave in Janet's mind, depleting her energy to speak. She slowly composed her posture and softly asked:

"Do I know her?"

"No."

"Is she more beautiful than me?"

"No."

"Then why?"

"I honestly don't know yet!"

"What, she's a test in the laboratory of your mid-life dreams?"

"Maybe!"

"Is that all you can say, maybe? You're supposed to be a highly intelligent man who easily outsmarts most people, and you say 'maybe'?"

"Success at work does not mean success in my personal choices or my emotions. Actually, I feel totally messed up psychologically in this regard. Perhaps I married prematurely… I told you I received neither love nor comfort from my parents… and how I was a focused student determined to succeed. Perhaps all this hard work and success was an escape to camouflage my troubled past. Perhaps I missed out on normal fun other young people my age had. Perhaps what's going on in my life now, is to compensate for what I lost in my budding years… I'm working on it…"

"What a drama! What do you expect me to do now while you drown in the confusing cobwebs of your mind? What? You want me to let you go and wait like an idiot until you finally grow up? Do you really believe I'm capable of being such a strong martyr? If you want a separate life, go do it, but at your own risk, there is no guarantee I'll be there at your beck and call."

"I know that," Jim said facetiously.

"What do we tell the children now?"

"We tell them the truth… that it is my mess, and I need some time to sort things out. All I ask is that you allow me to see them at least once a week."

"Will see!"

"I appreciate your understanding!"

"Yeah, okay! Go and have fun, and don't you worry about the kids or me. We'll all be fine!" Janet said, sarcastically.

They skipped dessert, and Janet was in a hurry to go back home to contemplate the outcome of this sad conversation and figure out which reservoir of strength she could muster to cope with the consequences of this bombshell that he threw in her lap. Neither one of them spoke a single word on the way back home. They both froze in a sea of ice so thick; no icebreaker could cut through.

◆

Jim jolted in his plane seat, remembering this nightmarish episode. He sat up and ordered coffee, an hour before the plane was expected to land. He suddenly cracked a peal of a little vicious laughter, saying to himself how his life has been floating like a dream, not real. He wondered why he allowed his life to be mind-made and controlled by the events of his past and the unknown future.

He recalled reading a passage in a book once, along the following lines: "there is no such thing called past or future as real, when all there is, is the present moment. It is the only thing that is real, there is nothing else. Life is nothing but a series of present moments. You can only live in the Now". This insight did not register in Jim's mind at that time, and he kept believing what he was doing was right. He was enslaved by his ego's solid grip on his mind which made him repeat his past thoughts of lack and kept him distant from living in the Now. Paradoxically, he must have enjoyed his hidden 'suffering' from the so-called 'fun' he thought he had.

◆

The plane landed at JFK on time, and Jim checked for messages on his cell phone. There were five messages from his friend Joe, all within seconds from one another. He listened to the first message and heard Joe shout:

"Where are you, man? I'm trying to reach you; I have some bad news. Your girlfriend, Tanya, was fatally hit by a fast-moving car while crossing the street five hours ago. She sadly didn't make it, and two other people got injured too. Call me as soon as you can!"

Jim tried to stay calm not wanting to believe what he just heard. He nervously called Joe who repeated the story and said that the accident was caused by a drunken driver, still alive, and being interrogated by the police. Joe added, "Tanya's parents called me, when they couldn't reach you. They're waiting at the hospital morgue to see you and to help them decide on what to do next."

Jim was utterly shocked, and his ego was smashed to pieces. He asked Joe to wait for him in the lobby. Saddened by the horrible news, he closed his eyes and went into silence, while being driven to his hotel from the airport. Tanya was a sweet young lady with a good heart and a loving personality. A good friendship was being developed between them.

Joe was at the hotel, waiting. Jim left his luggage with the concierge, and they both rushed to the hospital.

The meeting with the parents was very sad. Tanya's mother couldn't stop sobbing with tears. Jim was asked if he wanted to go to the morgue and see her downstairs, but he refused. He wanted to keep the memory of

Tanya's face the way he knew her. Arrangements were discussed, and burial plans were made.

The loss of Tanya was hard on Jim. It sent shocks to his entire being and created many unhappy signals to his tired mind. He kept asking himself:

Why am I experiencing a disturbing sequence of sad events lately, and was there a message for me to learn?

Am I being punished for the wrong I've done to my family?

Are these signs meant to alert me to turn my focus inwardly?

Is Tanya's death the final storm before the awakening that follows the thread of suffering?

After a restless night, Jim woke up from a strange dream that shifted his mind to another level of awareness. He dreamt of his wife, whom he still loved, and his children, whom he adored. They were all playing with him in the dream. He thought by loving Tanya, he would ease into a new life that would diminish his constant guilt leaving his family behind. He was wrong! All of a sudden, he realized he was lonely without anyone to love.

Tanya, whom he had met during a bank cocktail event, was not only beautiful, she was also a spiritually mature and compassionate woman. Her interest in Jim was based on his character, not because of his wealth, as she came from a rich family herself. He loved her peaceful smile and was amazed by her genuine love for other people, especially the poor. She left a gracious image imprinted in his mind.

That morning, Jim wondered if the loss of Tanya indirectly influenced his shift of consciousness towards the family. He thought of her spiritual practice that may have sent him a message to become aware of his inner Being?" He contemplated these positive thoughts and felt Tanya's soul roaming around the room. He was perplexed about what to do next.

Despite the glimpse of hope from his family dream, Jim continued to have sleepless nights battling with the demons of his mind. One night he felt so uncomfortable he started sobbing and breathing heavily. The mighty Jim was feeling lonely and desolate. The success of his business had lost its glamor and did not mean much to him anymore. The outer luxuries of life did not satisfy him either. He deeply missed his children and his family life, a priceless experience he hoped he can regain.

He struggled to get a peaceful sleep. He tossed and turned, often cursing the noisy thoughts in his mind, and cursing his success that caused him his unhappiness. The old heroic wings of prosperity were being cut and now he feels small and humiliated.

One restless night he woke up around 3:00 AM, hearing a voice within, directing him to write down his thoughts and feelings on paper. He got out of bed, drank a glass of water and sat at his desk holding a pen and gazing at his notebook, wondering what to write.

Several minutes passed before he was able to silence the troubling thoughts of his mind, allowing a conscious rise of self- awareness to click in. Then the voice within guided him, and he started to ask questions:

Am I but a foolish clown playing around like a loser in the game of life?

Where did the innocent days go when people called a shaman and thought I could see in the dark?

Did I blind myself, focusing on outer achievements that convoluted my understanding of what material success is about?

What strength have I built within me, as a shelter to protect me in times of adversity?

What do I know about true love, other than glimpses of my own selfish compassion?

How can I be in touch with my Inner Self, as it is said, to be the Source of all life to guide me?

What Did I learn from my escapes to the partying scene pursuing bodily pleasures that left my soul unsatisfied?

Personally? I did not succeed, I failed.

I confess I allowed the outer fruits of external illusions to destroy the internal house of my true identity.

I confess I allowed the monstrous ego in my mind to rule my life and misguide me.

I confess I allowed my greedy ego to take me deep into the valley of darkness to find my worthless treasures.

I confess I stopped listening to my soul's voice that used to embrace me with its Light on the mountain top.

I confess I foolishly deserted the family home I built over fifteen years, a nest of love and warmth.

All this cannot be called success, all this is failure.

Am I prepared now to invite heavenly angels to visit my heart and guide me in peace?

My body, soul, and mind are not my own; God loaned them to me for a while, will I invite Him now to dwell within me forever?

God is my only real 'friend' to lean on. Not Joe who took me partying, when God can take me to dance in His garden of Grace.

There, I can find the joy of life and the power to forget my past and forgive the people I hurt.

There, I can seek divine guidance to show me the way and find the real purpose for my being on this planet.

There, I can be empowered to kick the demons of my past out of my mind and substitute the fears of tomorrow with His Love .

There, I can build a strong bridge of faith toward a meaningful future that remains unknown.

There, in His Garden of Grace, I will find the strength to regain what I lost and live a life full of Love.

Chapter 2

Cleansing the Mind

Jim had a dizzying time since he returned from his trip to China and India. The cheer of his successful trip was offset by the sad news of Tanya's death, and the spinning of many repeated inner questions that were invading his mind. The turmoil affected his ability to focus well on his work. He relied on his staff to handle the execution of pending files.

He called his wife, Janet, from work and told her about the loss of Tanya. Janet went silent for a moment, and all she said was one word, "sorry". She did not ask Jim how he was doing. She was still suffering from the wounds of his sudden exit from her life which made her very angry. Yet, she hoped he would ask to see her and the children. Perhaps it was too early, she thought. Jim then asked her if he could pick up the children to spend the weekend with him. Janet agreed and abruptly said hung up the phone.

Jim's head was aching with no one close to talk to. He was not prepared to see a therapist. He yearned for some spiritual guidance that would lead him in the right direction. He preferred not to have the advice of a religious figure, and he did not belong to any church either. He believed in God as the Creator, and his exposure to the teachings of Christ was limited to his forgotten Sunday school classes as a child. He did not resonate with the church rituals that he believed were far from the core teachings of Christ.

Nevertheless, Jim found solace writing in his journal. He wrote every night and hoped the silent echo of his inner voice would never leave him. He also hoped the silent voice to be soon manifested in a physical form of someone worthy of his trust, a real person he could talk to.

◆

On Friday of that week, Jim's chief accountant, Brian Forthright, knocked on his office door to ask for his decision on a pending banking matter. Jim signaled him to sit down though he wondered why Brian wanted to see him, and not wait for his boss, Michael, the chief financial officer, to return from his trip.

"Hello sir, sorry to interrupt you, but there is an urgent matter I need to discuss with you, Michael is away as you well know!"

"It's alright, what is it?"

Brian went ahead and explained the issue in detail. Jim could hardly concentrate and did not listen carefully. Brian kept talking for five minutes, noticing that his boss was not paying any real attention to what he was saying. Jim's mind was somewhere else. Jim suddenly interrupted Brian and asked:

"Is this something that cannot wait until Michael comes back from his trip?"

"I don't really know, sir! I need to ask the bank if they can wait. I hate to bother you, but I noticed that you were not concentrating on what I was saying, is everything alright? Can I be of any help, or would you prefer I come back later?" Brian politely asked.

"No, that's fine. Do you, by any chance, know of a good spiritual therapist in town? You live around here, don't you?"

"Interesting, you ask! In fact, I do. I'm quite satisfied with the spiritual teachings I have been receiving from a non-denominational group three blocks away from here. I go there four times a week after work."

"You're spiritual, you?"

"Yes, Sir, I am. It has been three years since both my wife and daughter died from a tragic car accident, which tore me to pieces for a long time. For about two years now, I've been frequenting this center nearby, to ease my pain and to move ahead. The group has been extremely helpful and very loving. Why, do you ask? You have someone in mind you wish to refer to the group?"

"Yes, I do… Me!"

Brian couldn't believe what he just heard, he sat up straight in his chair with a dropped jaw and asked:

"You, sir?"

"Yes, me. I'm human like everybody else, no? Before I continue, allow me to say how sorry I am about the loss of your wife and daughter. This must-have happened before you joined us, right? I didn't know, I'm sorry."

"It's okay sir, I am almost fully healed now though I miss them very much."

"Listen to me Brian, please run the banking issue by me one more time, but I would appreciate it if you come to see me after hours, and we go together to meet your people."

"That's great!" Brian said and took ten more minutes to discuss the issue, and Jim told him what to do. It was agreed that they will meet again after work.

When Brian left and closed the door behind him, Jim sat back on his chair, reclined and put his hands behind his head smiling to himself, pleased that the Universe is responding to his needs. "Could Brian be the manifestation I asked for?" He wondered.

Brian returned to Jim's office around 6:00 PM, and they both walked out to go to the center together.

◆

On their way over, Brian asked Jim:

"Sir, I told you the reason why I needed the help of this spiritual group, but why do you need it, if I may ask?"

"Brian, please start calling me Jim! Well, I separated from my wife and two children five months ago, telling them I needed some soul-searching time alone. The truth was that I was looking for fun and partying with other women, so I left. Three months later, I met a lovely lady, Tanya, a spiritual lady, unlike me. Unfortunately, Tanya died from a car accident about 10 days ago, the day I returned from my long trip. So, one tragedy after another, and now I find myself quite lonely and sad. So, that's why."

"I'm very sorry to hear that, sir, I mean Jim. I assure you your wounds will heal faster than you think. I suffered for too long, but you don't have to." Brian responded lovingly.

"Tell me, Brian, what's so unique about your group? How would they open the door to peace and happiness in my life?"

"Well, we basically learn how to connect with the higher self, our consciousness, or God if you prefer. We practice going into silence or meditation. Also, we learn to live in the present moment, every moment of every day. We rise above the turmoil of mental thoughts from a past that does not exist in the Now, or an unknown future that has yet to come. We learn that Life is Now, not yesterday and not tomorrow." Brian explained.

" On what religion do you guys base your teachings ?"

"We do not follow any specific religion. The teachings could be derived from Zen teachings, Buddhist texts, Christ's teachings, the Torah, the Hindu Bhagavad Gita, the Quran, or the Tao Te Ching, by Lao Tzu."

"Lao, who? Never mind, these are mainly Eastern teachings, right?"

"Yes, though, you'll be amazed how similar they are in essence to the teachings of Christ. The leaders of the organized Christian institution, however, preferred not to emphasize these core lessons to their followers, even if they themselves understood them well."

"How long do the sessions last?" Jim asked.

"There is no strict time, it is up to the practitioner."

"Practitioner, huh?"

"Yes, there are also lectures you can choose to listen to. I normally try not to miss many, as I find the speeches very beneficial to my spiritual growth. Besides, I live alone now, so I don't need to rush to go anywhere."

"You don't have a woman to share your life with?" Jim asked.

"No, not really, I still love my wife, and I am okay, living alone. Maybe someday, who knows?"

"You are an interesting man Brian, you're how old, forty?"

"Forty-three!"

"Younger than me, by one year… How far are we now?"

"Just around the corner, less than two minutes."

◆

They arrived at the "Spiritual Awareness Center" or SAC which was located on the street level. Brian opened a big solid door, and they both walked in.

They faced a reasonably large hall with several rows of chairs in front of a podium. The room was well lit, and the music was soft and inspirational. The energy was positive, with a scent that felt like inhaling a fresh breeze. There were about forty happy-looking men and women mostly in their thirties and forties, standing and chatting quietly in small groups, sipping from teacups in their hands. Many of them recognized Brian and waved warmly at him. The people were mostly local residents. One black gentleman noticed Jim standing with Brian and he came over to greet him. Brian introduced him as Charles Green, the president of the center.

He welcomed Jim and then asked if he'll be staying for a short lecture planned to start in five minutes. Jim agreed, and Brian went to fetch a cup of tea. Jim told Charles, "Brian and I work in the same office, and he suggested that I come to visit."

"That's great, Jim, Brian is a great man and very loving. If you would like to learn about what we do here, I'll be glad to spend one-on-one time with you in the office, after the lecture."

It was time for the speech, and they all moved around and sat down to listen.

Charles went to the podium, greeted everybody, and extended a special welcome to Jim, a first-time visitor and a friend of Brian. He then announced Lama Bohdi, as the guest speaker for the evening.

Lama Bohdi was wearing an orange habit wrapped around his body. He was a good-looking man in his early fifties, with a shaved head. He said he was visiting from the Dharamshala monastery in India, the home of the Dalai Lama. He added that he will speak about 'spiritual freedom'.

Some of the points of his speech that Jim wrote down were:

- *To be spiritually free, one needs to avoid identification with the thoughts of his mind and the emotions of his heart.*

- *You are free when you are no more bound by the sense of 'me,' as separate from everybody else or everything else, and when you begin to experience oneness with the Universe.*

- *Freedom is when you experience self-realization with the practice of meditation and silencing the mind from thoughts.*

- *Freedom is a state of bliss and conscious awareness that brings peace into your life.*

- *Spiritual freedom is awakening your energy vibration of pure consciousness that exists in the core of your being.*

- *Join the fellowship of spiritual teachers and like-minded people. This will deepen your understanding and accelerate your experience of peace and joy.*

It was the first time Jim had heard such words of wisdom, and quickly started wondering how this could be applied in his own life. He did not fully understand some terms, but he did not mind, as he knew he could ask Brian or Charles to explain.

After the lecture, the members walked around in small groups again, and some of them chatted with the visiting Lama, asking him questions. Jim told Brian to wait a few minutes while he spends some time with Charles in his office.

Jim asked Charles about the organization, and Charles said:

"I started this center about ten years ago, together with five of my friends who were keen to follow this path. We do not belong to any organization, and we have no one to report to but ourselves. The six of us are executives with different jobs, mainly in the financial arena. Our membership is small, and it grew basically by word of mouth. We have about 125 registered members, and each one chips in, to the extent possible, to cover the rent and other minor expenses. You may ask if we can grow further, and the answer is yes, if we could attract benefactors to support our growth."

"I commend you on this endeavor, and I'm sure you will manage to expand your ministry if I could call it that," Jim said.

"Thank you! How about you, what do you do and how can we help you?" Charles asked.

"As I said before, Brian and I work in a commodities trading company, he is in the accounting department, and I am basically a trader in soft commodities. Our offices are only three blocks away from here, as you may know already."

"How can we help you, Jim? Evidently, you are looking for some answers. You can trust me and feel free to share what is on your mind. Consider me as your brother. First, tell me, did the speech on spiritual freedom mean anything to you?" Charles asked.

"Yes, thank you, and I do have some questions to ask, not only about the lecture but about my life in general. First, regarding the speech, it was the first time I hear such a meaningful message even though there are many words or terms that I did not fully understand…"

"Such as?" Charles interrupted. Jim took out his notes from his pocket and said:

"Such as self-realization, identification with thoughts and emotions, sense of me, silent meditation, conscious awareness, the core of being, and the like. These are all new to me." Jim stated. He then gave Charles a brief story about the recent events, including his separation from his family and the death of Tanya. Charles quickly understood that Jim was feeling sad and lonely, the reason for his presence with them that night."

"Jim, let me say without sounding arrogant, you came to the right place. Almost every one of us here had similar stories to tell. Together, we hold hands in love, and follow the teachings of masters and sages to straighten our walks in life. I personally am prepared to spend personal time with you, and I highly recommend you make Brian, your friend, and feel free to ask for his help too. Brian turned out to be one of the brightest and sweetest brothers we have. He learns fast, and his heart is full of love. He kicked out all his past fears, and again I say make him your brother too." Charles spoke with a passionate tone.

"Thank you, Charles, and I will follow your advice. I know our time is short now, I will ask Brian if he's free to have dinner with me tonight to get the ball of brotherhood rolling. I will also keep in touch with you, and here is my cell phone number. I will try to visit with you more frequently, and I thank you again for your warm welcome."

The conversation took a good twenty minutes. They both walked out of the office and found most of the members till around. Jim found Brian and asked him if they could have a bite together. Brian was thrilled, and the two of them walked out five minutes later.

♦

It was close to 8:00 PM, and Jim found a nearby restaurant that gave them a quiet corner table. Brian was thrilled that Jim was willing to befriend him.

"Charles said great things about you!" Jim began.

"Wow, that's nice of him. I respect this man. He spearheaded the establishment of this center, and he is truly dedicated to seeing it prosper and attract more people. He does not seek fame or glory, just to help and serve others." Brian said.

"I liked him too. He encouraged me to visit more frequently and recommended that I can ask you to explain things I don't fully understand. So, you could become my spiritual teacher, come to think of it." Jim said with a happy smile.

Brian laughed a little and asked Jim, "what are the things you don't understand?"

Jim repeated the words he heard in the lecture that he did not fully understand and asked Brian to elaborate. Brian took his time explaining each meaning one at a time. Jim interrupted him and asked the waiter for the menus to order some food first.

An hour and a half went by fast. Both were immersed entirely in the discussion at hand. Jim was highly impressed with Brian's spiritual knowledge and sweet demeanor. He asked him to hang around after work for a few days to follow through on the points discussed. Brian told Jim he is available this weekend if need be. Jim told him he'll be spending it with his two children, but Sunday evening is open if he can join him in his hotel. Brian agreed, and they both walked out to head home.

◆

Jim was nervous on his way to pick up the children on Saturday morning. He had not seen them for more than three weeks and wondered how they'll receive him. Back together in his two-bedroom hotel suite, they sat together for an update conversation before going to lunch. Laura, the fourteen-year-old, started the conversation asking her father:

"So, are you happy living away from home?"

"It's a good question, sweetheart, and as I mentioned earlier, I needed some time for myself to sort out the mess I inherited from my past. I confess I hurt you guys and your Mom, and I'm very sorry because I was blinded by my business success and wanted to explore what else was there in the real world. Well, I am quickly finding out that the 'real' world is not really real. What is real is true love, which I have for you and your mother but did not appreciate." Jim replied.

Todd, the younger twelve-year-old son, jumped in and asked:

"Mom said your girlfriend Tanya died in a car accident, how are you taking it?"

"I'm okay, son! Tanya was a good woman whom I knew for a very short period. She's gone now, and I miss her companionship. She was teaching me how to be true to myself." Jim said.

"Do you feel lonely you have no one in your life now?" Todd asked.

"To tell you the truth, Todd, yes, I do. I am working on loving myself first and use the time alone to grow spiritually."

"What do you mean, to start going to church?"

"No, not that, but to forgive myself for the wrong I did to you and your mother. I want to find out who I truly am and what is the real purpose of my life. It's more complicated than you think!"

"Do you still love Mom?" Laura asked.

"Of course, I do. Janet did not do anything wrong. I always loved her, and I always will. I'm the bad guy here. I hope she can forgive me one day!"

"It's been more than six months, Dad. How would you feel if she started seeing another man?" Laura was curious to find his reaction.

"I wouldn't blame her after what I did… why, is she seeing anyone?" Jim suddenly became curious.

"Why don't you call her and find out?" Todd interfered.

"It's not my place to do that, do you think I should, rascal Todd?"

"Yeah, why not? Maybe she still loves you, who knows?" Todd continued with the same theme. Laura then stepped in and asked:

"Dad, you mentioned earlier that you're working on growing spiritually, are you doing anything about it?"

"Funny, you ask! Actually, yesterday was my first day. It so happened that a colleague of mine in the office told me he is part of a group that helped him to grow spiritually after the loss of his wife and daughter in a car accident three years ago. So, I went to check it out, and I appreciated what I saw. The head of the group, together with my colleague, promised to explain how I could become an awakened person spiritually. It may take a while to shovel the old dirt out, but I am determined to go ahead."

"Are you looking to find another woman now?" Todd asked.

"Oh, heck, no, not again. My priority is to work on me now!"

Both Laura and Todd smiled when they heard that because inwardly, they hoped to see their father back with them at home. They loved him dearly and missed his jovial presence.

It was getting close to noon, and Jim suggested to continue talking downstairs and have lunch at the hotel restaurant. He agreed to take them see a movie before dinner. Then they would chill out or play video games before they go to sleep. Their mood changed for the better, and they all had a good time. Jim took them back home Sunday afternoon and thanked them for their visit with big hugs.

Jim appreciated the freshly injected doze of love from being with his children. The natural warmth of true love, coming from his own offspring uplifted his soul. He compared his thirst for affection from his own blood to a camel thirsty to drink from the well of his own oasis. The feelings gave him hope, and a fresh light that decreased the darkness in the chambers of his mind.

◆

Jim anticipated Brian to arrive within short. He was looking to enlighten his dry soul with heavenly raindrops that would awaken his true self. He had some questions to ask Brian, and the first on his mind was:

"Brian, did the thought of going to an ashram or a monastery overseas ever cross your mind after the tragedy?"

"Honestly, No! First, I needed to keep my job, it was my only source of income. Secondly, I thought that going away would not necessarily heal my wounds. Our souls, as I learned later, are with us wherever we are physically. I was lucky to come across this group whose name plate I noticed when I was passing by one day, and something inside prompted me to knock and find out. That was sixteen months ago, and that was it. They became my ashram. Its attributes are within us, and with the company my brothers and sisters, where I belong, grateful for their support."

"Hum… I hear you Brian, the thought crossed my mind, but I see your point now. I will do the work here then, as you suggested, no need to go far. We'll work on a schedule, and I promise to be your humble student, sir!" Jim said with a smile. Brian laughed and said,

"Sir? Huh… I will try my best, 'sir', and 'professor' Charles is there to help as well. Consider us your ashram" Brian responded, with fingers crossed.

Brian explained the process to go through. He reminded Jim, that it won't be easy in the beginning. "The ego will fight back and block your progress. I will write an outline on what to do, and bring you related books to read. You can write a list of any questions that cross your mind and we'll address them one by one." Jim was thankful and enthused to begin. They agreed on a convenient weekly schedule that included a couple of visits to the center to visit with Charles and the group. Plus, two private sessions together depending on Jim's travel program.

◆

Jim sat quietly in the living room, when Brian left, reflecting on the events of the weekend starting Friday with the introduction to a spiritual group, followed by the rejuvenating visit of the two children. He felt uplifted for a change, eager to work on his inner growth.

He opened his journal and asked himself:

Am I being sincere seeking a fundamental change to my current life condition?

Am I willing to learn how to transform my old thoughts and emotions to a deeper level of consciousness?

Will I succeed to silence the ego dimension in my mind and to liberate myself from the pains of my past, and my apprehension about the future?

Am I willing to seriously pursue the guidance from Brian and his group to lead me on the right path?

Will I exercise self-control and say no to the external worldly temptations of the night?

Will my suffering diminish during the process of my spiritual awakening journey?

I truly enjoyed spending quality time with my children.

Their positive expressions of love joyfully accelerated the blood flow in my veins.

Their smiles lifted me high with fresh wings to fly, and their hugs awakened my soul with alive vibrations of love.

I pray they will patiently tolerate my process of transformation into a better being, to regain our genuine bond.

I pray for their continued love and for their mother's forgiveness, to support the rest of my journey.

Chapter 3
Turn Your Telescope Around

Jim had a productive and meaningful weekend. He walked into his office on Monday morning with a smile, ready for the typical intensive operations of a physical commodities-trading company. His executive assistant, Mary, showed him the do list for the day, and pointed in particular to one serious item. It was about an accident that took place on a small refrigerated vessel chartered by his company to transport Anhydrous Ammonia, from a factory located in Donaldsonville on the Mississippi River to an ammonia storage terminal in Tampa, Florida.

The refrigerated tanker had a leak in one of its several spherical tanks. When the leaked ammonia was exposed to the atmospheric temperature of the air, its poisonous gas spread swiftly and inflicted serious injuries on ten crew members causing eye irritations, skin swelling, inflammation, blistering and skin burns, breathing problems, and corrosive damage to the mouth, throat, and stomach. The ship stopped at the nearest port on its route in the Gulf, for the hospitalization of the injured crew.

The title of the goods on board belonged to Jim's company, and though he had adequate insurance, his company was legally liable to any related claims that may arise. This, regardless to the investigation outcome, and even if it were caused by a mechanical error of the ship. Apart from the negotiations between the respective insurance companies for a compensation settlement to be reached, Jim was more concerned about the health condition of the injured crew. His executive VP, Thomas agreed to fly down and check the situation in the hospital on the spot.

Jim called Brian to his office to share his concern. 'there's no rest for the weary" he told Brian when he walked in. Brian comforted him, saying: "Please note such unfortunate events will always occur in the physical world, and the best way to overcome them is by silencing the mind with calm meditation." Jim looked at Brian for a while, and then closed the door. The two sat quietly to meditate with eyes closed for five minutes. The quiet time helped Jim realize the adage: "silence your mind and accept what happens 'as is'". He noticed how his awareness rose slightly above the egoic troubling thoughts of his mind and created peace instead of anger.

This was Jim's first tiny lesson as a debutant on his journey towards spiritual awakening: To accept events calmly when they occur and let the spacious silence prevail from within. With his change of attitude, the other business issues that came up during the course of the day became easier to handle. He also noticed a change in his stress level that normally invades his system. He smiled and gave himself a small pat on the shoulder before he and Brian proceeded to go to the center.

◆

At the Center Jim saw Charles and was introduced to several other members who welcomed him warmly. Charles said that he will be giving a short talk to follow through on the last lecture about Freedom, which was given by Lama Bohdi.

He started his speech referring to a book with the title 'Freedom', written by Osho, also known as Rajneesh. Charles said: "The writer, stated that there are three types of freedom:

1. 'Freedom From': psychological slavery imposed by society, parents, or religion.

2. 'Freedom For': a fulfilling creative life in the artistic or humanitarian field, and

3. 'Just Freedom' the ultimate freedom of simply being true to yourself and living in the moment."

- Charles emphasized the focus on the third type, and Jim wrote down some more remarks:

- Many people may not be true to you, but you should always be true to yourself.

- Let people value you for who you are, your true Self or your true eternal identity, not what possessions you have or the titles you hold. Then he added:

- Freedom is when your soul knows no fear, only love.

- Free yourself from noisy thoughts and go to Silence.

- Free yourself from unhappiness, or what people think of you. - Embrace God's love, and it will set you free.

- Freedom is serving one another in love.

Jim had his journal with him and noted the above remarks. He later showed the journal to Brian and asked him to check the list of questions he had written the night before.

The two of them stood together in a quiet corner sipping tea. Brian was going through the shortlist of questions that Jim had written. He looked at Jim with a happy smile and said:

"What you did is wonderful. In fact, this is an excellent way to follow in our future meetings. You write the questions, and then we discuss them together. Let me write these questions down and prepare some answers for us when we meet on Wednesday after work. Is that okay with you?"

"It sounds good to me. Let's do that, and let's meet in my hotel room to have some privacy. If we get hungry, I can order room service."

"Deal!" Brian confirmed.

♦

They chatted with other people for another twenty minutes, and then Jim excused himself to talk to his colleague, who should have arrived at the hospital by then.

Thomas, Jim's right hand, answered his cell phone when Jim called.

"So, tell me what's going on, and did you visit the injured people?" Jim asked curiously.

"Hi, Jim, yes, I did the round, and let me tell you it's not a pleasant sight. I could not see many faces clearly due to the burns and swelling of their eyes and mouth. They could not talk, but I had the chance to talk to the captain of the ship who was not injured. Two of his officers were hurt along with the sailors who were on deck. They tried hard to seal the hole where the gas was leaking, but to no avail. It took three minutes to find and use the masks to cover their faces, but it was too late."

"What did the doctors say, when will they heal?"

"Not sure yet, I didn't have a chance to talk to the doctors directly, but the captain told me the doctors did not know when and how the burns would heal. It could be a couple of weeks?"

"Was there anyone from our insurance company?"

"No, I didn't see anyone, but I checked with the office, and they're expected to be here tomorrow," Thomas said.

"When do you intend to fly back?"

"I was hoping tomorrow evening. I want to set up a special comfort room for the family members who show up and visit with the insurance people when they come."

"Please engage the services of some local psycho-therapists and spiritual volunteers to be available for consultation with the victims and their loved ones." Jim added.

"Okay, I will consult with the hospital administrator to help me find them. I'll call you tomorrow with an update. Take it easy and rest well, Jim."

"You too, Thomas, and thank you so much for doing this."

The news about the accident was on TV channels, newspapers and on the internet. Jim's company name was mentioned, along with his photo as the CEO. All he could do was to sit back and wish the injured crew well. He remembered from what he heard Charles say, to not let his mind be crowded with negative thoughts or sad feelings. He could only send the victims silent prayers wishing them a quick recovery and good health.

♦

The first session with Brian took place at Jim's hotel living room as planned. Brian came fully prepared with two books for Jim to read. He started by saying:

"I thoroughly reflected on the questions you wrote down Sunday night. Basically, you were expressing a keen desire to 'turn the telescope around'. Instead of looking at external objects that are meaningless, now you want turn the telescope to look more deeply at your inner True Self."

"Interesting analogy!" Jim said.

"You brought up questions about sincerity, transformation from old thoughts, silencing the ego, seeking guidance, self-control, and accessing spiritual awakening. All these are excellent questions to start the process of healing from within. By turning your telescope around you look closely at answers to these very questions with more clarity of a magnifying glass.

"For you, Jim, it won't be that difficult. All you need is to 'take your power back' according to Dr. Deepak Chopra. You did it successfully in your business world, and you can do it similarly in your personal life. Your powerful beliefs about yourself, and your strong personality are at your disposal. So far, your outer achievements were mostly motivated by your egoic self, now you can go beyond and use the same energy to discover your inner strength.

It will help you find your True Self, which in turn leads you to know who you truly are. That should be the 'freedom' you seek, the joy which is your birthright. And, that's what we will work on during these sessions."

Jim was taken aback listening to the wise words expressed by Brian. After a small pause, he asked him: "How do I find my True Self?

"Good question. One thing for sure is that you cannot find it looking in the bag of your past or waiting for it to appear in the unknown future. Both, past and future, do not really exist. You can only find your True Self in the present moment. Eckhardt Tolle, the great spiritual teacher (and I brought you here his bestseller 'The Power of Now' to read) wrote: "You say, 'I want to know myself.' You *are* the "I." You *are* the knowing.

You *are* the Consciousness through which everything is known. And that cannot know itself; *it is itself.*"

"What does he mean, can you elaborate?" Jim asked.

"You, yourself, are one as 'consciousness.' This means there is no duality, a subject, and an object. You are not an object to yourself. The ego created that as an illusion to give you a false identity when you say: "That's me." You simply cannot have a dual relationship with yourself when 'you and you' are one in the Stream of Consciousness. That is when you find your True Self, the One Life, and the only Self: the invisible and powerful Self. The one that connects you with God, the Source of all Power and Joy." Brian expounded with confidence.

"Wow, are you sure you want to continue working as an accountant? You make an excellent teacher!" Jim commented.

"I am grateful to my commitment to learn and improve my spirituality, that is why I read a lot, and why I frequently go to the Center. I love it, and I feel pleased doing it." Brian responded.

"Very good! How about we order some food while we continue this revealing discussion." Jim asked, and then ordered two chicken salads and some soup. While waiting for the food to arrive, Jim asked Brian why do people suffer and is there a way to end it? Brian replied:

"I'm sure you agree that suffering is not only created by physical pain or a chronic illness, but also from negative emotional feelings and mental disorders. The challenge is not to let each mental thought or unhappy feeling become the 'truth'. Physical pain does not necessarily make you unhappy as much as thoughts and feelings do. We invite our own misery into our lives. It took me a long time to overcome the loss of my family, which made me suffer a great deal.

"I learned later that the extended suffering period I went through, was caused by my false identification of my True Self. I broke my true identity for too long because I allowed my unhappy thoughts and feelings of anger to dwell deeply in my egoic state of mind. I treated my ego as my friend, not my enemy that had to be defeated. With the help of the people in the Center, I recognized that I should not feed my ego with more miserable thoughts and feelings."

"So, what happened, how did you end your suffering?" Jim interrupted Brian, who then replied:

" Yes, I learned how to live in the "Now", as I said earlier. "Unhappy feelings do not survive in the present moment. The Now shuts the egoic mind and your Consciousness shifts to the healing Presence of the Now. The Holy Spirit, as often mentioned in the Bible, becomes the bridge that connects you with God, and diminishes the level of your suffering. Mind you, suffering does not end overnight; it's an arduous process, but eventually, it goes away."

"So, why is it necessary to suffer?" Jim asked.

"Buddha said without suffering there is no enlightenment! We, humans suffer, it is innate and sometimes for unresolved reasons. So, instead of focusing on why we suffer, we just figure out how to end it. Just monitor and accept what causes suffering and monitor the thoughts in your mind and/or feelings in your heart. The unconscious mind creates your suffering, just be aware of suffering events, accept them as they happen, and rise above them."

"Accept? Isn't that surrender?"

"Yes, and as the teacher, Tolle, said: "Bring acceptance to your nonacceptance and bring surrender to your nonsurrender and see what happens." I tried it, and it worked for me, a big relief."

"Well, it is evident that spiritual growth requires a lot of work within," Jim remarked.

"It is harder when, on the inside, you resist or oppose 'what is'. When we 'accept' or, say 'yes' instead of 'no', our ego gets weakened and our negative thoughts diminish. This way you'll be free to enjoy the value of the present moment." Brian elaborated.

"We'll see how long it would take me to learn!" Jim wondered.

A waiter knocked on the door, and the food was placed on the dining table. They took a short break and drank the soup with freshly baked bread, then ate the delicious salads prepared by the excellent chef in the kitchen.

When they continued, Jim asked Brian the final question for the evening:

"How about silencing the mind, is that done with meditation?" "Now, this is a vast topic and an excellent question. As Deepak

Chopra says, "meditation bypasses thought, and awareness is the only reality". There are many books written about this subject, and I brought you one to read… Yes, meditation is a practical practice of stillness that takes you beyond the realm of thought. It is a practice of Awareness that does not always require closing of the eyes. Meditation can be short, twenty minutes or so, what then? The challenge is to maintain a meditative silent state throughout the awake hours of the day but with awareness and stillness. That should be the practice to follow!

"Many teachers practice Presence, or Awareness of Consciousness, as a mechanism to silence the mind. To get to that level, you need to invite Presence to grow in you. Presence happens in the Now and diminishes the egoic activity of thoughts in your mind. You arise to a higher level of Consciousness via the power of Awareness." Brian warmly expressed.

"So, again, this requires more work and practice," Jim said

"Yes, with practice, you improve and begin to feel the joy created with inner peace generated by Presence. I am still working on it, and I may continue to do so indefinitely. We are spiritual students for life. But, do not count the time it takes. Pure Consciousness, is a timeless experience. "

"Where do we find stillness then?" Jim wondered aloud. "Awareness is key. Listen to the Silence within you and around you, be it from a noisy source on the street or a calm surrounding in a garden. Awareness awakens your stillness, which you experience when you walk quietly in the forest or when you look silently at a flower and notice its alive Presence. Smell the flowers of your garden and enjoy their sacred scent. You can practice inner Silence even when you walk in a crowded area. Your 'aware' stillness is invisible, and its power resides in your core being, and its Presence dismisses all noisy thoughts. You will sense feelings of peaceful joy arise within your inner body. As such, you experience True Love, the Oneness with All Life."

"Brian, I am highly impressed by what you say, and I believe we should record these sessions. I'm sure it'll help me in my practice to listen to them again."

"Good! I will bring a small recorder with me when we meet again. By the way, when are you free?"

"How about Sunday evening, after I take the children home?" "Fine with me. Meanwhile, start reading one of these books and continue to take notes and write any questions that pop. Before I leave, do we go to the Center on Friday?"

"Yes, I'm free!"

"Good, enjoy the rest of the evening and hope to see you in the office tomorrow."

"Thanks a lot, Brian, I'm enjoying this work together. See you tomorrow and goodnight!"

Before writing about the day's events in his journal, Jim called Thomas to find out what was going on with the crew at the hospital.

Thomas told him:

"I'm staying another night to meet with a therapist and some volunteers in the morning. I arranged a large room for consultation, and I met with the insurance representative who told me not to worry, the negotiations started with his counterparts. A workable settlement should be reached soon. There is one particular crew member, however, who is in a serious condition suffering from breathing complications and a big damage to his lungs. The doctors were not sure he can make it.

"Sorry about that! Please do the needful and hope to see you tomorrow. Thanks again!"

"Sure thing! I should be back in the office tomorrow afternoon." Jim took a shower to unwind, then sat down and wrote:

It appears that to grow spiritually, I may have to learn how to handle the ripples of challenge that arise from a deep sea of uncertainty. It is said that 'adversity yields character'. It sounds contrary to what I learned today. The objective is not to resist but to 'accept' adverse conditions as an observer, to see them as is. Once you acknowledge adversity, you can then rise above it. Otherwise, the ego creates a character, which is the false self. And that, which the ego produces, gives a false sense of identity.

The disturbing episode of the ship accident requires me to be silent and to meditate. How am I going to experience stillness or Presence? I need to learn how to meditate and practice this process of Awareness.

Now, what can I do to help out these victims, beyond the settlement of the insurance companies? Why do I still have some guilt feeling though it is not my fault?

Life keeps throwing stones at me, when I yearn to see them as precious gems instead?

Am I being tested to see how much pressure I can handle from the adversities of the world before I surrender to the universe?

Brian says, 'turn the telescope around', to find my True Self inside my inner being. Am I afraid to start digging, to shovel out the mountains of dirt that have been accumulated in my past four decades and beyond?

Ironically, my compassionate feelings towards the injured crew members are strangely triggering revised feelings of love towards my family and others.

Wouldn't it be wonderful if I could talk lovingly to Janet and ask for her forgiveness? Why am I holding back and delaying my confession? It must be the tricky ego again?

Jim closed his journal and went to bed with a new book in his hand to read. The book, titled 'Your Erroneous Zones' by Dr. Wayne Dyer, seemed to fit his current state of mind. As written on its cover, the writer affirmed that there is a spiritual solution to every problem. The writer teaches that errors can be fixed by 'taking charge of yourself and make yourself happy with self-reliance'.

Jim delved into the first chapter and made sure he finished it before he went to sleep. It drew his attention to similar discussions with Brian on how to develop the ability to 'turn the telescope around', and search for strength from within.

Before he went to sleep, he contemplated simple phrases from the book that resonated well in his mind and hoped to re-live them in his dreams. They were thoughts like: "*You are a choice-making individual*", "*Eradicate the myths from your past*", "*take responsibility of yourself*" and "*love yourself and destroy any self-doubt.*"

♦

Jim had a restful night. On his way to the office the next morning, he called his assistant and asked her to notify Michael, Thomas and Brian to meet with him in his office at 3:00 pm.

The executives showed up on time and sat around the conference table in Jim's large office. He asked Thomas first to brief everybody about the situation at the hospital.

"I could have had a more enjoyable trip, but I did what any right person would do. The sight of these crew members can break your heart, and the pain they had to tolerate was excruciating. It's going to take them a while to heal hopefully with minimal facial disfiguration. Most of them are not comfortable talking yet, and one of them who suffered from damaged lungs went into a coma this morning.

" A consultation room to comfort the loved ones of the victims is in place now, and we found/hired a spiritual psychotherapist to be available every day in the afternoon. Other volunteers from the hospital will also assist.

"The insurance guys are diligently working on a settlement, and we hope it'll be satisfactory."

"Thanks, Thomas, the reason I asked for the meeting is to figure out how we can help these people, beyond any insurance settlement. What I have in mind is to create a fund dedicated to their case. I want to start by capitalizing the fund with the estimated profits expected from the two contracts I recently concluded in China and India. Brian, can you please look into that?" Jim asked, and before he could continue, Brian interrupted him and said:

"Interesting you ask, I have already done the estimates, and I was about to share them with Michael to include in our cash flow. The numbers are still fresh in mind if you care to know now."

"Go ahead, tell us!" Jim said.

"Based on an approximate total volume between the two clients, the revenue from sales should be around $62 Million. Since we purchased the goods in advance, and we know the cost of sales, the approximate gross profit would be around $2.9 million, other things being equal." Brian stated.

"I see! Michael, I would like to exclude these amounts from our business cash flow and allocate $3 million to a new account you will establish in the name of a non-profit organization you will also create, as a subsidiary of this company." Jim requested.

"I understand, but it would take several months before these profits get fully realized. Do I wait until we have them on our books first? Or…. Jim interrupted him and said,

"No, don't wait, take a short-term loan from our company reserve fund, and you pay it back when the profits are actualized. Also, if there is a shortage to reach the $3 million, I will pay it from my account. Are we all clear on this project?" Jim asked.

"Jim, who would manage the fund?" Thomas asked.

"I wouldn't mind doing it if you agree, Jim!" Brian answered

"Fine with me! Thank you, Brian."

"What do you have in mind, Jim, regarding the use of funds to help these people?" Michael asked.

"I don't fully know yet? Financially, it depends on the insurance settlement. If it's not adequate, we fill in the gap. These people should be paid the monthly income they normally receive, plus 20%, as moral support. If they are incapacitated and cannot work, we again fill in the gap. They and their families should not be cut short of their normal income. So, something along these lines… is that okay with you guys?"

They all nodded in agreement and were very proud of Jim's compassionate humanitarian gesture.

Chapter 4
Planting Seeds of Transformation

At the Center, Jim had a private meeting with Charles. He expressed how helpful Brian had been in the last few weeks. He then asked Charles about forgiveness.

"I must have deeply hurt my wife, Janet, by leaving her and the kids in pursuit of my meaningless physical pleasures. Do you think she'll forgive me and take me back?" Jim asked.

"Forgiveness, if you ask spiritual teachers, they agree with me that it is the highest form of Love. It is not easy, though! When you hurt someone, a lot of anger builds up, and that's not good for Janet either to be unhappy. To forgive you, she has to realize that she would forgive herself simultaneously. The fact that you betrayed her does not change, but her reaction to this fact might change, if and when she forgives you. What's important is that you are seriously considering it." Charles explained.

"She is a strong woman, and I know I broke her heart, I also believe I should take a chance and bet on her continued strength to forgive me in her heart," Jim said.

"This sounds good; how do you intend to approach her?" Charles asked.

"Either calling or I can send her a letter with the kids when they come to see me. What do you think?" Jim responded.

"Either way, it's good. What you should ask for is a meeting face-to-face! Is she spiritual, by the way?" Charles asked.

"If by that, you mean she believes in the power of Love without fear, the answer is yes. She is not religious, like me." Jim replied.

"Then go for it, Jim. Remember, Love and Forgiveness go together. Just don't push her to act immediately. I honestly believe you need more time to grow spiritually. Don't forget that you need to forgive yourself for the errors you did first, then hope Janet will notice the change in your character. You both have to forgive yourselves for your good, and she needs to regain her trust in you. So, continue your focus on your inner work, and the universe will guide you when the right time comes. For now, you may express to the children your desire to rejoin them at home soon." Charles said.

"If I wait too long and she meets somebody else, wouldn't that be a mistake on my part?"

"As I told you earlier, this is not up to you, leave it to the universe to take care of the timing, and whatever else Janet might do or not do. Focus on having peace within you first. Good things happen at the right time. Besides, in the process of forgiveness, you will also experience Freedom, what we discussed the other day." Charles emphasized.

"Thank you, Charles, I appreciate your advice and I'll keep you advised."

"By the way, you told me when we met that you and Brian work together, but you didn't tell me you were the owner and founder of the company. Brian told me about your decision to help the victims of the ship accident. That's very noble and generous of you, big boss! I hope with your entrepreneurial talent; you will be able to guide us with your ideas." Charles mentioned with a smile.

"I'll be happy to help in whatever way I can. Thank you, Charles,and we'll meet again soon!"

◆

More than two weeks had passed since the ship accident, and Jim met with his senior staff to get updated on the latest developments. Thomas said:

"The insurance companies reached a settlement agreement two days ago. The shipowners' insurance company will pay all hospital expenses, and each of the injured crew will receive a one-time payment of $100,000, plus all costs for continued medical treatments. One, unfortunately, died a week ago, three were lightly disfigured and will go back to work, four with medium-level disfiguration and would require plastic surgery, not sure the shipowners will keep their jobs. Two were severely disfigured or disabled and will not be able to work.

"The crew members earned an average salary of $35,000 a year. Their insurance did not cover disability for over three months. Seven of them were released from the hospital but closely monitored from home. The two that remained require hospital treatment for a while longer.

"The families, or next of kin, were notified of the settlement and were not satisfied. I have their full addresses, and we need to discuss what we should do on our part."

"Thank you, Thomas, how about you, Michael?" Jim asked.

"I created the non-profit and called it "Good wishes Inc." you can change the name of you like. The fund is ready as you ordered."

"Thank you, Michael. So, we need to consider a gift to the family of the deceased plus the two that cannot go back to work and make sure the shipowners hire back the four that require more treatment; otherwise, we help them too. Any ideas?" Jim asked.

There was silence for a while than Brian spoke:

"You decide the gift amount. Regarding the two disabled men and basis their salary plus 20%, they both come out to $100,000 a year. It will add up to one million over ten years, or two over twenty years. Then if any of the four do not keep their jobs, we calculate the same yearly cost of $50K per person until they are either hired somewhere or remain unemployed."

♦

Brian went to see Jim in his hotel room that evening. He shared with Brian the highlights of the conversation with Charles, whether Janet would forgive him and take him back.

"What do you think about forgiveness Brian, am I dreaming or is it for real?" Jim asked.

"It is a unique opportunity for you to heal, let go of the past and awaken to the present moment. When you forgive you throw away the burden of guilt and sadness. Forgiveness is the best proof of love, without fear. What else can I say? If the two of you want peace, happiness, worthiness to experience the beauty of life, then forgiveness is the answer and it will set you free. Jesus taught us that we are already forgiven. So, forgive one another and forgive yourself. Let go of the illusory past and live in the Light of Now." Brian said eloquently.

"It is not up to me; it is up to her too!"

"Don't worry about her, forgive yourself first and once you do, she will sense it and loosen up. The universe will make it easier for her to forgive herself, and then you."

"Wow! Did you and Charles go to the same school? He gave me a similar advice!" Jim remarked. Brian smiled and said,

"We are in the same group and share the same teachings."

"Why am I so eager to do it and get it over already?"

"Jim, this is not a business deal you can control as you wish! This is a delicate matter and involves another independent soul. Give yourself a break and be patient. You put your intention out there and God will take care of the rest. Please don't be so anxious! Focus on your own growth. How are you doing with the reading and writing, by the way?"

"I am quite diligent I should say. You're welcome to check my notes and this man Wayne Dyer is a blessing! I am now reading slowly chapter four 'Breaking Free from the Past'. It is amazing how all of you, spiritual people pretty much say the same thing: the past, free yourself from the past, and the past…" Jim said with a smile.

"It's an interesting exercise to be spiritual, isn't it?" Brian affirmed.

"I like it when he explained that the best thing is to *learn* from the sadness of the past and find out who you are now." Jim stated.

They spent another hour expounding on the spiritual benefits of inner stillness, and how to let go of useless thoughts and feelings, and how to make the right choices every day.

♦

Jim was looking forward, to spend the weekend with his two children. When he picked them up, they had big smiles on their faces. They sat together in the living room, tea and chocolate croissants were placed at the coffee table.

"I hope you guys had a good week! Anything new?" Jim asked.

Laura and Todd looked at one another and Todd said:

"I'm in the soccer team now, and Laura has a boyfriend!"

"Stick to your own stories, silly!" Laura said and poked Todd with her elbow.

"Interesting stories, who wants to elaborate first?" Jim intervened, smiling.

"I'll go first! The coach picked me up to play as a goalkeeper because I'm strong and tall. I love it! We had one game against a rival school, and I saved three strikes. You should come and see me play sometime." Todd said proudly.

"Of course, I will, just let me know when! How about you Laura, you have a sweetheart now?" Jim asked.

"Well, he's not a sweetheart yet, but a nice guy. We're just good friends. I like him because he's polite, funny and good-looking. Mom met him and she liked him too. We're about the same age and he's one year ahead in school. We go to the movies during the weekend, and he teaches me math sometimes."

"Dad, I saw them kiss too!" Todd intervened.

"Are you jealous Todd, you don't have a girlfriend to kiss?" Jim asked with a smile.

"Heck, no! I'm not interested!" and Laura added: "Yeah sure!"

Jim was enjoying this dialogue admiring how much they've grown in the last seven months. He also realized how Janet has done a great job bringing them up to be close and respectful of one another.

"How's school? Are you two doing well?" Jim asked.

"I'm doing well, I had an average of B+ on all my classes, but Todd did slightly better. He scored an average of A-, right Todd?" Laura asked.

Todd did not comment, but he heard his father congratulate them both and how proud he was. Laura was a beautiful young girl who looked very much like her mother. She had same color eyes and hair, athletically shaped and almost as tall as her mother, about 5:6 in. Todd was also tall for his age, about 5:8 in. athletic, funny and good looking.

"Are you all happy at home?" Jim asked curiously.

"We are! and we miss having you with us, though! Mom takes excellent care of us, and she only goes out on rare occasions with her lady friends. She does not seem to be angry with you anymore, and Todd told her you are becoming spiritual nowadays." Laura said.

"Is that so Todd? How did she react to your gossip?"

"She didn't say a word, Dad. I think she was impressed with the change in your life. Did you call her yet?"

"No, son! Not yet, and I hope to do so soon. I was advised by my spiritual teachers to focus on forgiving myself first, before I ask Janet to forgive me."

"Do it quickly Dad, we really miss you at home." Todd commented.

Laura was looking around and she saw the book "Your Erroneous Zones" on the dining table. She held it up and asked her father if he was reading it and what was it all about. Jim was happy she asked and said: "This book was written by a famous spiritual teacher named Dr. Wayne Dyer who recently passed away. He wrote more than thirty self-help books and many of them were bestsellers. This book in your hand was his first, which sold millions of copies, it shows you how to be happy. You can read a list of his answers on how to correct our errors or mistakes, as humans. I like it, and I'm not finished studying it yet."

"Did you say studying it?" Laura asked.

"Yes, my dear! Such books require focus and taking notes, which I also do every night before I go to sleep. To change old habits and thoughts is quite a process, and I'm determined to go through it."

"So, you're a student now?" Funny Todd, asked.

"Yes, young man! To live a better life, you never stop learning!"

"I'm quite impressed Dad! We all love you and can't wait to see you with us when you graduate, Okay?" Todd said, while Laura was still reading the cover-text of the book.

"Where are you in the book now, Dad?" Laura asked.

"I just finished chapter four that taught me how not to live in the past and focus on the present moment. I am now looking to study chapter five which will teach me not to worry and to stop feeling guilty."

"Do you feel guilty still?" Laura asked.

"Honestly, I do! When I walked out from home, I did not feel I was doing something wrong. That's how huge my ego was. It did not take me long to realize I was wrong. I was blinded and totally out of touch with my true self. Even when I met Tanya, as a good friend, I was feeling guilty about leaving you guys, and how much I must have hurt your mother. So, I need to eliminate this guilt by forgiving myself first and ask for your forgiveness as well. The chapter will give me specific ideas how not to feel guilty and I will note down the lessons I learn in my journal."

"Wow! You're on a roll, Dad! Good job!" Laura responded.

"Well, I want to fix things up so I'm learning how to go about it. Please be patient with me and give me some time."

"I know it will not take you a long time, Dad, you are a brilliant man and a fast learner. You succeeded in business and you will succeed in your personal life, I'm sure!" Laura emphasized.

"Well said, and that is very encouraging. You know the adage that says: *'if there is a will there is a way'*. I know I'm willing! Jim confirmed before he suggested to continue the conversation during lunch in a nearby restaurant. Todd then jumped in and asked his father if they can order room service for dinner and Jim agreed after checking with Laura who also said she would like that.

More meaningful questions and answers were exchanged during lunch, and the rest of the day was spent with a walk in the park, followed by watching a new Star Trek movie in the cinema.

When the children went to sleep after enjoying their room service dinner and playing some video games, Jim was inspired to write a letter to Janet, to be delivered by Laura. He wrote:

Dear Janet,

Having the children with me this weekend inspired me to send you this short note along with a sample of what I write nowadays. I enjoy the questions our children ask and the honest answers I reply. I confessed to them the mistakes I've done, and my determination to correct them.

Todd asked me if you and I talk. I said, unfortunately, not yet. I hope we can communicate soon, as I would like to ask for your forgiveness. I am working diligently on forgiving myself for the mistakes I did. I am learning from my spiritual friends that forgiveness can free us to regain the power of true Love.

I would appreciate it if you can find it convenient for us to meet and talk. Thank you!

Jim

(An excerpt from my journal)

My past mistakes

I created a gulf of space between us that blinded my eyes

I broke the vows of love that bonded two independent souls

I allowed the pillars of our temple to stand far apart

I allowed selfish fears alter my true meaning of love

I allowed my past fears empower my ego to lead me astray

I allowed a thick veil of false desires cover my clear vision

I sought false freedom to handcuff me and lay a heavy yoke

I sought freedom that chained me and fragmented my inner self

I allowed ego to enslave my mind and steel the joy of my soul

I allowed my nights to create dark wounds not lights of peace

I gave fear my honorable heart seat that used to belong to love

I lived in darkness and closed the curtains of my inner light

I let the clouds of mind invite the illusion of life pleasures

I silenced the music of my soul from the harp in my body

My dreams of tomorrow:

To awaken from my dark dreams and live again in the light

To restore the temple of true love that is the only Truth

To silence my ego and throw away the shadows of all fears

To replace my bitter tears of sorrow with fresh tears of joy

To regain the joyful peace bestowed by the union of my beloved

To confess my wrongs and live life only by what is right

To dwell again in the house of love, peace, and harmony

To wear new garment of freedom placed on the throne of Love

To dance to the music of my soul and sing new songs of love

To hug and caress those who fire up my day and still my night

♦

Brian arrived Sunday evening as scheduled. Jim told him about the pleasant weekend with the children and the letter he sent to Janet.

"Do you mind telling me what you wrote?" Brian asked

"Basically, I asked for her forgiveness and for us to meet sometime.

I also shared with her an excerpt from my journal. Here, you can read it!"

Brian took a minute to read the excerpts and with a big happy smile on his face, he said:

"Wow! We have a poetic healer in our midst. How wonderful? I'm so impressed, my multi-talented brother!"

"It's from the heart! I wrote it for me, then I thought why not share it with Janet? Perhaps it would soften her heart and help her to trust me again?" Jim responded.

"May the power of love heal her too!"

"Brian, do you think I'm rushing?" Jim asked.

"No, not really! You followed your intuition. You shared the truth about your thoughts and feeling. Wait and see how she'll respond. So, where are in the book?" Brian asked

"Interesting you ask! My daughter Laura asked me the same question when she saw the book on the table. I finished chapter four and ready to delve into the fifth. I believe I heard and read enough about the past and I've become an expert on freeing myself from the past grip on my thoughts and feelings." Jim explained.

"What was the most important lesson you learned from the chapter?" Brian asked.

"The fact that I don't have to make the same choices today, as I did before."

"Excellent!"

"The next chapter is going to be very interesting, it's about emotions of guilt and worry. I'm still feeling guilty about what I did, and it causes suffering that I must end." Jim expressed.

"Here, again, awareness is key. Acknowledge what happened, don't let it agitate you, and rise calmly above it. This is a practice that will empower a shift in your consciousness from fear to love, and from sadness to joy."

"You see! Your poetic explanation is what inspires me to write poetically as well. You're a good influence, Brian! If you're so good as an accountant, you deserve a raise!" Jim remarked.

"Thank you, sir! We all get inspired by fellowship of people who think alike."

"Back again to the letter I sent Janet, how do you think she will react?" Jim was still eager to find out.

"How do I know? We talked about that. Don't be so anxious wondering if she would approve or disapprove, whether she will meet you or not, to remain angry or to forgive you ? … you did what you thought was right. Now you give her the benefit of the doubt. Leave it to the Universe to guide her."

"You see, I'm not used to being let down. It's my damn business arrogance that taught me to always win. What if she closes the door permanently in my face? Will I then slide back in reverse, into my old fears?"

"Well, this is not a business deal. You are dealing with an independent soul who's entitled to her own choices, right or wrong, it is not up to you. You focus on your own healing and win your soul back first. If she does not want to have you back in her life again, you still have a new you, for yourself. Besides, when one door closes, other doors open. It's a win-win situation!" Brian said, compassionately.

"I hear you! I still don't like feeling rejected."

"You rejected her first, Jim. How do you think she felt then? Don't be so egotistical and selfish now. Give the lady a chance to digest what's on her mind, as you gave yourself the chance to work on yours." Brian sounded assertive and firm. Jim paused for a while then said,

"You're right, I'll shut up and wait, patiently."

Jim ordered dinner to the room and they continued discussing the issues of fear and how to turn on the power of love to beat it. Brian left an hour later, and Jim proceeded to his desk to write in his journal the eventful exchanges with the children and Brian.

Chapter 5

Overcoming Potential Setbacks

Laura handed her mother the sealed letter when she returned home, from an outing. Laura suspected that Jim was trying to mend fences and left the envelop unopened and put it on top of her bed. Janet sat with the kids in the living room and asked them to report the events of the weekend with their father.

"Todd and I are enjoying spending time with Dad. He's different than what we knew him to be as a busy man, serious and always on the run. He's cool, funny and very loving now. Right, Todd?" Laura said.

"Absolutely! He said he'd like to come and see me play soccer." Todd said.

"Did you guys talk about me and what I do with my life now?" Janet asked.

"Very little, other than Dad saying that he misses home, and hopes you'll forgive him for what he did," Todd said, bluntly.

"And?"

"And what, Mom? We believe he still loves you and wants us all back together!" Laura injected.

"What do you guys think?" Janet asked.

"If it were up to us, of course, we say yes, let's all be back together, but it is up to you. All we can tell you is that Dad is a different man now; he's spiritual and doesn't' see anybody. So, it is your decision. We'd love to see you two together again."

They all went silent for a minute, then Janet asked if they wanted to have some tea? The children said, "no, thanks" and went to their rooms after saying goodnight. Janet held the teacup and went to her room as well.

She sat on the chair in the bedroom and opened the envelope. She moved around the chair restlessly while reading the letter and trying to digest Jim's new poetic prose. She scratched her head a couple of times and read the message again and again. The contents of his analysis dumbfounded Janet. She sat frozen in her seat, looking at the ceiling with a curious smile on her face. She did not expect Jim to be so forthcoming and thought their marriage was on its final legs and the brink of collapse. Her mind was racing with all sorts of questions:

What do I do now? The children don't know that I am seeing another man during lunch hour many days a week while they're in school, and during the weekend when they visit with their father.

Even if no man existed in my life, how could I trust Jim again after what he did?

Jim is asking me to forgive him and take him back! How could I forgive him for the deep dagger wound he punctured in my heart? He rejected me and dropped me like rotten fruit, so why should I be at his beck and call?

The kids love him, and I may still love him, too, but I'm developing a separate life for me now. What do I do with the man I am seeing? He says he loves me, though I don't know if I do?

I need time, I'm baffled now, and I'm not ready to meet Jim any time soon. I'm still angry, and I will not rush!

I need someone neutral to talk to, other than my mother. I don't have a close girlfriend, and I don't go to church. I'll try a therapist.

Janet tried to sleep but couldn't. She was restless all night and realized she cannot sit calmly with Jim and talk face-to-face while she still holds a grudge. The next morning, she called the nearest therapist she found in the yellow pages. His office told her the first available time is in ten days. She booked the appointment anyhow. She also called her boyfriend, and with some phony excuse, she told him she's busy for the next few days. She needed time alone to reflect on the 'bomb' Jim threw in her lap. She spent her day pacing around, driving the car aimlessly, and re-reading the letter Jim had sent her.

The children came back from school around 3:00 in the afternoon and found a restless mother in the house. Laura asked her:

"What's going on, Mom? Is it the letter Dad sent you?"

"Yes, what else? He wants to confess his sins and ask me to forgive him. Can you imagine?" Janet said nervously.

"What's wrong with that, Mother? Even if you don't love him anymore and don't want him back, forgiving him is also good for you. It will set you free." Laura replied.

"The trouble is that I still love him, I think. How can I forgive him when I know I'm not ready to have him back?" Janet uttered.

"Mom, you're not making any sense from what I hear you say. You need some time to think things through and decide what is best for you. Don't linger on with too much analysis and suspicious thoughts. Think about it and let me know what to tell me when we see him next. You owe him the courtesy of some response, okay?" Laura said before she went to her room.

"Okay, smart elk, we'll talk later!"

♦

Apart from the usual business matters that occupied his days, Jim spent his free time reading, going to the Center, or with Brian. He was eager to hear back from Janet, but not too concerned, as he was focusing on his spiritual growth.

In one of his sessions at the Center, he had a chance to talk to both Charles and Brian together, and he asked,

"I have a question how do you define Consciousness? From what I read, sometimes it's defined as awareness, or Presence, or even God. I'm a bit confused. What is the nature of Consciousness? Is it a thought in mind produced by the brain?"

Charles took the liberty to answer Jim first. He said,

"An excellent question is not always easy to explain. Many spiritual teachers prefer not to use the word as a noun because then it sounds like an object. Consciousness is not an object, separate from our core being. It is an invisible source of All-Knowing, the full awareness of being, thus the essence of who we truly are."

"Sorry, I may be thick in the head, but I don't understand how to relate to it…" Jim was saying when Brian interrupted him,

"You don't relate to it! You don't have to understand it either. It is not an 'it' or a 'concept' or a 'thing'. A teacher once gave an analogy and said imagine an iceberg where you only see its tip, which is about 5% of the entire massive block of ice, which is 95% underwater.

"We only know and see the tip. It represents our identified thoughts and feelings. But that is not the whole being. The deeper part which we do not see or know represents a dimension of not-knowing. There is no ego or thoughts in the deeper part. It is where wisdom and love dwell in spacious awareness. Consciousness *IS* that vast, spacious awareness of not-know-ingness. We sense its 'presence' when we meditate and notice the rise above our thoughts to a higher level of awareness. I hope this analogy makes it more transparent for you?"

"I guess I understand it better now, and perhaps I would start sensing 'its Presence' when I meditate. So, what you're saying is that

Consciousness is always there, eternal and timeless because it has no form to identify with." Jim stated.

"Well said! Now you're getting the picture, Jim. Brian told me that you sent a letter to your wife. Did you hear back from her?"

"No, not yet, it's only been three days. Give her time. I'm sure she's perplexed with an ocean of thoughts at this moment."

"Are you nervous? Eager to hear from her? What if she turns you down, will you be disappointed?" Charles asked.

"A good question, I don't know yet! I am optimistic, and I can only send her positive messages of love. So, we'll see!"

"It's a spiritual challenge, Jim. I just wanted you to know that we are here as your brothers, and we share your trust in the Universe that whatever happens will be for a good reason." Charles expressed.

"I appreciate your love, and I'm holding up quite well so far. I'll keep you advised."

Jim spent another twenty minutes with Brian elaborating on the discussion they had and wished him well.

♦

Meanwhile, Janet talked with her two children when they came back from school on Wednesday. Laura avoided confronting her again with the same questions since their last conversation. Todd just tagged along to join them with a long face.

"I'm sure you both are eager to find out how I should respond to your father's letter. Right?" Janet asked.

"You bet we are! Why do you need so much time?" Todd voiced his anger.

"Well, it's not as easy as you think. I hope you guys will never be hurt as I was when your father walked out on us. I am still holding a grudge against him; the reason why I'm finding it difficult to forgive him and see him again." Janet explained.

"But, Mom, we all make mistakes. Yes, he made a big mistake, but he regrets it and blames only himself for it. He's a very responsible man. I'll be lucky to find a man like him one day. He takes excellent care of us, he loves us all, and he'll never turn his back on us, as many men do. He's down on his knees, asking for your forgiveness. Why can't you do it for good old times' sake, our sake?" Laura expressed how she felt.

"He's also coming to see me play soccer tomorrow despite his busy schedule. Why don't you come as well, and you two can talk?" Todd asked.

"I hear you guys, and I decided to see a therapist next week to help me. Meanwhile, I also wanted to tell you something I've been hiding from you. For about one month now, I've been seeing a male friend a couple of times a week, for lunch and dinner when you go to see your father. I'm not in love, I want you to know, but he's a very good companion and a great listener. I told him I'd not be able to see him this week. That's another reason I'm taking some time before I respond to Dad's letter." Janet explained.

Laura and Todd looked at one another, surprised and silent for a short while. Laura then asked,

"Who is this man, do we know him?"

"I'm not sure you do. He is the bank manager in this area, and he handles my account. He's eight years older than me, divorced, and has two children who live away from home."

"He's just a friend, you said?" Todd asked.

"Yes! Not as intimate as you might think, Todd!"

"Are you saying that you will be seeing a therapist to help you, what if it drags on for a long time? Why don't you write Dad back and explain what you told us? He'll understand!" Laura suggested.

"Why don't you guys tell him when you see him this weekend?" Janet said.

"Are you going to see your friend this weekend too?" Todd asked.

"I might! Mainly to tell him that we can't see each other until I clear my head, first."

"Okay, Mom! We wish you well, and please keep us advised."

"I will, and I love you guys very much!" Janet said, and the children went to their rooms.

◆

Todd was thrilled to see his father come to watch the game between the junior school team and their opponents from another junior high. They waved at one another, and Todd looked athletic in his soccer outfit, wearing a no. 1 jersey. Other parents were present, and Jim had his baseball cap on also wearing dark glasses not to be recognized by people who may know him.

The whole game lasted one hour, thirty minutes each half. Todd saved two-goal strikes and only missed a penalty kick. The final score was 2:1, and Jim was very proud of his son. He waited for Todd to shower and then join him for a drink nearby. After a big hug and congratulations, they sat together and had some soda on ice. Todd thanked his father for coming and said he asked his mother to come if she likes but didn't.

"I don't think she's ready to meet you anytime soon, Dad!"

"Did she explain why?"

"She talked to us yesterday and said she'd be seeing a therapist next week to help clear her head."

"That's a good idea, I understand, no rush!"

"Dad, what did you write in that letter that shook her up so much?"

"The Truth, my son, nothing more and nothing less!"

"You love her still?"

"Yes, I do! We have great memories together."

"Dad, I hope you guys make up and get back together soon. She said she has a new male friend she's been seeing for the last four weeks. She said they're only good friends, whatever that means?"

"I also understand that she's not supposed to be alone, after the hurt

I caused. Anyhow, do you like the man, did you see him?" Jim asked curiously.

"No, we don't know him! Laura and I only hope to see you guys back together."

"Great, I'm so happy I came to see you and will see you on Saturday. Give me a hug!"

They hugged goodbye, and Todd walked back to be with his friends.

◆

Jim went back straight to the Center for the 6:00 pm get together.

He saw Brian and Charles and then sat to listen to the message of the evening: "True Love". The speaker was a well-known pastor of a Unity church in the neighborhood. He started by saying that he has two primary references that inspired him for the words he will share:

- Saint Paul's first letter to the Corinthians chapter 13, and

- Gibran's chapter on Love from his best-seller, the Prophet.

Jim was highly focused due to his current hunger for a spiritual understanding of the power of love. He took quick notes and highlighted:

In the contest of the entire message that Paul sent to the people of Corinth, who were pagans before they became followers of Christ, it is essential to read the last sentence of the chapter before this famous chapter on love. He said: "Now let me show you a way of life that is the best of all."

Paul had stated in Chapter 12, the various gifts that people have.

He emphasized, however, that all these great gifts, talents, and wealth are useless without love. Without love, we have nothing.

Love is patient, kind, not jealous, and not angry.

Love is forgiving and hopeful. Loves helps us to know God as He knows us.

True Love is a transcendent love beyond emotions, thoughts, or physical relationships.

Faith, hope, and love last forever, but love is the greatest of them all.

The Pastor then shifted to the 'Prophet' by Gibran.

He said that it would be best to read the three short pages that Gibran wrote about Love. He mentioned that millions of copies sold in more than 30 languages. He read the chapter slowly and poetically. With every added sentence or phrase, Jim would drop his jaw lower with awe. Jim noted:

When love beckons to you, follow him.

When he speaks to you, believe in him.

When love crowns you so shall he crucify you.

He frees you from your thorns and makes you naked.

Love helps you to know the secrets of your heart.

Love and fear do not co-exist.

Love gives only love and takes nothing back.

Love does not want to possess any nor can he be possessed

Love's only desire is to fulfill itself and knows no pain but joy.

You cannot direct love; it will direct you if it finds you worthy.

Jim was elated to hear such gems of poetic prose and was determined to buy the book the next day. The depth of his expressions resonated so well with his current love story. Two phrases remained vivid in his mind: '*how love can crown me and can crucify me*', and '*how I cannot tell love what to do, love leads the way if love finds me worthy.*'

When the speech was over, Jim applauded the speaker from all his heart. All he wanted to do was to rehash what he learned with either Brian or Charles. Brian was free, while Charles was busy talking to the Pastor. Jim suggested they go and have a light meal outside to go over this message of love. Brian did not say no to Jim's request especially when he found him so excited about the subject.

As soon as they were seated in the restaurant, Jim immediately asked Brian,

"So, wasn't that a great speech?"

"Indeed, it was, and I can see how it resonated with you."

"I tell you I'm going to download Paul's chapter on love, and look up the 'Prophet' online, tonight still. I want to read them again and again until they sink deep in my brain and in my heart."

"Is there a specific part of the speech that registered the most in your head?" Brian asked.

"The fact that love is so strong it can take you high or smash you down if you mistreat it. Love can crown you like a mighty king or crucify you with utmost pain. Another thing, you cannot order love to just tag along and do what you want. On the contrary, love leads the way and makes you happy provided you are a good man. So, I also had my days of glory and my days of suffering. I should only trust in Love, as trusting in God, and not to worry about what happens next."

"How about Paul's chapter on Love?"

"Another amazing set of poetry! The power of True Love is above all things and all talents and money. You cannot buy love; you can only practice it as an ultimate divine gift. True love is unconditional and intuitive, the essence of being within any formed or physical relationship."

"So, you see Love as a divine and eternal power that you cannot mess around with, right?" Brian asked.

"You bet! I messed around with it, and you know what happened.

Now, I learned how to respect Love and be loyal to the people I love. Gee! Love is so powerful!"

They took a break and ate their dinner quietly. After finishing with the main course, Brian asked Jim,

"Good food! Any news from the home front?"

"Yeah! I saw Todd this afternoon and watched him play ball. He told me that Janet would see a psychotherapist next week, and also she's been seeing another man the last several weeks."

"I see, how do you feel about that?"

"I thought about it, and honestly, I feel okay with it. I have no right to tell Janet what to do. She's a smart girl; she knows what to do."

"Are you jealous?"

"Of course, I am! I love this woman, and she knows that too. The key here is to stay calm and confident that whatever happens, it would be for a good reason, for her, me, and the children. So, I'll keep the good faith and wait patiently. Love is patient and kind, no?"

"Jim, I'm truly impressed with how fast you're learning and growing spiritually. It's fun, isn't it?"

"Yes, it is my friend. Tonight, I will read, write, and meditate. And I will see you in the office tomorrow to talk about our humanitarian work.

Thank you for joining me this evening; I needed to share how happy I felt with someone I trust."

"I consider it an honor to be trusted by you, Jim. Thank you and have a restful night."

♦

When Jim was alone in his hotel suite, the first thing he did was to look for the material online. He found both references and managed to file and print them out. Jim re-read them and got teary while he was reading. He discovered a level of sensitivity within him that had been suppressed by his ego and the harshness of his business life. He enjoyed the awakening of these sensations that enhanced his satisfaction with the spiritual realm.

He appreciated his positive thinking and the new construction of strong pillars in the temple of his life. He patted himself on the back for not getting angry with Janet's new adventure or the delay of her response to his letter. He became grateful to the shift in his consciousness and to destiny that knocked on his door and woke him up from his deep slumber. Jim realized that the detour he took to indulge in the world since he left home, was nothing other than, an experience with a lesson to learn.

He thought of his revised feelings as a wave of joy that arises after a storm of sorrow. He determined that night to dwell in the garden of true love and say goodbye to the shadows of fear, and the tricks of the egoic false identity.

Jim was unusually calm that night about the possibility that the relationship with Janet might not realize the way he wishes it to be. He surrendered to the Universe to take care of him regardless of what happens.

He's now allowing the power of love to lead the way. Jim surrendered also to a future of not-knowing and felt at peace with it.

He wrote these expressions in his journal and was grateful to the spiritual growth he was experiencing. He meditated in silence for ten minutes and then went to sleep peacefully.

◆

Jim felt energized and fully alert when he got out of bed the next morning. Everyone he greeted warmly everyone he saw on his way to his corner office. The staff noticed a new shining face, an image they had not seen before.

His managers briefed him on what was going on with work. Brian and his assistant, Mary, showed Jim 'thank you' letters, not only from the victims of the ship's accident, but also from the shipowners expressing how stunned they were by his compassionate gesture.

Before he went home after work, Jim told Brian he would delve into the chapter on "Guilt and Worry" this evening to prepare for the discussion they will have on Sunday evening.

◆

The weekend with the two children was quite revealing. Laura found her father at peace and calm when she told him that mother was seeing another man.

"I'm upset with Mom that she could do such a thing without asking us first." Laura said.

"No, my dear, don't be upset. Mom is simply experimenting with the real world and has no intention to hurt your feelings. She wanted to find out first if her friendship with this man was worth sharing with you guys."

"Dad! Wouldn't you be upset if things turn around and wipe out your and our hope for some reconciliation?"

"Sweetheart, and you too, Todd, please be aware that I am a different man now. Why get upset? I don't intend to change Janet's life choices. If she needs time to decide, let her have it. If she wants to be with another man, then so it is. The good gesture I did by writing her my poetic letter was more for my sake than hers. I abide by the Truth to cleanse *my* soul and leave the rest to Destiny. So, let us be patient and continue to be loving towards her. She needs your support at home, not your anger. She needs your love, not judgment. She is swimming in an ocean of perplexity now, and she needs to know you are there by her side to calm her down."

Laura jumped out of her seat and ran to hug her father, followed by Todd as well.

"You are an amazing man, Dad. We love you! Did I hear you say a 'poetic letter'? what do you mean you wrote her a romantic poem?" Laura was curious to know.

"Oh no! not romantic, I wouldn't play with her feelings at this stage. I just shared with her an analysis of what I was going through, that's all!" Jim explained.

"Then you can share it with us too, and we're entitled as well, No?"

"Fine! I'll let you read it. I kept a copy, let me get it but promise me you don't laugh when you read my prose! Okay?"

Jim pulled out a copy from his desk. He gave it to Laura and Todd, who sat next to her on the sofa. The brother and sister started reading the letter with wide eyes and were highly focused. Two minutes later they looked at one another, and Laura said,

"Wow! What other gifts have you been hiding from us? It's an amazing piece of truth and honor. No wonder why Mom was restless for two days after reading this sacred message. If that doesn't shake her up, and make her jump to forgive you and take you back in her arms, I don't know what else would? You have changed, Dad, and we are proud to have you as our father, right, Todd?" Laura said, looking at Todd's wondering face.

"Now you understand why I wrote it. It is both a confession for my past mistakes and an invitation for a new beginning." Jim confirmed.

"Can we tell her that we read it and feel her out ourselves?" Laura asked.

"I suggest not to do it yet. It is supposed to be a private letter. You may ask your Mom if any of the contents disturbed her and see if she takes the initiative to tell you herself."

"Dad is right, Laura. Wait and see! As Dad suggested, she needs our support and understanding now, not our curiosity that might shift her attention around."

"Wisely said, Son!"

"Okay, fine! The saga continues, and we all have to learn something from this, I guess!" Laura said, affirmatively.

"Let me repeat, whatever happens, or whatever Mom decides, we both love you very much and for as long as we live."

The room turned lighter and songs filled the air with gentle melodies of love. Father and children stood together and hugged in silence, enjoying the exchange of 'secret' crowns of affection on each other's head, decorated with fragrant flowers and eternal beauty. The joy that shined in their faces was ascending to new heights, like eagles ruffling their wings high over the mountaintop.

♦

Brian showed up around 6:00 pm on Sunday and found Jim in an excellent mood.

"It seems you're still overwhelmed with the Love speech," Brian remarked.

"Not only that! I had the bonus gift of having the children with me this weekend. They first were upset why their mother did not respond to my letter yet, and I cooled them down. They thought I wrote Janet a romantic letter, and I corrected them. They asked if they could see it, and I let them read the copy I saved. They admired my truthful confession and my poetic prose. We had a lot of fun, and we laughed and hugged often." Jim explained.

"Great news! Did you have a chance to read chapter four on "Useless Emotions?"

"Yes, I did during the last hour, just before you came, Professor Brian. So, it is useless to feel guilty about the past or worry about the future, huh?"

"It simply is!" Brian confirmed. "Can you elaborate a bit?"

"To learn from your experience in the past, it's not worth it to feel guilty about what you did or did not do. Why ruin the present moment with past events that are gone? Dr. Dyer wrote in detail about the origins of guilt. He said guilt feelings are embedded within conversations and attitudes between family members. Then he talked about related guilt in a couple's relationship, "if you do this, then I do that, and if you don't, then I'll be angry". Dyer stretched the guilt realm to schools, companies, and even social sexual expressions." Jim stated.

"Does he say how to eliminate guilt from your life?" Brian asked.

"Yes, of course! He said: 1) Events of the past are over, and no present guilt feelings can change what happened. 2) Admit your mistakes and do not live in denial and try not to make the same mistake twice. 3) Write your lessons down in a journal, which I do. And 4) teach the ones in your life that normally make you feel guilty, that you will not succumb to their attempt to make you feel guilty."

"Excellent! How about future worries?" Brian asked.

"He said People worry about things they have no control over. I do not worry about the future of my business or its success. I do not worry about my children, and I'll always be a good parent. I don't worry about my health though I should work out more seriously and so on. The only thing I need to be careful about is not to worry if Janet decides to go on living without me!"

"So, even though you said you wouldn't be jealous if she chooses to be with another man, you are still somewhat concerned if her choice does not include you, right?" Brian is digging deeper.

"Well, sort of… May be, hum, yeah, it's possible!"

"The thing is, now you are patient and quite confident believing that she'll take you back. How long can you wait, and what if she decides not to comply with your heart's desire?"

"Good question? I don't know Brian, and I hope I don't have to swim in an ocean of jealousy, anger, and despair again. I may come and cry on your shoulder, or Charles if it annoys you! I can always turn the telescope toward my inner self, to draw on the strength that dwells within, to keep me focused on the connection of Love with my True Self."

"Bravo, Jim! Meanwhile, keep your fingers crossed, and the best will happen.

Chapter 6
Disappointing Expectations

Janet met with her friend, Martin, on Saturday for lunch. She told him that Jim is asking her if she would take him back, and the children are on his side. She expressed her confusion about the situation and asked Martin if they could stop seeing each other until she clears her head.

"Do I take it that you still love him?" Martin asked.

"I was madly in love with him until recently. How can I say I love him now when I have not forgiven him for what he did to me?"

"You know you cannot stay in a state of confusion for too long, you'll be hurting yourself this way. On one side, you're not sure you want to forgive him, and accept him again in your life, and on the other side, you're not sure you are capable of loving me as long as his shadow keeps haunting you wherever you go." Martin said.

"That's why I will consult with a therapist on Wednesday."

"Who is it, if I may ask?"

"Dr. Moynihan, here in our area."

"I know her! She's good, but also known as an advocate of separation, and wants her clients, mostly women, not to go through the agony of guilt and wounds. She believes once a spouse cheats, the wounded partner continues to feel the pain, even after they reconcile. She believes pretensive and temporary patchwork is unadvisable.

"Are you saying she is not conciliatory, and the victim should not forgive the offender?" Janet asked.

"That's what I hear! Find out for yourself. The good thing is she does not drag you on with many sessions. She lets her client hear her opinion after a couple of sessions only."

"I see! That would suit you better if she advises me not to fix my marriage and remain independent, right?"

"That's not true, Janet, I will not impose myself on you. You are free on your own any time you like, before or after the consultation with the therapist. What you're going through is a serious matter and watch out for the ego that may mislead your direction."

"What do you mean?"

"The ego wants war, not peace, the ego loves revenge, not love, the ego thrives on conflict and could steer you away from the truth."

"Tell me something. You got divorced two years ago, did you consider going back with your wife after the separation?"

"No, because there was no real love between us. That relationship was patchwork most of the time. We were not true to each other, and we sacrificed our earlier freedom for the sake of the kids. You may have a different situation here. In the end, with or without professional help, you are the best judge of what you should do."

"Okay, Martin, I will keep in touch, and I appreciate your understanding."

"Understood, Janet, you know where to find me. I'm not going anywhere."

♦

A whole month went by without any word from Janet about her decision regarding Jim's appeal to reconcile. The children kept asking her if her sessions with the therapist are helpful to consider a positive response to their father's letter. Janet kept saying "not yet" and "it is a long process." They asked if there was anything in the letter that offended her, but Janet refused to comment. They stopped asking and patiently decided not to disturb her until she was ready. Inwardly they were agitated, but their father kept encouraging them to be supportive.

Janet was battling with demons in her head and saw them like invisible chains firmly tied in the crevices of her egotistic mind. She often asked herself during her restless nights,

How can I find Love that refuses to enter the dark chambers of my heart to show me the light?

Where are the angels of daylight to help me see clearly how to win my battles against the demons of darkness?

Did I create those little devils in my mind, or were they master-minded by my ego?

How long can I cover the façade of calmness to hide the fire of anger burning within me?

Why do I lack the power of Love to forgive Jim, and why do I continue to mistrust him?

Why do I contemplate revenge, or am I yearning to experiment with the temptations of the world as he did?

Am I burying a chance to be freed by Love, or am I getting addicted to suffering living in the abyss of my soul?"

The therapist says, 'it is, what it is,' 'you either live independent of others or surrender the control of your life to others.' Could this be right? Have I been so dependent on him?

I spent my life 'loving' others. Am I capable of loving myself now and honoring my search for freedom?"

Am I going to feel this way all my life, will I succeed to kick the demons out and live in the light again?

Janet was immersed in the turmoil of her repeated thoughts of self-doubt and fear of the unknown. She found that the sessions with the therapist more disturbing than helpful. Janet had no desire to dig and shovel the accumulated dirt from her mind. The therapist wanted Janet to chart her own future instead of relying on Jim to decide for her.

Her ego that got strongly activated by the break-up threw a thick veil covering her eyes and blurted her clear sight from understanding that forgiveness can set her free. Janet's freedom could only be realized by winning the battle against the demons in her head. She was heart-broken and didn't have the strength to fix it alone by herself. After a month of therapy, her condition, psychologically, got worse, not better. Her therapist told her she can only rise to see the light after cleaning the dark rooms in the basement of her heart.

♦

In the interim, Jim was focusing on his business and his private sessions with Brian and Charles. He finished reading the book 'Your Erroneous Zones' and discussed the lessons learned from each chapter with Brian. He mainly reviewed Chapters nine and ten that explained the issues of procrastination, and declaration of independence. Charles was involved in that discussion too.

On the procrastination side, he wanted to interrupt his elongated patience waiting for Janet to decide and to change his own laid-back assumption that *"all is well, I'll wait, and it will get better"* as he used to say. He thought he should do something to shake things up and create a change. The meeting with Charles and Brian was to share his thoughts on how to end procrastination. Jim asked,

"Why am I waiting for Janet to decide? I know her, she cannot decide on her own."

"But you said she is seeing a professional to help her?" Charles asked.

"Yeah, but that is not sure will help her because she hates digging in her past. Janet is too shy to hold herself accountable."

"So, you can't hold your patience any longer?" Brian asked.

"It's not that! Humbly speaking, I think I'm the only one that can help her by putting her on the spot and induce her to speak the truth about what she wants. It would be a constructive confrontation to end her suffering from 'no decision yet,' or 'wait and see' attitude!"

"What do you have in mind, Jim?" Charles asked gently.

"I want to surprise her with an unsolicited visit. When I take the children back home on Sunday, I'll ask her to let me in to talk." Jim said confidently.

"What do you expect her to say or do? To immediately jump and hug you or tell you to please leave? Or, you two may agree to communicate until a final decision is made?" Charles asked again.

"Perhaps one or none of the above. I just want to tell Janet that I'm willing to listen to whatever is on her mind. She's welcome to demean me, or even slap me on the face, to scream and call me names… that doesn't bother me! She needs to shoot her bitter anger out directly in my face and stop pretending she's fine. I have nothing to lose. I'm prepared to continue with my new life regardless, with or without her."

Charles looked at Brian, who was rooted in his thoughts. "I don't see any reason why Jim should not try to end the procrastination on Janet's part. He's entitled to face the truth and assess the state of her mindset after all." Brian told Charles, who responded saying,

"I agree with you both. You are a courageous and loving man, Jim. Do it and remember the angels of heaven will be with you to guide you."

"Thank you both, and if I may add, a quote Dr. Dyer used in chapter ten about independence, and the fact that the union marriage is based on two independent souls,

"In marriage, independence between a man and a woman is equal, dependence is mutual, and the obligation is reciprocal."

"You see, we experienced this independence when we got married. What happened between Jane and me since then is Jane becoming dependent on me, and I was obliged to protect the union as such. We allowed dependency to creep in like a snake, which eventually ended the independence of the two equal souls in our holy union. Dr. Dyer suggests that for marriage to work again, each one needs to write a new declaration of independence and hope to re-institute the union to its original state." Jim expressed.

Charles and Brian heard Jim and wished him good luck. They appreciated his willingness to share his personal feelings and seek their advice.

◆

Jim had another happy weekend with his kids, and on their way back, he told them he was going to escort them to the door and surprise Janet and ask her if they can talk. He explained to them he believes it's the only way to end her silence. Both children agreed and admired his courage to break the ice.

Janet was stunned to see Jim with the two children standing outside the main door.

"Hello, Janet, how are you?" Jim greeted Janet, who had a hard time standing straight and who muttered a few words:

"Why are you here? What do you want?"

"To talk a little, that's all! Do you prefer we talk inside, or we go somewhere?" Janet hesitated to respond for a few seconds, then said,

"Okay, come inside, and kids, please go to your rooms and shut the doors behind you."

"With pleasure, Mom!" They both said at the same time with a happy smile on their faces.

The couple went to the living room, and Janet asked Jim if he wants a drink. He asked for a glass of water then sat in his old chair, remembering the ugly scene they had in that same room before the break-up. Janet brought him a glass of water and sat across on the sofa, looking nervous.

"Did I write anything in my letter that may have offended you?"

"No, on the contrary, I found it informative, and it instigated an attempt to dig more deeply at what happened. I congratulate you on your poetic expressions too. I did not respond because I decided to consult with a professional, as you may know already." Janet said.

"Are you still seeing the therapist?"

"I had my last session with her last Wednesday. I think it did me more harm than good. It added more salt to my wounds. I'm on my own now."

"So, are you prepared to consider a conciliatory talk between us now?" Jim asked.

"No, I don't think I'm ready!"

"Is there anything I can do to help? Don't you think if we communicate more regularly, a solution may be reached to stop the procrastination that has prevailed thus far?" Jim asked.

"I'm not so sure, I'm still angry at you!" Janet expressed her feeling. "I understand, and that is why if you vent out your anger directed at me, you may feel better. I can take it, and as I said in my letter, I confess that I did something wrong and stupid. I am a different man now."

"Yeah, the kids tell me you are a spiritual man now, how amusing?" Janet said, sarcastically. That made her relax a bit when she said with a wry smile.

"That is not something to joke about. I'm proud of the new journey I'm on now, and you can make out of it whatever pleases you." Jim affirmed.

"Well, that's good for you, but I don't see how this can help me regain my trust in you, and eliminate the deep anger within?"

"Why don't we find out? Why close the door to civil communication in person, or on the phone, as I also would like to know, sooner or later, where you stand in this regard. I do not intend to push you to reconcile, and if you need more time, I understand, as long as we keep the dialogue going between us. What do you say?" Jim suggested.

"I appreciate your gesture, and I will think about the communication part. Give me one week, and I will let you know. I am eager to move on too." Janet said.

Jim then stood up after telling Janet he'll be in touch after one week and thanked her for this first talk. On his way out, he said:

"I'm so proud of our children. We're having the best time together, and they love you very much." He was eager to ask her for a hug but chickened out the last second. He waved goodbye and left.

On his way back to his hotel abode, Jim noticed the ego creeping in to alter his conscious mind and turn his thoughts to the outside realm of disappointment. He was aware of his ego's attempt to make him feel rejected. Jim scolded his ego and pushed its tricky games down, allowing a rise in his level of consciousness to overtake any attack by the false self. He turned his thoughts to gratitude that he at least succeeded in sitting down with Janet and showed her in person that he still cared for her well-being. He believed it was a good start, remembering the words of St. Francis of Assisi, who said: *"Start by doing what is necessary, then do what is possible, and suddenly you are doing the impossible."*

Jim did not feel he wasted his time visiting with Janet. He did what he thought was necessary, relying on the power of Love to speak on his behalf. He did what was possible, and he had faith in the Universe to eventually reveal the Truth, which is not impossible. He wished he could hug Janet, not because he pitied her, but to extend his sincere and loving arm to get her out of the sea of self-doubt and despair. She looked thin and desolate, and that motivated him to help her get rid of the demons in her mind.

He later sat at his desk and wrote a few words of gratitude before Brian's arrival at the scheduled meeting:

I thank you, God, for this opportunity to open a new door leading to a world of peace and harmony.

I am grateful to the reception I had from Janet and pray for her continued interest in communicating with me.

I am grateful for our children and their continued support to enliven the dormant power of Love in their mother's heart.

I am grateful to your silent guidance and the advice I receive from Charles and Brian.

I pray that Janet will open her heart to hear your Voice and rise above the shadows of her mind.

◆

Brian was eager to hear how the visit went with Janet, and Jim told him in detail. He also expressed his gratefulness that the visit took place and how he squashed the attempts by his ego to rule his mind with feelings of rejection.

"The thing is, Brian, I cannot feel rejected by Janet when I was the one who rejected her eight months ago and introduced the demons of sadness to her life! So, no, I'm grateful and do not feel rejected by her. I want to keep living in the present moment." Jim declared.

"Glad you brought this up, did you have a chance to start in the book I gave you, "The Power of Now" by Eckhardt Tolle?" Brian asked.

"No, not yet. Who is this author that I hear a lot about?" "Eckhardt Tolle, of German origin, now living in Vancouver,

Canada, had a depressing childhood and was hopeless until the age of 29 years old when he says he experienced a shift of consciousness. From that moment on, he dedicated his life to the principle of awareness and living in the present moment. His book, which you have was a best seller and inspired millions of people to change their lives. You will learn more about his message when you read the book."

"I will! What briefly is it about?" Jim asked

"The Now is all that you have. Whatever happened in the past or will happen in the future happened in the Now- the present moment. Work and accept the events of your life in the present moment, not against them.

All forms of fear are caused by future thoughts. And all forms of non-forgiveness are caused by too much past and not enough presence. He emphasizes silencing the thoughts of your mind and experience awareness within, it transcends time and space. Anyhow, you will enjoy it and apply more of what you've already done to grow spiritually." Brian explained briefly.

"I see! Thanks, I will delve in it starting tonight. Back to Janet, in the last chapter of Erroneous Zones, one characteristic of eliminating errors is to be independent, not dependent. How is Janet going to do that? She depended on me all her adult life!"

"I wouldn't be so presumptuous yet, Jim. People change, just like you have changed. She knows that if she does not want you back, she has to rely on herself, and that is independence. If I were you, I wouldn't assume that she wants you back because she couldn't survive independent of you. That's ego, not Love, talking. I'm sure you can wait another week and find out what she wants. You said it'll be alright one way or the other, so, stay the course!"

"You're right, Brian, I will focus on Love, not fear. Anyhow, I have a lot to apply from the lessons I learned from the book, in my everyday life. I need to be always aware of the ego's games and make sure he's not empowered to creep into my life again." Jim affirmed.

"Right! It is easier said than done. We're human, and mistakes will happen. The challenge is how to handle them not to stop them from happening. Dr. Dyer admits that not everybody can claim immediate success from reading the book. Consistent awareness is key to success, and if we fail, we can rise again."

Brian stayed for a short while, and they skipped dinner together that evening. Jim was eager to start reading the "Power of Now" and silence his mind with more thoughts about Janet.

♦

Jim was thoroughly immersed reading the first few pages of the first chapter, titled "You are Not your Mind." His cell phone rang at 9:30 pm, and Laura was on the other line.

"Hi Laura, is everything alright?"

"Yes, Dad, I just wanted to ask you about the talk with Mom, she wouldn't tell us, and I saw her crying an hour ago. What happened?"

"Oh, I wouldn't worry about it. The talk was short and went well. Janet told me she doesn't need to see the therapist anymore, and that she's not yet decided about me. I offered to help by being a good listener without any pressure. She asked me to give her a week to decide whether we can at least communicate by phone or in-person until she makes up her mind. I hope she would agree to that simple request. So, we'll see how she responds in one week."

"Are you okay with that, Dad?"

"I was a bit disappointed as a first reaction, but I got over it five minutes later. At least we talked, and that's what matters." Jim reassured her.

"Why then was she crying?" Laura asked.

"I don't know, I didn't say anything to hurt her feelings. It could be just a reaction to have seen me after such a long time. Maybe she misses me, who knows?" Jim said with a light laugh.

"I'm sure she does, I bet you she's still madly in love with you. You're the greatest, and she won't find a better man, ever!"

"Oh! You're so sweet, my dear! She should go out and try, I'm sure there are many better men out there."

"I'm sure she won't. She stopped seeing the other friend, and she prefers to sulk and suffer if you're not in her life."

"If so, this is wrong. She has a life to live. She should either forgive and forget the hurt I caused, or to get over me and go out to find someone she can fall in love with. I hate to see her suffering like this, and I'm not going to feel guilty about it anymore. I confessed my sins, and it's time for atonement now." Jim expressed his thoughts passionately.

"Fine, Dad, stay well, and we'll see you next Saturday. I love you!"

"I love you too, sweetheart. Please continue supporting Mom, and goodnight!"

Chapter 7

A New Vision

Jim had an interesting dream on Wednesday night after his return from the Center. He dreamt the big room at the Center was packed with no less than one hundred people, and all seats were taken. He saw people standing in the back, listening attentively to an inspiring speech by an Indian Guru about Inner Treasures of the Soul. Jim also saw himself at the podium, sharing his story of inner transformation to a multitude of listeners, eager to hear him speak. He remembered his dream vividly when he woke up and wondered what it meant.

He sat down with Charles in his office one evening and told him about the dream. Charles smiled and said he has similar dreams on occasion.

"What does this tell you, Charles?" Jim asked.

"It is a positive message that keeps encouraging me to expand our mission. I believe we have a unique spiritual platform that appeals to a large number of people searching for a different environment than traditional religions. There is a new wave of awareness and genuine interest in similar spiritual teaching like ours. This unconventional approach makes it easier to familiarize the members with non-denominational spiritual practices and encourages them to search within for their self-improvement and self-love. And, you, Jim, is an excellent example of that.

"I know we can grow and expand, but as I told you before, we need financial support and a fulltime leader to spearhead the expansion," Charles explained.

"Did you consider merging your ministry with another group of similar beliefs?" Jim asked.

"The closest that is non-denominational is the Center of Spiritual Living, a Religious Science Group that was started by Ernest Holmes, who wrote the well-known book "Science of Mind." It is said they have 400 churches across America now. We differ in that they focus more on the spiritual 'mindset,' whereas we believe that spiritual healing resides more in the heart and soul and less in mind."

"I see! Tell me then, since you've been contemplating this 'dream' of expansion, have you designed a specific plan on how to implement it?" Jim inquired.

"Yes, I did, I have it written down in a notebook which I keep here in my drawer. Do you want to see it?"

"Yes, Please! It would really help."

Charles pulled out the notebook and showed it to Jim. He saw five neatly hand-written pages. Jim flipped through the pages and noticed the organized sections, covering the objective and the strategy for its fulfillment. He looked at Charles and asked him if he could make copies of these pages to study calmly at home. Charles made the photocopies and gave them to Jim, delighted by his interest in looking into the project. Jim said he will revert with his remarks next week and left.

Jim ordered room service that evening. He read the contents of the expansions plan more thoroughly. Jim was impressed with Charles' train of thought and decided to reread it in a couple of days for further consideration. He wanted to spend the rest of the evening, reading more pages from the "Power of Now." He recalled reading a quote by the famous Russian writer Leo Tolstoy that said, *"There is only one time that is important – now! It is the most important time because it is the only time when we have any power."*

" Ironically, Jim was holding a book in his hand with a similar message that was inspired many decades before.

♦

The next day in the office, Jim asked Brian to brief him on the movements in the account dedicated to helping the injured crew members. Brian replied:

"If you recall, we start paying the monthly costs to sustain the two people who were severely disfigured, and considered disabled, within one month, when their disability insurance expires. The four who were not severely injured, and the other three who needed further treatment, were all hired back by the shipowners.

"So, other than the one-time donation to the one family, our commitment now we only help the families of the two disabled members. We can set aside one million dollars to cover their costs for the next ten years, and still have approximately two million dollars in the fund. I am investing the money in a secure interest-bearing account for now."

"Very good! Have we booked the profits from the two deals, as we discussed earlier?"

"Not fully yet, we should be able to complete the execution of the two contracts within the next two months. Given the fact that we don't need the whole three million dollars borrowed from the company reserve account, should I refund some of it?" Brian asked.

"No, don't, I may have other ideas in mind?" Jim replied.

"I see! Would they be additional donations to new projects?"

"I'll tell you soon, I'm not fully decided yet. I'll see you on Friday evening." Jim answered.

Brian wondered what Jim had in mind when he left his office, and discretely walked out.

◆

Jim couldn't wait to see Brian Friday at 6:00 pm to discuss the "Power of Now," which got him really excited. He liked how the author, E. Tolle, explains his message. Jim told Brian he didn't go to sleep until late last night as he didn't want to stop reading and contemplating the points raised in the first three chapters. He was thrilled that he read about seventy pages already with many underlined parts to remember.

"So happy to hear, Jim. What particular parts you remember the most." Brian asked.

" In a few words, how one can live more happily if he stops listening to his mind. This man was suicidal before he got enlightened and shifted to a higher level of consciousness. We can all be enlightened if we don't listen to our noisy thoughts. We can all taste the shift from a false identification of the old self to a true identification of who we truly are by the timeless conscious Presence in the Now." Jim said confidently.

"How impressive! Did you understand his guidance on how to experience such Presence?" Brian asked.

"Yeah, interesting how he prefers to use the term Presence, instead of the word God which to most people creates an image of an object, an old man with a white beard, as someone who is outside you vs. Presence which is inside you. He brilliantly explains how to free our self from shackles our mind and not listen to the useless thoughts of the past. When you do, he says, you feel liberated in the soul, and spacious awareness rises uplift you."

"How do you rise above your thoughts?" Brian asked. "Through stillness. You quiet your mind either by meditation or taking a walk in Nature, as an example. He does not say to stop thinking altogether, but to be aware of our thoughts and make sure they don't control us. He said the same thing about our emotions too."

"How did this relate to your love story with Janet?" Brian asked. "Ah-ha, now I see where you are going. I used to dwell on my past.

Now, I try to focus on the lessons I learned from my past with Janet." "Such as what, Jim?"

"Well, not to procrastinate when her deed disturbs me, such as taking me for granted and turning her back on my good suggestions. Another example, taking the kids on vacation, or to send them to a sports camp, stuff like that.

I allowed her to stop me from pursuing such plans. Then a price was paid that led me to leave. So why have such memories?"

"Don't you think that this kind of behavior will re-surface again if you're back together?" Brian asked.

"It's possible. I changed, and I will not tolerate negative behavior anymore, but I'm not sure if Janet can unless she miraculously changes too? I turned the telescope around as you know, I don't know if she's even aware that she has a 'telescope' to turn and look within?" Jim said.

"I bet you she will, sooner than you think, not by choice because that's what suffering does. She would reach a level where you have no choice but look inwardly with the telescope of life. Tolle experienced that himself as he wrote in the introduction of the book."

"Who knows, I'm going to see her again tomorrow, and she's supposed to tell me what she wants to do with us."

"Only if she's ready, Jim, and don't be disappointed if she doesn't give you a positive reply. She may enjoy seeing you suffer along with her, who knows because she still operates from an unconscious mind."

"That's her prerogative. Unconscious minds experience pain, but I will not experience pain anymore, I am consciously aware of who I am now, and I am developing strong faith in my true self to uphold me. Ego wants identification with pain, especially emotional pain, to keep us afraid and weak. Not me, my friend, thank heavens, I surpassed that." Jim spoke proudly.

"I hear you, but you know the famous words, 'the spirit is willing, but the flesh is weak.' We're not superhuman, and you still love Janet, let's see what she'd tell you tomorrow, and we go from there, step by step." Brian stated.

"What I am truly studying now is the third chapter of the book, about not allowing the mind to take over and to surrender to the power of the present moment. You see I'm used to rely heavily on my mind in business, and time was very precious to me. Now I'm learning that all this is an illusion, and the only thing that exists is the Now. That should be my daily practice, to evolve consciously and sense the joy of true being." Jim remarked.

"Excellent, I see how much you're enjoying this book and you'll enjoy it more and more as you continue reading it. It is a new spiritual dimension that's good for all of us to practice." Brian concluded.

"Thank you, Brian, to be continued! And I'll keep you advised with what goes on, both with Janet and with the book study." Jim said happily.

♦

After a lovely weekend with the kids, Jim drove them back home early afternoon on Sunday. Todd, his son, asked him if he was going to see his mother again. Jim replied:

"I hope so! She said she will let me know how she feels in one week, which is today."

"She's been acting strangely, all week. She paces around the rooms aimlessly, and she rarely talks or smiles. She's quite depressed, I think! What's wrong with her?" Todd asked again.

"It's a process, son! When something big happens in your life, different than what it used to be, it can be unsettling and makes you restless. I went through it in the beginning, but now it's gone." Jim explained.

"They say you can only rise after you hit bottom, and Mom must be going through that now." Laura intervened and said.

"That's true, but that should have happened earlier, shortly after I left. Now she's more confused because she has to decide whether she still wants to take me back. So, we'll see!" Jim said.

"What if she's stubborn and closes the door in your face? What would you do, Dad?" Todd asked.

"It's possible, and if she does, I'm okay now and will be okay always. I'm prepared to accept the possible and the impossible. If she doesn't want me back, I will still love her and wish her well."

"You're amazing, Dad!

"We're here now if I don't see you to say goodbye, I wish you a great week ahead, and I love you!" Jim told the kids while parking the car in the driveway.

They walked toward the main door, and Janet was there waiting to receive them. She kissed the kids and asked Jim to come in. Jim hugged the kids and said, "see you next Saturday."

◆

Jim had his glass of water and sat in his usual chair. They looked at one another and exchanged little smiles before they talked. Jim started and asked, "how was your week?"

"A lot of digging and shoveling still. I go through spells of ups and downs, feeling helpless and depressed. I don't remember having had such feelings before. I am often perplexed to tell you the truth. I can't decide what to do yet." Janet delivered her message with a slow and low voice.

"I understand what you're going through. I went through it too the first fourth month of living alone. Take a deep breath, feeling unsure about the next step, is part of your journey. There is no light without darkness first." Jim stated.

"What is this thing with your philosophical poetry nowadays?" Janet asked facetiously.

"I have a lot of free time, so I read a lot. Which reminds me of what the great poet Khalil Gibran said about being confused. He said, *"Perplexity is the Beginning of knowledge."* He also said, *"Sadness is but a Wall between Two Gardens."*

"What do these sayings mean?" Janet asked curiously.

"The first means basically that when we are down, there is only one way to go, up. Look at Perplexity as living in the dark and knowledge as the light. Or, we become wiser and learn from our mistakes. I like the second phrase even more. It means that whether we want to go right or left from where we stand now, there is a garden waiting for us. Again, sadness is dark;

the garden on each side is light. Darkness does not last forever, and the sun will always come out the next day. Is it clear now?" Jim explained poetically.

"Are you sure you don't want to drop the business and become a poet?" Janet said, somewhat sarcastically.

"It crosses my mind sometimes. Allow me to tell you what helped me a lot in the last two months. I made friends with a couple of spiritual friends, and we are all part of a small group called "Spiritual Community Center." I read self-help books, and I go to lectures and have regular discussions with Brian, my chief accountant, who introduced me to the whole thing. These people helped me a great deal. Perhaps you can find such a group around here?" Jim suggested.

"I appreciate what you say, and I truly would like to have a clear mind to guide me. I still have a lot to shovel out. I ask you to be patient, and we continue to visit for a while and hope for the best, okay?" Janet stated.

"I understand, and there is no rush. If there is anything I can do to help, please ask. I can recommend some books to read if you want, but the best is to find a spiritual person you can confide and hang out with." Jim suggested again.

"What books have you read?"

"The first one is "Your Erroneous Zones" by Dr. Wayne Dyer, and the second which I have not finished yet is "The Power of Now" by Eckhardt Tolle. I can write them down for you, and you can look them up online."

"Okay, I'll do that, the second one rings a bell because I heard him talk in one of Oprah's tv shows and she highly recommended him."

"I'm happy to hear you will consider reading these books. They are amazing."

"Well! This was a good visit, and we'll keep in touch. See you next Saturday." Janet said and stood up to usher him out with a handshake.

Jim looked up to the second floor from his car and saw the two kids waving at him from the window. He waved back with a smile and thumbs up before he drove away.

♦

Jim drove slowly back to the City. He wanted to contemplate the contents of the short visit he just had with his alienated wife, Janet. It's evident that she's still fighting a war with her ego and yet to decide whether to accept him back. Nevertheless, Jim noticed some Improvement with her attitude based on her tone of expression in the limited conversation they had. Jim thought she still needs more time, and he should not come to any conclusions prematurely.

At least, Jim had a chance to show Janet a glimpse of the spiritual transformation process he went through. He encouraged her to find a spiritual friend and recommended books for her to read. Janet was more amenable and open to positive ideas and did not appear to be as nervous. He figured that if True Love is his aspiration, then it is worth waiting for. Jim was still working on loving himself, and patience is a characteristic of love.

Though the unhappy days Janet had been going through affected her body language and added little wrinkles to her face, Jim found beautiful still. He wanted to help her. He remembered what Rumi said about helping a beloved soul to heal, *"Be a lamp, a ladder, and a lifeboat, and be a shepherd."*

Jim smiled, visualizing Janet delving into self-help books and seeking spiritual support from people she can find and trust. He paused and wondered if he's the one chosen to guide her? Perhaps destiny can map such a possibility for them to reunite under a new banner of true love, and grow together in the spiritual realm of harmony and peace?

♦

While Jim immersed in the basin of hope for a magical reunion with his wife and family, Janet was walking around the house with more smiles than tears this time. Jim's suggestions to read and seek spiritual support were jumping up and down in her mind.

The children noticed a different look on her face when they sat down around the dinner table that Sunday night. Laura couldn't stay silent and had to say something.

"You're looking different after Dad's visit, Mom, how did it go?" Janet looked at her daughter suspiciously and said,

"Well, I'm battling with the new image of your father, from the big businessman I knew to some sort of a spiritual guru I have a hard time understanding! This new image of him unsettles me. He's becoming too sweet and soft for my taste. I prefer his old rugged personality as a strong businessman. Now he's saying I should become spiritual like him, and suggesting books for me to read, and to find spiritual friends, blah… blah…blah, I don't know, it's not me, and I find this a bit bizarre coming from him!" Janet said what's on her mind, though it sounded strange. At least she did speak, instead of remaining silent as she used to.

"You don't have to be like him, Mom. He's still running his business anyhow quite well, but he wants a different peaceful personal life that balances his business headaches and keeps him connected to his inner self. I wish we can all be like him! It's so much more enjoyable to be around him nowadays than before. Anyhow, if you're not comfortable with it, tell him so, and let the chips fall where they may." Laura expressed her opinion without reserve. Todd was quiet, listening to stuff he couldn't fully understand. All he wanted was to see his father back at home. He was the 'ironman' in whose image he wanted to grow.

"Anyhow, I told Jim I needed more time, and he didn't seem to mind. He said there is no rush." Janet stated.

"That's exactly what I mean! Where can you find a man that would be as considerate and patient as Dad has been? He confessed his wrongdoing to you and asked for your forgiveness. Others walk away and never look back, or give ultimatums, put their foot down, scream and then leave, but not Dad. He's a gem of a man, please do not underestimate the advantage of his spiritual pursuits." Laura said.

♦

"Why don't you marry him?" Janet said, facetiously.

"I would, in a second, if he were not my father. A man like him is rare to find, Mom. He's my idol for the type of man I want to be with. The separation between you for the past several months did a wonderful job on him. He's a much better person now that you've ever known before. Please wake up and smell the roses." Laura was on a roll with her courageous delivery. Todd got enthused, he stepped in and said,

"I agree with Laura, Mom. I love Dad much more than I did before. He's not as weak and soft as you think he is. This spiritual thing he's into has made a strong man, stronger than his personality as a businessman."

"Okay, guys, I heard enough. I'm glad you love him, but please don't hate me for my procrastination. You have to give me the benefit of the doubt. It's my life, after all! If I can't trust him, how can I love him again? That's my battle, and I need to sort it out if I can." Janet expressed her stand.

"Fine, take your time, and let's hope for the best," Laura said.

Jim was back in his hotel suite, reading while waiting for Brian to show up at 6:00 as planned. He learned about the delusion levels of uncon-sciousness and how to shift to a shining level of consciousness. He noted how to always look inside and observe traces of fear caused by unpleasant thoughts and emotional feelings.

Brian was punctual, as usual. Jim briefed on the visit with Janet and said,

"Janet hasn't decided whether to take me back or not. Her reception was cordial and asked for more time. I told her I'm not in a rush, it is her decision and her life to think about. I used the opportunity to recommend that she reads the two books you gave me and to look for some spiritual friends in the area that can support her. I'm not sure she'll follow through.

"She's not eager to understand the difference between spirituality and religion, and she's not religious at all. Anyhow, I felt better to impress upon her the transformation I'm going through, and perhaps this will help her to step out from her confusion and awaken to a new level of higher consciousness."

"This is going to be a good test for your patience level," Brian said. "I'm aware of that, and I won't let it bother me. I'll keep busy working on myself. Thanks again for the book that I'm truly enjoying. I finished Chapter four and ready to get into the next one."

"What stood out from what you recently read?"

"I understand better the delusion of unconsciousness and the shift to conscious awareness into the now. I also noted not to resist the continued attempts when ego attacks. Just simply observe with awareness what the ego is trying to do and rise above it.

"What I appreciated, in particular, was his clarification about the purpose in life that it does not refer to a future journey but to the inner purpose which can be found by living in the present moment, where fulfillment resides. I was touched when he said that the outer purpose of achieving success will ultimately fail because it is not permanent. He quoted when Jesus talked about rich on the outside and poor on the inside. *"You gain the world but lose your soul."* I know I don't want to lose my soul!"

"Anything else?" Brian asked.

"Yes, I have an idea to discuss with you, but before I forget, I want to add how simply Mr. Tolle defined the 'power of now' as the 'power of Presence' that liberates us from our thought-forms.

"Now, I don't know if Charles told you that he and I met and discussed the expansion plans he has in mind for the Center?"

"No, he didn't."

"Okay, maybe he wanted to keep it private for the time being. He had detailed notes about his plan and his strategy and gave me copies to review. The method may need some tweeting here and there, but mostly, it is good. The key to its implementation requires money, which the Center does not have.

"Charles would like the growth to be in three phases, and phase one is to branch out in three major cities: Chicago, Denver, and Los Angeles. He proposes to hire a fulltime leader to spearhead the growth and a budget of not less than two million dollars for phase one to complete within two years from now. The other two phases to follow in sequence after that with an ultimate plan to reach ten Centers all together, including New York. What do you think? Jim explained briefly.

"I think it's a great idea, and we are all aware in the Center that he has a plan, but you know better than us since you have seen the details. What do you think, Jim?"

"I'm not advanced in the knowledge of your mission as you guys are, but I'm all for it as long as it does not become a huge organization that eventually loses its essence, as many others have before. Otherwise, I'm in favor, which brings me to my question to you about donating the money from our fund. It is sitting there doing nothing, and you're keeping one million as a reserve for the disabled ones anyhow. Why not donate that to the expansion of the mission?"

Brian didn't believe what he just heard, at up and told Jim, "If you were a woman, I would jump up and kiss you. What an amazing idea? Yes, we have the money, and I'm sure we will succeed in attracting many followers in these three cities. Who will spearhead the project is the question. We're all busy with our jobs, and we need someone who understands the goal of our mission." Brian remarked.

"How about you?" Jim quickly asked.

"Me? I work for you, remember? Besides, I am not an expert like Charles and his original partners, they are the visionaries."

"Brian, firstly, don't underestimate yourself. Secondly, you'll be guaranteed the same income you now make, and thirdly, you are available, you have no family, and you are a great speaker. So, what do you say?" Jim asked with a big smile.

"Wow, you are throwing a bomb at me now. I need to think about it." Brian said.

"Let me know soon because I promised to get back to Charles this week. You have twenty-four hours, okay?"

"Jim, you know this job entails a lot of traveling, what will happen to our meetings together?"

"You'll still have your home base here, and we can meet when you are back from your trips. Brian, I don't know anyone else that can do a better job, and you know how much I trust you and respect you. So, think hard and let me know, please. Thank you!"

"Fine, I'll sleep on it, you… you, trouble-maker!" They both laughed before Brain left to go home. Jim gave him the copies to read overnight.

Chapter 8

Expansion vs. Diminishing Hopes

Jim had an eventful Sunday. He sat behind his desk and wrote:

I Realize the sky in my mind may not always be clear, and thoughts of uncertainty may cloud the sunlight of my days and cover the shining moon of my nights. I seek Presence in stillness to remove these clouds and restore the light to my life.

I chose to take this road and invited my alienated wife to walk it with me. I'm not asking her to walk the path for me, but with me.

Her unfavorable decision will not take away my inner peace. The cure to her pain is within the pain. She needs to hear its message from within her soul.

I pray she'll be guided to connect with the center of her Being to know who she truly is, and to find what she really wants.

Despite my patience to wait, I now ask myself, if she suddenly says she'll take me back, would that be sufficient? Will she accept to join me on the road I already chose for my spiritual awakening?

Is it meant for us to remain apart and if she chooses not to abide with me in the same spiritual realm? I will continue to be kind and compassionate, but then I will not succumb to her outer and shallow choices of living.

He went into the silence for a few minutes, then closed his journal and went to bed, feeling one with himself.

♦

Early in the morning of the following day, Jim received a call from Laura, sobbing, and Jim asked her what was going on.

"I had an argument with Mom last night, and I don't think she's ready to take you back. She said she doesn't trust you, so how can she love you again."

"That's alright, my dear, you don't need to cry for that reason. Mom is still confused and needs more time." Jim said to reassure Laura.

"More time for what? She is so blind she cannot see how great you are! All she cares about is how to be revengeful and unforgiving. Todd and I want you back, Dad! This house without you has no life anymore. Isn't there something you can do to change her mind?" Laura pleaded.

"Sweetheart first, let me tell you I am always there with you in spirit. Second, and if your Mom refuses to look within her soul and find True Love and Inner peace to transform her life, I am not so sure I would want to share the rest of my life with a non-spiritual unconscious partner.

"This thought crossed my mind last night, and I am at peace with it. As it is said, 'you can take the horse to the water, but you can't force him to drink.' I gave her a chance, and I hope she awakens soon; otherwise, I will set her free to live the way she wants. It may not be ideal in the short term, but it would be better for all of us in the long run." Jim said, affectionately.

"I cannot imagine living here without you in case you two don't get back together. You have to find a solution, Dad. I don't have the nerve to tolerate this continued procrastination much longer." Laura said, while still sobbing.

"Sweetheart, calm down, of course, we'll find a solution. The Truth will prevail and show us the way. Relax and go to school now. You can call me any time you like. I love you and try to be supportive for a while longer, my love."

"Okay, Dad. I love you, too, and we'll talk soon!" ♦

Around noon on Monday, Brian asked to see Jim for a few minutes. He walked in, carrying the copies of the plan in one hand and a happy smile on his face.

"So, what's the verdict, Brian?"

"Briefly, and other things being equal, I believe this is my calling! I'm ready, and I feel this is the real purpose why I'm here on this planet."

"This is great! I knew you would find the courage to take on this task. You are the perfect man for the job. What are some of your concerns?"

"Nothing that cannot be modified. I will not take more of your time now. There are minor changes to the strategy, which can be discussed with Charles when we see him."

"Good, please arrange for a meeting today or tomorrow after work. I'm pleased with your decision, thanks!"

Brian called Charles, and they agreed to meet today at 6:15 pm. He informed Jim, who said they'll walk over together.

◆

Charles was waiting for them in his office when they arrived. Jim started:

"You may ask why Brian is with us for this meeting. After reviewing the plan copies you gave me, the thought crossed my mind that Brian would be the right person to spearhead the expansion program. He would be a good representative of the mission. He is knowledgeable, bright, and diligent, and we all trust him.

"He happens to be managing a non-profit fund I created that has a balance of about two million dollars that I would like to donate toward the branching out plan. I would like you to consider both the money and Brian as one package proposal. I discretely asked Brian last night to consider and review the plan overnight, and this morning he agreed with great enthusiasm. So, what do you say?"

Charles was pleasantly surprised to hear this presentation from Jim, and without further contemplation, he immediately said:

"This is an amazing proposal; how can I say no to both your generous contribution and the best guy for the job?" He stood up and shook their hands and then continued,

"But Brian is your chief accountant, you would not mind seeing him leave his work?" Charles asked. Jim right away responded,

"Oh, I was going to fire him anyhow!" Jim said and looked at Brian's face that turned pale for a few seconds, then Jim laughed and said: "it is easier to find an accountant than to find the ideal man for this mission." Brian's face relaxed, and Jim was kidding.

"I don't know if you were serious for a minute!" Brian said.

"Okay, good! I am happy to see that we all agree. I leave the details to be sorted out between the two of you, and God bless!"

"Before you go Jim, any news from the home front?"

"No fundamental change, Brian knows the latest he can brief you. I am eager to go to the hotel, eat some salad, and continue reading Mr. Tolle's book.

They shook hands, and he walked out with a jovial bounce.

◆

Jim had his notebook ready to write down the highlighted points of the chapter on the state of Presence.

- You are in a heightened state of Presence when you are free of thought.

- You experience Presence when you are present, in the state of no-mind.

- You experience Presence in the gap between thoughts or when you see the essence of beauty in formed objects.

- When you experience Presence, your core Being becomes conscious of itself.

- Presence is enlightened consciousness, not identified with physical or mental forms.

- Stillness, or meditation in silence, is a reliable carrier of Presence.

- Christ is your God-essence or the Higher Self, which is your awakened divinity. Christ is not a personalized identity.

- Presence is One, not mine, or yours though collectively, it generates an intense energy field.

Jim had some questions to ask Brian about Presence when they meet in two days on Wednesday. He took a small break from reading and contemplated how Brian appeared in his life and helped him to become spiritual and how this led to his acceptance to spearhead the centers' expansion program. This clarified the real momentum of evolution in the realm of spirituality. How one good thing leads to another good or better idea. Jim felt grateful that he could help out financially, it made the fruit of his hard work for many years more meaningful and worthwhile.

After the brief break, Jim went back to read and take notes from this inspiring and practical book. He read the first couple of pages twice to try to understand the relationship between the body and the realm of Being.

- Being cannot be explained to the human mind as water cannot be explained to the fish.

- Being is the ever-present *'I Am,'* the invisible that has no name or form.

- Being is a state of enlightenment that frees us from the illusions of the body and mind. It frees us from fear and suffering and liberates us from being captives of the mind.

- Feel your inner body and transcend beyond the limitations of the outer body.

- Use your inner body as a bridge to connect your outer identity with your essence identity, your True Self.

Jim had to stop before finishing the chapter as it was getting late, and he needed to digest these new lessons he was learning to figure out how to apply them in his daily life.

♦

Jim woke up at 7:00 am the next morning feeling good after a peaceful sleep. He took a shower, and while still drying up, his phone rang. He ran to answer with his towel around his waist. It was his daughter Laura,

"What is it, sweetheart?"

"Sorry to bother you so early. Mom had an emotional outburst last night during dinner, and it scared both Todd and me. We remained calm but couldn't understand why she was so angry for no reason we could tell? I asked if her anger had to do with us, and she said no, "it all has to do with your father." I asked her to elaborate, and she loudly said,

"He wants me to read self-help books and hum… find a spiritual teacher and stuff like that. I don't want to do these things, and I don't like the fact that he pretends to be spiritual himself.

"I told her that you're not pushing her to do these things and that you are not pretending to be spiritual, you are who you are! So, it is getting worse, Dad, what should we do?"

"Laura, my dear, this is to be expected from someone struggling with a request to change certain aspects of her character. Her perception of me is giving her mood swings because she thinks I have a dual personality now: the businessman and the spiritual man. She does not understand that they are both merged into one. I am who I am, even during the full business hours. My staff noticed the change, and they admire me manifold now.

"Anyhow, back to your Mom, her outburst is caused by a behavior change, created by her perplexed thoughts and mixed up feelings. It is a temporary divergence of suffering, we hope, could be the step before her eventual awakening. Janet is still frustrated, angry, and hurt. She needs time to develop enough strength to face the facts of life and make the right decision. Then, and only then, can she stop having these mood swings, and get rid of the fears that she's bottled up with."

"You always see things from a positive angle, Dad, and I hope you are right. It is easier for you to assess her situation from a distance, but we live here, and she's becoming unpredictable. Anyhow, thanks for hearing me out, and it's always good to talk to you. Have a great day!" Laura said.

"I love you guys and keep in touch!"

Jim dried up and got dressed while still thinking about Laura's call. *He pondered the words that registered the most about Janet's refusal to read self-help books and seek spiritual guidance. He wondered if that was a short statement caused by anger or a definite stand to close the door to her inner transformation. He never asked her to do this for his sake, but for her own sake, regardless of where she stands about a possible reunion.*

Besides, Jim thought, *Janet had no right to judge him for his choice of a spiritual path. This is unconscious behavior on her part, created by her ego, and he refuses to be drawn into it. If she cannot see that love can join them together in the 'Now,' into a state of Being, beyond the human form, then it could be better for both to live separate lives. Love to Jim is to intensely feel the Presence of the One Life, which is God within.*

♦

Brian met with Jim in the office and briefed him on the discussion he had with Charles. "The plan is to trigger the implementation in three months. We changed the three cities in phase one closer to us now. They are Philadelphia, Miami, and Chicago in that order. We will search for candidates to interview and recruit. I will submit my three months' notice and tender his resignation. Michael and I would recruit a replacement to take my position, or promote from within, we five accountants in the firm."

Brian then asked Jim how he's coming along with the book, and Jim said he has a few questions to discuss on Wednesday. Jim changed the subject and told him, "my daughter, Laura, called me twice to say that her mother is throwing fits of anger and frustration."

"What do you mean?" Brian asked.

"Janet, who had been silent, not expressing her feelings to the children before, is now bursting with angry emotions ever since I started visiting her. She told the children that she rejects to read self-help books or to look for a spiritual teacher. And she also thinks I am pretending to be a spiritual man."

"As you know, it's going to be a challenge for you to control your calm and not go on the defensive. The ego would love for you to defend yourself, but I'm sure you are aware you will not give the ego a chance to turn your open and loving attitude into a negative attack. You will remain conscious." Brian stated.

"I understand, but in the end, if she wants to continue being unconscious, I will not let her drag me into her realm. As you very well know, oil and water do not mix. I will see her again this week, and I will be consistent with who I am, and I will relinquish any judgment about what she said to the children."

"That sounds good, I will see you on Wednesday!

♦

The meeting on Wednesday focused on few points besides the clarification Brian gave to Jim regarding the state of Presence and how it is the same as Being or pure consciousness.

The discussion shifted to the fact that if you shut your mind, it does not mean that you stop using it. When you are in the present moment, the mind is creative and free from the thoughts of the past. You can plan and create as you please but with awareness to keep the ego out of the process. With stillness, the mind will be fresh and creative as you learn how to think, not with your head but with the whole body.

Brian then asked Jim what he thought about the art of listening. "One should listen not only with his mind but also to feel the energy field of the inner body, where stillness resides. This way, you give the other person space to be. When you are in the state of Being, you can then feel the state of Being of the person you're listening to. I will practice this when I listen to Janet. Her mind is running her life now, and with Presence, I can ease her conflict and strife in her current situation."

"Very well said! Pray that she will soften her stance and calm down her prejudice toward spirituality." Brian said.

"I know I'll be gentle and kind, I leave the rest to the universe to decide."

"Excellent!"

"Now, any idea of how you plan to fish for candidates?" Jim asked. "There is a Center for Spiritual Living in Philadelphia. I will start there and see what I can find. I may have to visit more than a couple of times to befriend the people and ask around."

"You know you will be missed by the company. The staff associates us already as spiritual brothers. I am grateful for the continued growth of our business without working under the stress and intensity I experienced previously. This proves the soft power of aware consciousness is a free present around the clock, regardless of where we are or do." Jim concluded.

"By the way, I heard Charles talking to his first partners about offering you the position of honorary chairman."

"I don't want any acknowledgment of this kind. That's very kind, but I do what my inner Being inspires me and what my soul guides me to do. Giving is from the heart, and the joy it gives me is my great reward."

♦

Jim picked up the children for the weekend as planned. They looked forward to spending their time with their father, away from the dark moments at home.

"We really enjoy being with you, Dad." Young Todd said. "Me too, Son! I hope you guys are experiencing an improved environment at home!"

"Not really! Mom has some quiet moments, but she rarely smiles and sometimes gets mad at us for no reason." Todd complained.

"She projects the inner battles of her mind on us, mainly to vent out her frustration, not to hurt us, because she quickly apologizes after her outbursts." Laura clarified.

"I am certain that this uncomfortable experience you're going through will normalize soon. We all have to be patient and support Mom lovingly. She will eventually awaken from her slumber and learn how to mute the aggressive spouts of her ego." Jim explained.

"What do you mean, Dad?" Todd wanted to know.

"The battles in her unconscious mind restrict her vision to see clearly because she's empowered by the ego that is controlling her thoughts and deeds. Ego loves resistance and conflict, and that is what distorts your mother's true identity. You know she loves you and does not mean to hurt you. But she gets over-ruled by the ego that induces her emotional outbursts.

"I encouraged her to read certain books and find a spiritual teacher to help her silence the attacks generated by her ego and live in peace. I will continue to do so despite her refusal so far. Why? Because she keeps listening to the voice of her ego."

"I see! What I don't understand is that you can be her best teacher to live in peace again. Why doesn't she realize that and welcome you back at home?" Todd asked.

"I don't know! So far, she doesn't even want to admit that I am spiritual myself. She thinks I'm fake, and that makes it difficult for her to cooperate.

We'll have another talk on Sunday, and let's have fun meanwhile." Jim was eager to change the subject.

♦

Jim and the two children had a great time as usual, and they were reluctant to go back home. He drove them back and parked the car in the driveway and walked them to the door. Janet greeted them and asked Jim to go in.

"How was your week?" Jim asked his long-faced wife.

"Not so good, perhaps the kids told you about my occasional outbursts!" Jim remained silent and wanted her to do the talking. Janet continued,

"I find these short discussions we have together disturbing my state of mind in a negative. You are asking me to change the way I live, I won't. I'm not interested in your suggestions to read self-help books or seek spiritual help. I don't need that, I have a great mind, and I am not weak in the heart, like you." Janet said.

"I'm happy to hear you're so strong. If I understood you correctly, you have no interest in what I say, or even who I am, as a changed person. That's fine, it is your prerogative. As I said earlier, I am *Not* trying to change you. You are who you are and free to choose your own thoughts and deeds. You mentioned that these meetings irritate you, are you suggesting that we put them on hold?" Jim said calmly knowing that her ego is till ruling her mind.

"Perhaps, we should. I still need more time to decipher the course of action that is best for me. You go on with your spiritual life, and I go on with mine, if that is okay with you!" Janet said with a glimpse of sarcasm about Jim's 'spirituality.'

"Okay, that is fine! I'll be around if you change your mind. I just would like to say I still believe you can unburden yourself from the pain you're still carrying. Just try to turn the telescope of your life towards your inner self. Your pain will disappear, and your suffering will end, by your inner power. That's all I wanted to say! I thank you again for seeing me, and I hope to hear from you soon." Jim said calmly, with a gentle, happy smile on his face before he stood up to leave.

"Please, don't tell me what to do, or not do. I don't need your help to know who I am and what I want from my life."

"I hear you I won't bother you anymore. The ball is in your court. All the best!"

Jim drove back wearing a vicious smile, but feeling disappointed, nevertheless. He had hoped Janet would have been more amenable to follow his advice. She was still mired by the grip of her ego, holding her hostage for her lack of interest. He surrendered her case to the Universe and determined to continue on his own journey of spiritual awakening. His main concern was the impact of Janet's stubborn procrastination on the children. They were being dragged into the shadows of her suffering for no fault of their own. They wanted him to find a solution, but how?

Jim later met with Brian and shared his disappointment. He reiterated the apparent possibility that they will not re-unite again. Brian remained silent and could not comment on his concern about the children. Jim thought they could eventually move in with him, but that would appear selfish, and create a huge war with Janet. The only solution was to continue being patient and hope for a miracle that would awaken Janet.

He then discussed chapter seven in the book, that explains the different portals that lead from the manifested bodily forms, or objects, to the unmanifested, invisible forms, be it deep inside the body, or surrender, or silence and meditation.

Before Jim went to sleep, he meditated and with an energized mindset, he wrote,

> *May my frustration and disappointment diminish to see Janet's suffering from emotional pain diminish as well.*

> *May her reversed feelings of love not burden me or alter my prayer for her to find God's Love.*

> *May my concern about the children be dismissed by seeing Janet's awareness to seek the Light.*

> *May the strength within me restrict me from compromising my chosen path or get affected by her unconscious behavior.*

> *May her stonewalling me be reversed to understand the Truth, not directed by revenge or disappearing love.*

> *May I be inspired to find whatever unknown possibility yet unrevealed, to soften Janet's stance and open her heart to the realm of happiness.*

> *May I find the way to assure our children they're alright regardless what Mom decides to do.*

> *May I find the strength to tolerate feelings of rejection should Janet refuse to re-unite with me in marriage.*

> *May I be the first to bless her decision and not judge the choice for her life journey.*

Chapter 9

Silence and New Developments

Two months went by with no word or favorable decision made by Janet Mayden. She became loyally enslaved by her ego, accustomed to the dim light in the dark chambers of her mind. Suffering is generally perceived as standard to many, becomes just a practice to survive. Janet shunned away and turned down all attempts by her loved ones to snap out of her reclusive life of despair, and move into the garden of hope and light, but to no avail.

Jim could not understand Janet's silence and her preference to self-imprisonment and self-pity. He found it hard to cope with his children's constant complaints about their mother's mood and closed personality. He sent Janet loving letters and suggestions to see a marriage counselor together, but she remained silent without comment. The ego tried to seduce him to react with anger, but Jim did not allow it to succeed. He consistently manifested true love toward his children, and that helped them to sustain their devotion to their mother. The odd vibrations they carried with them from home turned into waves of love from their father.

Neither Jim nor Janet brought up the subject of divorce, as a final decision to stay apart. A big void of communication prevailed and created a valley of awkward silence, that distanced the hope for reconciliation. Neither

Jim nor Janet had any interest in pursuing new relationships with others. Janet bathed in a sea of misery and abstained from socializing, while Jim was happy honoring his revised wish to remain patiently loyal.

Summer school vacation was near, and the children begged their father to move in with him. Jim insisted that Janet had to approve as it may not be wise to leave her alone in her current depressed condition.

◆

Meanwhile, Jim advanced well spiritually. He read several other self-help books and articles about modern spirituality. He took advantage of Brian's fulltime presence before shifting his attention to launch the branching-out campaign. One of the senior accounts was promoted to take his place as chief accountant, and the staff gave Brian an honorable farewell party.

Jim was more deeply involved in the expansion program for the community spiritual centers. His business savvy contributed good ideas to the plan. He appreciated the brotherly love received from the members at the Center, and Charles considered him his mentor. Jim's company continued to grow successfully, and the only glimpse of stress he felt was from the home front, and the condition of his alienated wife, Janet.

One morning, Jim, while busy working with his work in the office, unexpectedly received a call from Janet.

"Hello Jim, we need to talk!" Janet said, coldly.

"Okay! How have you been, is everything alright? Jim responded. "As I said, we need to talk!"

"Fine with me, when?"

"Today, if possible, I can come to the city, and we meet for lunch in the French restaurant close to your office," Janet suggested.

"Okay, I'll meet you there at 12:30 pm."

Jim asked his assistant to book a quiet table for two at his favorite restaurant, then sat back, wondering what does Janet have in mind? Will she ask him to come back home or start a divorce case? Five minutes later, he went back to his work without feeling stressed and told himself to relax, and he'll know why in two hours.

♦

When Jim walked into the restaurant, he saw Janet seated at a table in a quiet corner. It had been three months since he saw her last. She looked thin and well-dressed with make-up on her face that accentuated her good looks. With a gentle smile, she greeted Jim, who sat on the chair across from her.

"I'm glad you wanted to talk, here I am, all ears!" Jim started.

"Thank you for agreeing to see me. I have given what I am about to say a great deal of deliberation and thought. I want to end this relationship. I suffered enough from my inability to forgive or forget your breach of our vows. And, I am not prepared to follow your advice to seek spiritual help. It's good you chose that path, but it is not for me. So, I hope we can figure out an amicable modification to our relationship, bearing in mind the welfare of our two great children we love." Jim listened carefully, and though he expected Janet's decision, he was surprised. After a short pause, he smiled and said,

"I hear you, though sad, it has become clear that you now prefer we go our separate ways. I had hoped you would find a way to save our marriage, but your forthright request explains it differently. Perhaps, we are destined to live apart. I respect your decision and I will not beg you to change your mind. The challenge before us is to implement this situation in a friendly and loving manner. I can go along provided we don't start with a legal divorce proceeding and leave it to lawyers to mess things up. We can pursue our discussions spiritually." Jim responded calmly.

"What is this spiritual thing you keep bringing up?" Janet remarked. "People call it civil I call it spiritual. Meaning: to reach a settlement agreement in a responsible and just manner without anger or greed, and without the involvement of lawyers until we agree and tell them what to write. Is that a clear way that explains what I meant?"

"Yes, I understand! How do you suggest we proceed?" Janet asked. "First, we inform the children together. Either we take them out to dinner, or more privately at home. We underline the friendly manner we discussed, which should put them at ease, knowing we will continue to be friends. Second, you may want to write down on a piece of paper what you believe you need to continue having a good life based on our joint custody of the children until they reach eighteen. Third, you and I to agree on major decisions related to their education, summer vacations, and visiting rights. How about that?" Jim enumerated.

"It sounds okay, to me. When do we start?"

"How about informing them first when I bring them back on Sunday afternoon? Then you and I will continue talking, and if ready, you may give me the list of the things you want. Do you agree to proceed peacefully and lovingly now?"

"I do, can I order some salad now? I'm starving." Janet asked with a genuine smile.

"With pleasure!"

◆

Jim had a meeting with Charles and Brian at the Center to discuss some central ideas regarding the expansion when he also told them about the meeting he had with Janet.

"Many of us here have gone through a divorce, some ugly yet some friendly. It is good you are on a friendly path. Don't get too disappointed; there are no perfect relationships. The line between love and hate is very thin, and the difference between pleasure and pain is getting wider. You can only pray that she would awaken from her worldly dreams in due course!" Charles remarked.

"At least we agreed to be civil about the process, and I wish her all the best," Jim affirmed.

"How about the children?" Brian asked.

"We agreed we meet with them this Sunday and assure them of our friendly break-up. They might be relieved to see the end of pain is near, who knows?" Jim reacted.

"I remember the words of Khalil Gibran, who said, *"let there be a moving sea between the shores of your souls…And the oak tree and the cypress grow not in each other's shadow."* These words also prove that there are two independent souls in every relationship, and the only thing that lasts forever is the soul." Brian said, eloquently.

"Have you been to Philadelphia yet?" Jim asked.

"Yes, twice already, and I am befriending the minister of the Living Center there, he seems willing to leave the church. I heard him complain about the red tape in their organization, which restricts his freedom. I will see him again next week. I am also discretely looking for a place to rent. It's exciting!"

"Brian, you've been handling my accounts, I may need your help to update me, please. I need to figure out how to respond to Janet's future demands."

"No problem, I have him on my private laptop. I'll print out a copy and hand it to you soon."

"Jim, I meant to ask you if you would be interested in sharing your experience with the members one day, many still don't know you and eager to hear your story firsthand," Charles asked

"What do you want me to say?"

"What you do and how you experienced the transformation and shift in your consciousness! I believe it could inspire many." Charles replied.

"I'll think about it and will let you know. I'm a private person, normally. This group is different, though."

"Fine, I look forward to hearing from you. Meanwhile, stay cool, you hear?"

"I will! See you guys later!"

◆

Jim went to his hotel, aware of disturbing thoughts created by the after-shock of Janet's decision to end the marriage. The creeping ego of his mind wanted to play, but Jim would not let him take control. He wrote,

Life's garden has now revealed the truth. Some of it shines with livelihood, while the other side is withering from fear. The gift of life, as manifested by the work of man, can only be appreciated when we sense the unmanifested hand of creation behind its beauty.

Our limitation of failure, loss, or pain could turn out to be a great teacher to let go of our false self-image and ego-dictated desires.

I do not see the cross-roads designed by Janet as an unfavorable wind blowing in my face. The in-depth lesson concealed within it is real and positive. There is always a higher good in every event; there is no good or evil in life. The pain grows when forgiveness is rejected.

The sight of Peace becomes blurred when not viewed beyond what is happy or unhappy. There is always deep serenity underneath the sadness, and the sun still appears after the storm.

I accept the decision by Janet for us to be apart, woven by threads of destiny that cater to our needs. I relinquished resistance and adopted the power of forgiveness to arrive at inner Peace and dwell in my Being-con-

sciousness. I do not judge Janet for not following suit. She has different lessons to learn and now awaits the right time.

Through forgiveness, I recognize the useless values of the past, and I allow the present moment to transform me within and without. Being one with my true self is my reward, and it empowers me to withstand the storms of this impermanent life. All formed objects I have will not last, and as Jesus said, "the treasures of this earth will not last, and will be eaten by moth and rust."

I am determined to smoothly go through this process of marriage farewell and open a new door to our friendship. I will be fair and considerate, with no grudge or judgment. I will reassure the children with our love though we share different roofs for our shelter. I will move on carrying the flag of love and peace to all.

◆

Jim went to pick up Laura and Todd on Saturday morning. Janet was standing near the door. She asked Jim if he could stay for dinner when he brings them back to pursue their talks, and Jim agreed.

"What was that all about, Dad?" Laura was curious to know.

"Your Mom and I talked, and she offered to include me at the dinner table with you tonight."

"Cool, are you guys going back together then?" Todd asked.

"Not necessarily Todd, it is a nice gesture on her part; that's all! We will enjoy another weekend together and discuss where you would like to go on vacation with me, now that school will be over in two weeks. How about that?" Jim smartly changed the subject.

"Yay! A vacation together?" Todd asked

"We need to clear it with Mom first. Anyhow, we have time. Meanwhile, you can think about where you want to go, and we discuss it." Jim said.

"Can we go see a movie this afternoon?" Lura asked.

"Of course, as long as it is PG13. I am not allowed other ratings! Right, Todd?"

"I know what Laura has in mind, it's okay, Dad!"

Another weekend to remember, and it passed quickly with a lot of fun and laughter.

When they drove back and entered the house, the children were so happy their father was having dinner with them. It was close to 6:00 pm, and Janet was getting the table ready in the dining room. Jim could smell the aroma of the roast beef, a specialty he missed.

◆

They sat around the table shortly after, and there were smiles all around. The dinner was delicious, and after the second course, Jim looked at Janet and noticed her readiness to talk.

"Children, may I have your attention, please? Dad and I have some news to tell you. He and I had a productive meeting in the city earlier this week, and we have come to terms with our future relationship. I told him that we should be friends and not continue to live together as a couple. You are our main priority, and though your Dad will not be living with us, he can come to see you anytime he wishes." Janet said, and Laura cut her off,

"Are you two getting a divorce?"

"We don't call it a divorce, sweetheart! It is an agreement to live apart because we both have changed and chose a different path for our life. Your Mom is not comfortable with my spiritual interests, and I'm not interested to go back to the way I used to live. So, we agreed to move on independently, but we will continue to hold one another in great esteem, and you will always be loved even more." Jim helped Janet out.

"There is no way to reconcile?" Laura asked while Todd was sitting quietly in shock.

"We both tried and tried, but we couldn't honestly find a compromise that would satisfy both of us," Jim said.

"Listen, please don't hold it against me, I initiated the request to be apart. It is time to move on for me, I want to find myself again, and I am grateful to have known your father all these years. He's truly a great man, but on a different path now. I ask that you please forgive me if I hurt your feelings. I'm sorry!" Janet admitted.

"You're asking us to forgive you, and you refused to forgive Dad, who confessed to you down on his knees. I find this to be quite selfish, don't you think?" Laura reacted.

"But Laura, my dear, I didn't leave you as he did, I didn't break the marriage vows as he did. I accepted all of that now, the reason I wanted out. He dared to forgive himself and rise above his wrongdoing. I don't have such courage to forgive and forget, and that is why I prefer to live alone. We're both okay with this change, isn't it, Jim?" Janet explained.

"Honestly, I would have preferred to be back home if you had agreed to choose a spiritual path with me. Mom tried, but couldn't go along with it, so I have no other choice but to succumb to this change in our relationship. I cannot deviate from the path I chose, and yes, I am okay with Mom's different choices. At least, your Mom and I will be good friends, and our priority is to continue loving and taking care of you." Jim elaborated.

Todd excused himself to go to his room and hugged his father before he left. Laura was sad her parents could not find a workable solution to live together and followed her brother to go to her room. The parents moved to the living room to drink their coffee and talk for a while. Janet gave Jim a sheet of paper for him to read later and asked him to reply at his convenience. Jim took the sheet of paper and said goodnight, promising to call Janet the next day.

◆

Jim's heart was aching, not that he regretted the agreement with Janet, as much as the impact this break-up would have on the children. They were minors, and Jim felt guilty; it was his stupid mistake that created such an upset in their lives. He couldn't control his tears from falling, sobbing for a couple of minutes before he arrived at his hotel.

He took a hot shower, relaxed, and sat to meditate to mute his troubled thoughts and block the ego's tricks that tried to make him feel sad and guilty. A short time later, he sensed the spaciousness of Being within, lifting him above his thoughts and feelings. He eagerly pulled out his journal to write.

I have now learned the value of no resistance to what is; I allow the present moment to help me accept the new change and experience the Peace and Joy of Being within me.

With conscious awareness, I know I can handle the unknown future, without concern or struggle on my part. Negativity is not natural for me anymore.

The garden flowers, the forest trees and the dolphins in the sea are always happy, and so it is with me. I sleep with melodies of Peace, and I awake with songs of joy.

The love that initially triggered our relationship in the physical and emotional fields has transmuted to the spiritual realm of compassion and kindness. On a deeper level, I experience true love.

I pray that the world Janet wants to embrace, created by her egoic mind, dissolve and transform into a search for her true self within. May her impermanent fear be replaced by the power of Love.

I need to remember that I will be regularly tempted by the ego to return to worldly appeals, yet I rely on my connection with my soul to combat such temptations with the spaciousness of my inner Being.

I yearn to build a new world for my family and me, a society rooted in the Unmanifested Infinite field of Reality and Truth, a world of Peace and Harmony. I leave this dream to the Universe to provide.

◆

Jim was finally able to have a good sleep. He went to the office the next day and called Brian to see if he could drop by to see him anytime that suited him. Brian arrived around 11:00 am, greeted the staff he saw on his way to Jim's office.

"Good morning Jim, I hope you had a pleasant weekend! What can I do for you? I brought with me the figures you asked for."

Jim told him briefly what happened and the impact of the story on the children. "Apart from that, all went well. I struggled a bit with troubling thoughts before I managed to get a good night's rest.

"Here, I have with me this sheet that Janet gave me. I did not even read it. Take a look and tell if we can manage to honor what she wants." Brian took the sheet and spent about five minutes reading it.

"Come on, Brian, is it so complicated?" Jim asked. Brian looked at Jim and smiled before he said,

"I don't have experience in divorce settlement agreements, but I can tell you that Janet is very reasonable. Apart from property taxes, any mortgage you may have that you continue to pay, she asked for a relatively small amount for herself as alimony, and the child support to cover education and other sundry expenses is reasonable too. Yes, you can afford it is my answer! And, you have plenty of money in your private accounts as well, if you care to see."

"Fine, I don't want to see anything. Please write a nice reply to give to Janet and add twenty percent over the amounts she asked for." Jim asked Brian.

" I'll have the reply ready before the end of the day, and I'll email you the attachment. Anything else I can do for you while I'm here? I trust all is well, and if you are free Wednesday after work, I'm in town still."

"Good, let us meet after a short visit to the Center. Thank you for your good help, Brian. Your coaching made me stronger to cope with this undesirable change in my marital status."

"Don't mention it and will see you in two days!"

Janet didn't believe what she saw when she received the reply to her financial support sheet. She cried grateful to Jim's generous heart. This man must be spiritual, she thought. She called him right away and thanked him profusely. Jim took advantage of her call and asked her if she would be okay to take the children on vacation for one week when the school closes for the summer.

"Where do you intend to take them?" Janet asked.

"Not decided yet! Either to the Grand Canyon and Gethsemane Park, to see beautiful nature or to some beach in the Caribbean to have fun. What do you think?"

"I bet you they'll choose the beach. I know you don't like to be in the sun for more than a few minutes, but if you give them a choice, that'll be it." Janet said.

"I can tolerate the sun for their sake, and I'll use a lot of sun-screen."

"Why don't you then take them to St. Barth where you and I went once? It is clean and classy!"

"Good idea! I'll check it out and let you know. I wish you could come with us?' Jim teased.

"Take it easy now! Thanks anyway."

"Okay, I'll tell them, and I'll see you on Sunday then. Bye for now!"

"Thanks again, Jim, for everything!" Janet said before hanging up the receiver.

Jim felt rewarded for the attributes of compassion and kindness, realizing the miraculous work of the present moment.

Chapter 10
Another Spiritual Test

Laura had not called her father to complain about her mother's behavior as she did before. He saw they were more at ease when he picked them up for the weekend. He noticed that Todd preferred to remain silent. To cheer them up, Jim said, "We have a new project to discuss today. I spoke to Mom, and she's okay for the three of us to go on vacation the week when the school closes for the summer. That depends if you have good grades, of course! Otherwise, we are all grounded! Make sure you study hard and do well, okay?"

That story excited Todd, sitting in the back seat of the car who asked, "Where are you taking us?"

"To the jungles of Africa, a safari, perhaps!" Jim answered with a serious tone.

"No, please, no!" Todd reacted, and Laura confirmed too.

"Why, you don't like to see wild animals?"

"No, again, no!"

"Okay, how about we stay here in America and go see the Grand Canyon and Gethsemane Park?"

"Dad, why do you want to punish us?" Laura spoke

"Fine then, we either stay home or go to the Caribbean, you tell me."

"Yay! yes, the beach, Dad, the beach!" they both shouted happily.

"Okay, you know how much I love the sun! Never mind, I love you more, so the beach it will be! I'll take you where your Mom and I went once."

"Do they have a lot of water sports?" Eager, Todd asked.

"Yes, of course, water skiing, surfing, jet-skiing, stuff like that.

"Thanks, Dad, when do we go?"

"The first Saturday after school is closed and return the following Sunday."

"That will be in twelve days, then, yippee!!" Laura shouted

That discussion illuminated their hearts, and they could not wait to hug their father when they got out of the car at the hotel.

◆

During dinner that evening, Laura asked her father,

"Dad, now that the two of you reached an agreement of sorts, does that mean you both can start going out with new people?"

"I have no such interest. I'm still busy working on my inner growth, and for me, it is a priority over any relationship with other people. I can easily wait until one day I'm lucky to find someone who has a similar life purpose."

"What do you mean by inner growth?" Laura asked again.

"The human being is two parts, the human and the being. The human is the outer part, which is the physical (our body), the mental (our mind), and the emotional (our feelings). The human part refers to our senses, what we see, hear, smell, or say. Our thoughts that we cannot see fabricated in our minds and our feelings get developed the same way. Thoughts and feelings become the handy tools our ego uses to thrive on past stories or build fears about the future. Are you with me so far?"

Both Laura and Todd nodded a yes. Then Jim continued,

"Now, the second half of the two-word description of people is being. Being is where our soul or spirit resides. That is what spiritual teachers tell us is the invisible domain of our Being, the immortal part of our existence, the home where the mind of God, or the Universe, resides. That part does not die; it is eternal. Our bodies die but not our souls.

"So, you may ask why the Being part is more important than the human part to me, for example? Because that is where peace, joy, and love reside. I want to live a peaceful life, be happy, and cherish the feelings of true love. There is no True Love in the physical form. You may get some pleasure, but it fades away quickly. True Love, however, is eternal, like the love your Mom and I have for you, our children. It is unconditional love. We don't love you because we ask for something in return.

"Briefly, (because I can go on for hours) when I say I'm working on me I mean I am learning the method of connecting with my 'Being' part. To experience peace, joy, and love. This method is called a spiritual practice.

"I practice meditation, or the stillness of my mind, by muting negative thoughts and sad feelings. I sense the power of the present moment. I do not focus on what happened in my past or what will happen to me tomorrow. I sense the Presence of God in the flowers I see, the forest trees, the animals, and the fish in the sea. Nature is a great portal to find God. I am aware. This awareness connects me with my higher self, or my soul, my True Self, not the false self, which is created by the ego.

"So now you know why your Mom and I could not find a compromise. She is not into it, at least, not yet." Jim took a breather and Laura jumped in to ask,

"Why is Mom not into it, it sounds wonderful the way you explained it, also you live it, and we notice the positive change in you ourselves, why can't she see it too?"

"That's a good question. Buddha said that we go through suffering before we are enlightened. I suffered from the mistakes I did, and the hurt I caused. That suffering became the foundation, or the launching pad, for me to awaken. Thanks to Brian, my colleague at work who helped me to live in this spiritual realm, I explained. I am really happy, my beloved!" Jim concluded.

"So, you're not religious, Dad? Todd asked unexpectedly.

"No, my son, I'm not. I belong to a neutral spiritual group that does not follow any religion or denomination. We learn from the teachings of great masters and sages, like Christ, Buddha, and others. There is a new wave going on increasing the number of spiritual people noticeably."

"Is this why church membership is diminishing as I read?" Laura asked.

"Yes, that could be true. Modern societies are hungry for open-minded, spiritual guidance, much more than listening to the same old rituals still used in churches or temples."

"Thank you for this quick course on spirituality. It certainly sounds amazing and a mind-opener. I hope Mom can get interested in trying it. You can be her best teacher!"

"We all hope she does, and I hope you develop an interest too!"

They finished their dinner and went back to rest and watch a tv series in the suite. Jim was very pleased with the questions asked and was eager to express his feelings on paper.

◆

The children were excited to tell their mother about the planned vacation with their father. Jim asked his assistant to book a three-bedroom villa for one week at Le Sereno Hotel on the beach, in Gustavia, St. Barth, and round-trip business class. He desired to give the children a great vacation.

The school was over, and both Laura and Todd did well with grades from B+ to A-. They proudly showed their grades to their father. Janet took them shopping for beach attire, and the mood at home was noticeably improved.

A limousine picked the children up Saturday morning and drove to the city to pick up Jim at the hotel. The flight was at 1:00 pm from JFK airport.

Jim was elated to see his children so happy. They knew that Dad is a classy person who wanted to spoil them. The flight took off on time, and they arrived at the airport of St. Marten to connect with the ten-minute shuttle flight to St Barth. About six hours of flights, they checked in to a spacious hotel-villa which they admired. They showered and went to have dinner at the restaurant right on the water. Jim told the kids the time in St. Barth is one hour ahead than NYC.

The panoramic views of the calm turquoise water tempted Todd to jump in, but he had to control himself and wait until the next morning. Laura found the place as beautiful as Paradise and could not wait to stretch and bask in the sun on the white-sand beach. It was a long time ago since Jim had been with the children on vacation, and this one meant a lot to him. They all ate a variety of grilled fish served on a large tray with grilled vegetables on the side. They were tired after a lovely dinner, and all slept well that night.

Breakfast was served on the terrace, and the waiter showed them the program of activities for the day. Todd was the first to finish eating. He ran to the beach to join other kids his age for some water sports activities. Laura and Jim took it easy and slowly walked to the beach, equipped with sunscreen, journals, and books to read. Jim found his spot under the umbrella, close to Laura, who wanted to sit in the sun. The morning was spent leisurely between sunbathing and dipping in the water for a few minutes every hour until Todd joined them again around lunchtime.

Todd was so happy he told his father,

"Dad, I had the most amazing fun ever! The guard took us surfing first, and then we went on jet-skis for thirty minutes. It was the first time I do these two sports, and I love it. I fell from the surfing board a couple of times, learning how to go with the wind standing straight. I bet you I'll master it before we leave this place."

"So, you must be hungry now, right?" Jim asked.

"You bet! What did you guys do? Just sit around, lazy, doing nothing?" Todd said sarcastically.

"Yes, we did, you, hyper hero!" Laura said.

"Okay, let's walk over to have lunch, in two hours we all go on a boat to show us the area around here. Todd, you may also learn how to water ski while you're here. I'll go with you; I did it before. How about you, Laura, would you like to learn?"

"I'll give it a shot, why not?" Laura said.

That was the program for the rest of the week, from water sports mainly enjoyed by Todd, and relaxing on the beach, mostly enjoyed by Laura and Jim. The goal was to rest well, eat well, bond, and play together.

◆

On Saturday morning, while enjoying an early breakfast on the terrace and evaluating the enjoyable vacation as it was the last day before they return home, Jim received a call from his assistant,

"Hello Mary, what is it?" Jim asked.

"Sorry to bother you on your vacation, I had a call from the hospital in Rye. They said Janet had an accident; she hit a tree while driving back home late last night. She must have had one drink too many, the report said. She's now in the intensive care unit observed for some concussions and internal bleeding. I knew you might want to return earlier with the children, so I booked you on a flight that leaves St. Barth in forty minutes to connect in St. Marten an hour later. If you agree I will send you the booking confirmations by email. I will have a limo waiting for you to take you straight to the hospital."

"Oh, my goodness! Okay, I will notify the kids, and we pack and leave right away. Children, Mom had a silly accident last night on her way back home, she's being treated in the hospital, and it's best to leave right away and catch the flights that Mary booked for us. Sorry to cut your vacation short by one day. Let's go!" Jim said.

"Is she alright, will she make it?" Laura asked.

"I believe so; I will call the hospital from St. Marten before we take off. Hurry, let's go!"

Jim checked out, and they took a taxi to the nearby small airport to catch the shuttle flight to St. Marten. They checked in on the flight for the second leg to JFK and had forty minutes to spare. Mary also sent Jim the number for the hospital. He called and asked to speak to the doctor treating Janet. He waited two minutes before they connected him with the doctor.

"Hello, I am Jim Mayden, Janet's husband, who you are treating as I heard. Sorry I was away with the kids on vacation when I got the call this morning. How is Janet now?"

"Yes, I am Dr. Smith, and your wife is now in the ICU. The airbag, when the accident took place, protected her head but not her abdomen. The steering wheel smashed her belly and injured her liver and a couple of lower ribs. We're mainly monitoring the liver. We took a CT scan, among other tests, and found a contusion in her liver. This a bruise that sometimes can be serious, not shallow. It appears to be more serious than we thought due to some internal bleeding that showed in the blood tests." The doctor said, and Jim interrupted him and asked,

"Will she make it, Doctor?"

"Yes, we've seen many cases like this before. A serious bruise takes longer to heal, perhaps a couple of weeks, we now need to stop the bleeding, and we began the procedure already."

"What kind of a procedure? Will she need surgery?"

"That's what we need to determine. We will know by noon if the steps we took already are diminishing the hemorrhage. If not, we may have to operate to fix the affected blood vessels, take out the excess blood, and make sure no clots are formed that may cause damage to other organs."

"Thank you, Dr. Smith, we should be there around five pm this afternoon, can we see her then?"

"Yes, I'll notify the reception, and I might be around to update you. Thanks for calling."

Jim turned around and shared the highlights of what he heard from the doctor, who assured him they're taking the necessary steps to heal. Jim then changed the conversation and said,

"So, Todd, you were supposed to receive your certificate as an accomplished surfer and water-skiing graduate, are you disappointed?"

"Dad, they can always mail it to me. At least I did it! What's more important now is Mom's condition."

"You're right! There will be a car waiting when we arrive. We'll go straight to the hospital to see Mom; she'll be alright."

"Dad, I didn't know Mom drinks alcohol?" Laura asked.

"She only drank some wine socially. This is a different story now. The report says she must have dozed off and closed her eyes when the accident took place. It's okay we all make mistakes. Don't worry now and enjoy the flight back." Jim concluded.

◆

The flight landed at 4:00 pm, and the limo was waiting at the luggage belt. They drove up straight to the hospital. The children were nervous on their way, and Jim did his best to calm them down. They arrived at 5:10 pm and went straight to the ICU unit but could only see her from the glass partition. Janet was hooked up with tubes connected to the machine, and her face could hardly be recognized. Dr. Smith and a nurse were standing next to her bed. Jim waved at him, and the doctor walked outside to talk to him and the children.

Jim introduced himself and the children. The doctor said,

" We had to perform a small surgery this afternoon to close the injured blood vessels and take the excess blood around the liver. The bruise will take time to heal. She will be in the room you now see for three more days to monitor her progress or any other complications closely. You won't be able to see her or talk to her now. She's sedated and needs to rest overnight. You may see her tomorrow around noon."

"Thank you, Dr. Smith, will watch her for a few minutes and then go. We'll be back tomorrow, as you said."

It was a sad sight to see. Jim asked the kids to go with him to the hotel, and they'll return the next day before noon. They were concerned that Janet might suffer for a while, and Jim assured them that he'd take all the steps required to make her comfortable while healing at home. They were not in the mood to go out and ordered a light dinner in the room. Shortly after dinner, Jim excused himself and went to his bedroom while the kids watched a movie on TV.

Jim went into silence for a while then opened his journal and wrote,

I am now engrossed in a new test for my spiritual journey.

I will not allow blame, fear, or guilt to penetrate my space.

I will not question why this accident happened the way it did. I accept what happened and surrender Janet's health to God. I send her energy to heal fast with the least pain possible.

May the provisional suffering and pain open the door to her new journey of inner awakening.

May this unexpected test make me stronger and more loving toward her and the children.

May the children witness the practice of True Love and become aware of the inner source of its power.

May I become aware of the lessons to learn from this experience and adjust to its new revelations.

May all the doubt, physical and psychological pain be transformed into enlightenment and finding her True Self.

May Janet's painful experience empower her to crack the shell of ego and rise to taste true feelings of joy and inner peace.

They all got up on Sunday morning, eager to get dressed and see Janet. They had breakfast in the room, showered, and got dressed, ready to go by 11:00 am. Jim told them to leave their luggage in their room as Janet may need to stay in the hospital for a while longer.

They were at the hospital at 11:40 and went straight to her room. The nurse recognized them and let them in. Janet was awake, and tears fell down her cheeks when she saw them. They could not hug, but the children reached out and kissed her hand. She wore neck support due to a concussion. The nurse said they can talk to her though she may not respond with a clear voice yet. They told her about the great time they had, and her tears turned into smiles.

Jim held her hand and told her he spoke to the doctor, and she will soon be well enough to go home. He said not to worry about the children; they will stay with him until she goes home. The nurse told the children they could remain for a maximum of thirty minutes as their mother need to rest. Jim said he'll be right back and walked out. He quickly went to the local police department to get the report about the accident.

The police officer showed him a report that indicated the location, the condition of Janet, a photo of her with her head over the steering wheel, and her body slipping forward. There was no one else in the vehicle that they towed to the police garage.

The report stated it took the ambulance five minutes to get there, responding to a 911 call from an anonymous person. Jim took a copy of the report and rushed back to the hospital. He collected the children from the room and wished Janet a quick recovery. The nurse told him they could be back tomorrow around noon to see her and have an update from the doctor.

On the drive back to the city, Laura asked, "Why did this happen to Mom?"

"I wish I know, sweetheart. Accidents happen! The Universe works in mysterious ways, and we don't always understand why things happen."

"Why do you think she drank so much? Was she depressed or just having a good time?"

"We don't know, and please don't bring up the subject of drinking anytime soon, unless she deliberately brings it up. We cannot judge other people's behavior." Jim said.

"But, Dad, she's our mother, we need to know!" Todd intervened. "I know how you feel, son! Please show her some respect and be patient. One thing for sure, she'll never drink like that again. I know her. She's a very disciplined person!" Jim responded.

"Do you think she was with other friends, a man, perhaps?" Todd asked again.

"It's not important, and it is none of our business. Your Mom is free to live the way she likes. She will always love you first, for sure!"

"Okay, fine. I wish this accident didn't happen, and I could have enjoyed another day on the beach and got my certificates."

"Todd, that sounds very selfish on your part. Please take it back and learn how to be compassionate for a change. She's your mother, after all." Jim said firmly.

"You're right! I'm sorry, Dad. That was stupid of me to say it." "Okay, let's go have a bite to eat, and you can go see a movie or do something this afternoon. I called my friend Brian, my spiritual teacher, to come to see me around 4:00 pm for a private lesson while you guys are out there."

"What lessons are you taking, Dad?" Laura asked.

"He gives me a spiritual book to read, I write questions, and we discuss them together for about an hour or so. It is part of the practice for my spiritual journey."

"Wow! I'm so impressed!"

"I love it, sweetheart! It keeps me alert and makes me happy!"

◆

The children left around 3:00 to go see an action movie, "the transformers." Brian showed up on time, and Jim briefed him on Janet's accident, the reason why they came back one day earlier.

"How are you and the children taking it, Jim, I'm sorry!"

"The children are asking questions about why it happened and stuff like that. They're okay otherwise and will stay with me until Janet goes home. Me? I take it as a test to my spiritual growth and a chance not to allow ego to creep in and disturb my thoughts and feelings. I am learning to accept the situation as it is."

"That's the point! Do you still remember what Eckhardt Tolle said about Surrender in the last chapter of his book, 'The Power of Now,' which you read some time ago?"

"Of course, I do! I wrote about surrender last night! I recall vividly when Tolle refers to an accident as a 'limit-situation,' that also provides an opportunity for miracles to happen. Perhaps now, the suffering Janet is going through can oblige her to accept the unacceptable.

"For me, I use this episode as a surrender to a state of grace, which is the other side of suffering. As such, I experience peace and serenity that originates from the Unmanifested Self. The Bible refers to it as 'the peace of God that surpasses all understanding.'"

"Wonderful, Jim, you have learned how to turn negative life events into a positive gain to help you become more mature spiritually," Brian commented.

"I'm also trying to use this situation to teach my children lessons about awareness, true love, and forgiveness. They're beginning to understand better who I am, and the reason why Janet and I could not reconcile. Laura, in particular, seems to be interested in my spiritual experience."

"Do you feel that Janet might awaken with the realization that her suffering could end and transform into enlightenment?" Brian asked.

"That will be great, don't you think?" Jim said

"Then, what if she experiences a shift of consciousness, and starts understanding your situation, sending you hints toward reconciliation based on her transformation process? Would that be something you would respond to favorably?"

"If I notice a reversal from an unconscious mind to a conscious being, eager to look within and grow spiritually, why wouldn't I be open to consider reconciliation? I never stopped loving this woman anyhow!"

"Good to hear! Just be aware of what goes on, trust and let the Universe handle the rest." Brian confirmed.

Then they talked about the expansion program, and the excitement of the members at the Center. Brian also told Jim about the condition of the two disabled crew members. Plus, the fact, that the minister in Philadelphia came to meet with Charles and his partners at the Center this past week. And, that he's going to meet him tomorrow to hopefully finalize a definite deal.

At 5:30 pm the children walked in, and had a chance to meet Brian, their Dad's spiritual teacher. They chatted together for five minutes before Brian said goodbye.

"He seems to be a nice guy!" Laura said.

"He is, my dear, he is more than just nice. He is honest, loving and wise. He lost his wife and daughter in a car accident three and half years ago. He suffered for more than year he said until he finally opened the door to go within. His inner journey helped him find his True Self . Now, I consider him a wonderful friend and my spiritual teacher."

"Wow! What a story?"

"How about you guys, did you have fun?"

"Well, time to think about mundane things, and not to think about Mom suffering in the hospital."

"I go to the office for two hours in the morning then I come to fetch you guys, and we all go to see her again, okay?"

"Okay, Dad. Can we order room service again, we don't want to go out, to eat?" Laura asked

"Fine with me! Go ahead, order a tuna salad for me, please!"

♦

They drove up to the hospital the next morning and arrived around noon. Janet was less sedated and was able to talk to them freely. Todd told her about the water sports he did, and how Laura learned how to water-ski also. Janet was happy to see them both sun-tanned and looking great.

The doctor walked in ten minutes later and told Jim, Janet and the children, "the hemorrhage is pretty much contained after the surgery, though she requires close monitoring in this room for the next forty-eight hours. If all is well, she will be moved to a normal room and we will perform another CT scan to check the impact of the bruise on her liver. I believe she will be with us for at least five more days before she goes home. At home she needs a nurse around the clock to help her with her medication and to move around. I will then ask to see her two weeks later for another check-up, okay?"

"Thank you, Dr. Smith for the update and the wonderful care the staff has shown." Jim said before the doctor left the room.

Again, half an hour later, the attending nurse told them they have to leave to let Janet rest. Jim told Janet they'll come back tomorrow around the same time. They told their mother how much they love her and wished her speedy recovery. That triggered some tears to fall. She thanked Jim with a smile, then held the children's hands tight before they left.

On the way out, Jim reassured the children that Mom is getting better and she'll be home within short. He drove them back to the hotel to have some lunch and he said he'll be back around 5:00 pm. Meanwhile they can walk in the park or stay in and watch TV.

Chapter 11

A Process of Transformation

Janet was released from the hospital five days later, and nurses were assigned to take shifts around the clock for a week or two.

Jim went to see her and the kids every day after work. Janet was getting better by the day but had to take pain killers to alleviate the excruciating pain in her abdomen and her lower rib cage. She strolled for a few minutes around the house twice a day. Laura and Jim had fun preparing food certain evenings, and the rest of the time they ordered in. Janet had soup and some soft food, helped by the attending nurse.

One evening, after a week at home, Janet asked to see Jim alone in her bedroom. The nurse waited downstairs with the children watching TV. Jim walked in and sat on a chair next to her bed.

"Jim, I can't thank you enough for your true love and care. I'm sorry that I had to put you through all this and to cut the children's vacation short.

"The accident was a stupid mistake which I brought to myself. I felt lonely at home that night, and I went out to a bar for a drink, hoping to feel better, and to see some people be ordinary again. I asked the bartender for a stiff drink, and he gave me tequila shots pushed down with beer.

"It was around 10:30 at night when I walked in, and I had not eaten any food. An hour later, and after three shots of that drink, I felt quite drunk and tired. I decided to leave right away, and I thought I could easily drive the short ten minutes from home. Suddenly I felt nauseous and tired, I turned and hit an oak tree on the side of the road. I must have passed out until I faintly heard the sound of sirens and people talking around me. The rest, you know!"

Jim was listening with a smile. He did not scold or criticize her behavior. He remained quiet until she spoke again,

"I also wanted to tell you how sorry I am for turning my back on you and asking for our separation. You don't deserve that, Jim, you are the same wonderful man I knew when I fell in love with you. You are even better now, and I appreciate your truth about your choice of a spiritual path.

"I did not understand it then, but I know it now. It seems that I had to suffer first before I awaken on the inside. I was indeed captive to my dark thoughts and refused to see the light. This accident opened my mind to be more positive. The fear of losing you and the children woke me up.

"I ask for your forgiveness for the way I treated you and made you feel rejected. I must have foolishly wanted you to feel the way I felt when you walked out on me. I've been crying every night, the last three nights, thinking about the damage I caused, to you and myself. I hurt you many more than you hurt me. So, again, I'm sorry."

"Janet, what you just said, is music to my ears! God knows how much I prayed for you to see the light, as you said. I am delighted that you are seeking enlightenment after the unfortunate taste of suffering. The emotional pain is deeper than physical pain. Let us now keep a positive communication between us, please focus on getting well physically, and the Universe will guide us to what is next. I'll go down now, and you rest, okay?" He took her hand and kissed it before he left the room. She smiled at him with her teary eyes and asked to send the nurse to take her pills.

Jim went downstairs and told the children that he's leaving. Laura jumped up and asked, "Is Mom okay?"

"Yes, we had an excellent talk. Mom is resting now. Good night guys and I will see you tomorrow after six, and maybe we'll order some pizza!"

"Now you're talking, Dad, love you!" Todd said.

♦

The conversation Jim just had with Janet shot arrows of positive thoughts and feelings to his mind. The powerful realization was the positive shift of consciousness that started Janet on her journey toward spiritual awakening.

In a meditative state, he wrote,

I am grateful for the transformation I witnessed in Janet's mind today. She's learning how suffering can be her launching pad for her enlightenment. She spoke of her mistakes and asked for forgiveness.

I am grateful that she is responding to the healing power of True Love and looking within to embrace wisdom from her soul and drink from flowing rivers of awakened affection in her heart.

I am grateful to the Universe and the timeless secrets of turning what was unacceptable before to what is acceptable now. How true it is not to dwell on the past and to enjoy the present moment.

I am overwhelmed by the revived feelings of hope and a renewed sense of stability. How beautiful it would be, to regain a life of peace and joy, to a family that hungers for love.

I will monitor Janet's desire to search within, lovingly, and patiently. I will not rush her to speed up her process of healing and let her talk with a welcoming smile and warm understanding.

I could imagine the happy impressions on our children's faces when they notice the transformation of their mother's mind, and attempt to heal not only physically, but emotionally and spiritually as well.

It is vital to surrender our destiny to the Creator, who knows the secrets of our hearts and who guides us to take the necessary steps to remain faithful to our calling.

Jim had a very restful night with pleasant dreams of hope and love. He went to his office early with a fresh mindset to perform his duties.

◆

Brian called Jim in the office and asked about Janet's condition, and Jim briefed him on the conversation they had yesterday.

"Wow, so soon! That's interesting, and you must be pleased to observe the beginning of her transformation." Brain said.

"Of course, I am. Unfortunately, it took an ugly accident to bring Janet around. The Universe operates in mysterious ways!"

"Good, the minister in Philadelphia, is on board and spotted a fitting space available to rent. He's ready to start in one month after furnishing the place." Brian confirmed.

"Does he have potential members to start with?"

"He said many members of his congregation would join, so we'll see!"

"Good work, Brian, what else?" Jim asked.

"We have a good speaker tomorrow at six if you have time to come."

"Yes, I will come, Janet is feeling better, and I don't have to go there every day. I will see you tomorrow then! Who is the speaker, by the way?"

"Dr. Goodwin, minister of the Community Center for Spiritual Living here in the city. She has a degree in Divinity and a student of Science of Mind."

"What is the lecture about?" Jim asked. "How to balance work with spiritual living."

"Okay, that's interesting! I wish I heard her before I walked out on Janet and the kids. Anyhow, I'll be there!"

◆

Jim went up to the house after work, and as promised, he ordered two pizzas chosen one by Todd and the other by Laura. Janet was upstairs in the bedroom, resting. He quickly went up to say hi and asked if she cares for a slice of pizza? She smiled with an expected no. He said he'll come up to see her after he eats with the children. He told the nurse he'll bring two slices for her.

Laura had prepared some salad to eat with the pizzas, and they all had fun eating together. Jim could not remember when he ate pizza last, and this time was extra special with the kids.

Laura was curious to know about what is going on between the parents holding private conversations together. Janet had not said a word to her children other than what a great father they had.

"Dad, all Mom said, is how great you are! We know that how come she's fond of you all of a sudden?" Laura asked while Todd was busy focusing on finishing his second slice of pizza.

"Sweetheart, maybe it's the pills she's taking? I don't know?" "Come on, Dad! You can't fool us," Laura said.

"Do you remember the conversation we had about suffering that could lead to enlightenment? I believe Mom is experiencing a similar transformation. I hope she does because that eradicates all past thoughts and feelings of anger and fear. Sometimes we may go through suffering before we see the light of Life." Jim explained.

Jim's words sounded promising to busy-eating Todd. He paused and asked his father,

"Does this mean you will make up and come back home for good?" "Easy does it, Tiger! We're just talking. Transformation can be a

long process. We are talking positively together, and that is key. I don't know what destiny has for us, ahead!" Jim remarked.

"Dad, you create your destiny, come on, do it guys, and let's finish this drama!" Todd said while Jim and Laura laughed.

"That's very sweet of you, son! The pizza must be truly nourishing your heart, not only your tummy! I promised to check on your Mom when we finish here. Can you put two slices on a plate to take to the nurse?" Jim asked.

"Of course! Laura give him two from your pizza. I may get hungry later, who knows?" Todd instructed.

Jim loved these happy moments with the children who were noticing a different but pleasant atmosphere at home.

◆

Jim went upstairs again, gave the pizza to the nurse, and went in to see Janet.

"Did you eat?" Jim asked.

"Yes, the nurse gave me some soup and mashed ham potatoes, how about you?"

"Yes, we ate pizza. It was fun watching Todd so excited, holding on to the last two slices of the big pizza he chose. We had fun! They asked me what's going on between us, and I told them we're having friendly conversations."

"What did you think about my confession last night?"

"It's not a confession, as much as an invitation from your soul to take you on a pleasant journey to find your True Self, the source of all Love and Happiness in life."

"Will I be as poetic in my statements as you've become? I love the way you speak. It irritated me in the beginning, but I love its tone and its sincerity. Will you teach me to speak like that?"

"I don't think anyone can teach you; it is innate within you; you will learn how to get in touch with the Source that teaches you."

"Jim, I want you to be my spiritual teacher!" Janet demanded. Jim was quiet for a while then said,

"Seriously? I don't know if I qualify! I'm still a novice myself. Maybe I can find you a better-qualified teacher?"

"No, I want you! I'll be honored to learn what you have learned so far. Please don't turn me down!"

"Janet, it is a responsibility; I wouldn't know where to start!" "Start with what Brian taught you and repeat the same with me. I learn fast, you know! I hear voices in my head telling me to start on this journey; please don't let me down." Janet pleaded.

"Alright, I guess I can continue to learn while coaching you? Next time I come, I bring you the first book that Brian gave me, its title is "Your Erroneous Zones" By Dr. Wayne Dyer. You can look him up on the internet."

"I heard of him, he wrote several self-help books, and many were bestsellers," Janet said.

"Good, I'll get you the book to read that first. I studied it chapter by chapter with Brian. You write down any questions, and we discuss them together. I will charge you $250 an hour, is that fair?"

"Come here!" Janet grabbed his hand and kissed it passionately and said, "thank you so much. I can't wait!"

"I'm going to the Center tomorrow evening; I'll come the next day with the book, okay? Rest well now; you're going to need a lot of energy to keep up with me."

"Yes, sir! I'm ready," Janet said before he left the room.

♦

The next evening Jim went to the Center to see his friends and listen to the lecture. He saw Charles talking to a good-looking young lady, and he signaled him to join. Jim walked over and greeted Charles, who introduced him to Dr. Sylvia Goodwin, the guest speaker this evening. He introduced Jim as a recent member benefactor of the Center. Charles had to excuse himself to answer a call on his cell phone.

"So, you're the one who is financing the branching out plan that Charles was telling me about?" The young lady asked.

Jim was shy and did not comment. He asked her,

"What do you do and what did you study for your Ph.D.?"

"I am a minister of a spiritual church in town, and I studied Divinity associated with the church of Religious Science and New Thought. How about you, do you belong to any church?"

"No, I don't, I consider this Center to be my church. It is where I began my spiritual journey, and the members have become my extended family."

"Do you have a family?"

"Officially, I'm still married though we've been separated for more than nine months now. I have two children who live with their mother. You?"

"No, I'm single! I've yet to meet the right person?" Sylvia said. "Who is the right person to you?"

"He should be primarily spiritual, not religious, but an open-minded, spiritual man. The rest is secondary. How about you?"

"My wife has yet to go on a spiritual path, one reason why we went our separate ways. She recently had a painful car accident that seems to help her awaken and search within. I heard you'll be speaking about a balance between work and home for a spiritual person, right?" Jim asked.

"That's right!"

"I'm eager to hear your speech. The imbalance I had before is what caused the friction between my wife and me. I wish I heard your speech before I walked out on her!"

Sylvia was looking at Jim with a big smile expressing admiration of his forthright words, honest demeanor and his good looks. Charles returned and told her, "we're ready in five minutes. How do you find Jim, isn't he great? We all love him around here, particularly Brian, who used to work for him and now spearheading our expansion program I told you about."

"Where is Brian, I don't see him around?" Jim asked.

"He'll be here in a few minutes; he got stuck in a small errand. It was him who called."

A minute later, Brian walked in and came straight to talk to Charles and handed him a package. He then got introduced to Dr. Goodwin and greeted Jim, who right away told the guest speaker, "he is my spiritual guru!"

"I see! Perhaps we can have some tea after the speech," Brian suggested.

Everyone was seated, and there were about sixty people present. Charles took the podium and said,

"Before I introduce you to our guest speaker this evening, I would like to tell you Brain has finalized the deal with the future head of our new Philadelphia Center. You all met him when he came to visit us two weeks ago. Which brings me to honor the man who made this and future growth possible. He donated $2 million to support our mission. Jim, come on up for a minute, please."

Charles unwrapped the package and pulled out a plaque with the words ***"Thanks to our honorary chairman, Jim Mayden"*** embossed in Gold. Everybody clapped, and Jim walked to the podium to receive the plaque and hug Charles.

"I do not deserve this honor. The honor is to see our mission grow, encouraging more people to experience spiritual awareness and enlightenment. Thank you!" Jim said and moved back to his seat. They all applauded him in appreciation.

◆

Dr. Goodwin was introduced and walked to the podium to deliver her speech.

She first congratulated the group on the "evident solidarity and brotherly love." She added they're welcome to visit her church and influence the congregation the adoption of such a beautiful spirit. Jim took out a small notebook for the highlights of her message:

To be spiritual is to be the same person everywhere, at work, at home, or in society.

Never hide your true self from others. Be proud of who you are and let the manifested truth touch the lives of others.

If you're successful at work or in business, it is good to make money as long as you remember to help those in need.

Make sure you do the work that rewards your soul, and as Gibran said: "when you work, you are a flute through whose heart the whispering of the hours turns to music."

Be honest in your dealings, avoid shortcuts, and reject bribes. Also, remember that work is meaningless if not done with love. "work is love made visible," Gibran also said.

At work, it is not what you do, but how and why you do it. Put your heart in what you do, and the tree will bear good fruit.

When you go home, go early and enjoy time and dinner with the children. Play with them and read them stories before they sleep.

Embrace your spouse with love and affection and leave matters of the office behind.

Respect the weekends and share spiritual stories with the family, for them to learn.

Look around and give to your community, by offering voluntary assistance, or charitable donations that would improve their lives.

Always hold your spiritual flag high for others to see, the world is hungry for our simple message of love, so don't be shy!

The speech lasted about fifteen minutes, and the members gave her a good round of applause.

Charles advised that beverages will be served and to feel free to roam around and socialize.

Brian came over a few minutes later and found Jim speaking with two of Charles's partners. He took him aside and said, "I was talking to Dr. Goodwin, and she asked me if you are still around. Come talk to her."

"Why, what does she want?" Jim whispered.

"I don't know; maybe she likes you?" Brian said, facetiously. "Brian, she's a gorgeous spiritual woman, and her looks are very tempting indeed. I'd rather avoid exploring this situation. I have a sick woman, the mother of my kids, who needs my love and attention at this moment."

"Okay, just come and talk to her for a minute and then leave, I'll go have some tea."

"What you became a matchmaker all of a sudden?" Jim said in laughter.

Jim walked around and saw Sylvia talking to one of the female members, an older lady who's always in the Center. Sylvia excused herself and walked over to Jim. She asked him,

"How did you find my speech, any questions, or remarks?" "Great, I took several notes, and again I wish I had heard you before. I see you are an admirer of Khalil Gibran, my favorite poet, who was quite spiritual as well."

"That's true; he's one of my favorites too. What kind of business do you do? Brian told me you own a successful trading company."

"Yes, but what he didn't tell you is what the monstrous success did to my ego, which in turn shattered my self-esteem. Luckily, Brian showed up and helped me to awaken from the illusory dreams of my outer success and turn 'my telescope' to look within."

"Well said! Do you plan to continue with the work you do now?" "Yes, unless you have other ideas! I enjoy my work, and now I enjoy sharing the fruit of my hard labor to help the needy, as you just said." "That's wonderful! I thought perhaps you might want to become a fulltime spiritual teacher! I see it in you!" "Are you offering me a job, Doctor?"

"Sylvia…I can't afford a man of your stature. But think about doing it even if you postpone it. I am psychic in these things."

"I truly appreciate your observation, and I take it as a great compliment."

Sylvia gave Jim her visiting card and said, "Call me if you want to discuss this further." Jim took the card and gave her one of his own. He thanked her and excused himself to leave. He walked around eager to dispose of the plaque he received, he said goodbye to Charles and asked Brian to call him later.

◆

Brian called Jim at 7:30 pm, and they talked for a few minutes. Brian said he was invited to join Charles and the speaker for dinner nearby. Jim told him,

"This lady suggested that I should become a spiritual teacher. She's psychic, she said, and I fit that role of a teacher! I thanked her for the compliment. What you and Sylvia don't know is that Janet asked me yesterday to be her spiritual teacher, and I said I'll try. So, there you go! Two women asking me to teach, how about that? Do I look qualified for such a sacred task? I wonder!" Jim said.

"Yes, you are, Jim! You have it in you. It is innate! It's like you were born with this gift, but you didn't know you had it. Anyhow, I am happy to hear Janet asked you to be her teacher. Please do it, we all learn from the lessons we teach. As for Dr. Sylvia, I bet she liked you as an outer person too. She gave you her card. I saw that, so are you going to take her out? She is also stunning."

"Brian, why don't you take her out yourself? I am in the middle of reviving a reconciliatory relationship with my wife. I had my share with beautiful women already. That is my priority now, the family, okay?

"Fantastic! I'm truly happy for you. I wish you God-speed!" "Okay, buddy! Enjoy your evening, and we will talk soon!"

◆

The next day Jim drove up to the house after work. The children asked if they could go out to eat; they've been sitting all day at home.

"Fine, pick a restaurant you like and reserve a table in thirty minutes, I'll go up and see Mom now, and I'll be down shortly."

"Hey, how do you feel? I brought you some books to read." "I'm better, thanks. Come show me what you have," Janet said.

Jim handed her the book by Dr. Dyer and "The Prophet" by Khalil Gibran and said, "This one is serious for studying, and this one is poetry, yet spiritual. Gibran inspires me with his loaded phrases of deep spiritual and philosophical understanding of the human being."

"Wow, thanks! Come closer; I want to kiss you on the cheek."

Jim obliged, and then told her he went to the Center the night before and saw his old friends again. He also told Janet about the speaker, a minister who spoke about having 'a spiritual balance between work and home.'

"Did you learn anything?"

"I took notes, and I told her afterward, I wished I heard her speech before when I was foolish and egoistic."

"The speaker is a she?" Janet was curious to know.

"Yes, she's the minister of a spiritual living center in town." "Did you like her, how old was she?"

"She spoke well, and yes, she's a beautiful young woman in her late thirties, I would think! She said she's psychic, she gazed into my eyes and thought I would make a good spiritual teacher. I took that as a sign of confirmation that it's okay to teach you."

"Good to hear! Are you going to keep in touch with her?"

"No, my dear! As I told Brian, my priority is to help you and the children. I have no interest in having new lady friends, no matter who they are and how they look. By the way, the children asked me to take them out to dinner, and I said yes. Can we get you something to eat?"

"No, I'm fine! I'm still on this special food for my liver. Next week we need to see the doctor again, will you take me?"

"Of course, I will. Please Let the nurse fix an appointment any day in the afternoon, and I'll come to take you. I see you are walking better now, and no neck support anymore, good! Okay, let me go downstairs and take them to dinner, and I'll see you before I return to the city."

◆

Jim and the two children went to an Italian restaurant in town. The manager recognized them and seated them at a lovely table.

"We noticed an improved situation with Mom since the accident, what's going on?" Laura asked.

"There is always the positive side of cases of suffering like the one your Mom went through. She expressed more interest in the path of spirituality. She realized that it had done me well, and now she would like to try it out for herself. She asked me if I could teach her the way I learned."

182

"What a difference a day makes?" Laura recited. "How do you plan to teach her, Dad?" Todd asked.

"I give her self-help books to read, she writes down the question, and then we discuss together a couple of times a week."

"So, we will see more of you here, then!" "Yes, I'm afraid so!"

"This is great; we're happy to see the two of you on such good speaking terms and communications. Honestly, it is a big relief for both Todd and me." Laura said.

"Who knows, this may develop where they'll be together again for good, Laura!" Todd projected.

"Perhaps you should become a fortune teller, son!"

"Why not, Dad? The two of you are a beautiful sight to look at and have around. Don't you agree, Laura? Say something!"

"Todd, we stay out of it. They know exactly how to make their own decisions. Yes, you can pray and hope for the best, but at the end of the day, it is not up to you and me."

"You're both so sweet and considerate! Naturally, the decisions Janet and I make will always take you guys as a priority with serious consideration. There would be nothing better than to see our family reunite and live together under the same roof. We all have good intentions, and hope destiny will lead us to make the right decisions." Jim explained.

They each ordered their favorite dishes, and Todd cracked two jokes about his slim shape despite his healthy appetite. Laura said that she had lost her interest in the boyfriend she was seeing because she found him to be shallow and flirtatious.

"Are you disappointed it didn't work out?" Jim asked.

"Yes, I was, because I thought he was more mature than that. Besides, he possessively wanted to know where I am every hour of the day. Give me a break! I don't need that. Even my parents don't do that, I told him, but to no avail."

"Don't worry, Dad; I'll keep an eye on her!" Todd joked. "Shush you, sneaky beaver!" Laura said.

"So, you told him you don't want to go with him again?" Jim asked. "Of course, I did! I'm not anxious to find another also. I can wait until I find a man like you, Dad. You are my idol!" Laura said, which prompted Jim to get off his seat and kissed her on the head.

"How about me, too, Dad? You are also my idol!" Todd asked, and Jim moved toward him and hugged him from the back.

"You guys make my day and bring real joy to my heart… Laura, sweetheart, don't wait too long. It's alright to meet others, and if they don't work out, you learn from your mistakes and do better the next time."

Todd changed the subject and asked, "Dad, did you and Mom kiss, or hug yet?"

"What's with you and these questions, Todd?" Laura asked. "It's alright, you know we cannot easily kiss and hug, given her condition now, Todd! You will be the first to know when we do that, okay?" Jim replies with a peal of gracious laughter.

The children had dessert and thanked their father for a lovely dinner. They drove back home, feeling happy. Jim went upstairs to check on Janet and found her eagerly waiting for his return with a massive smile on her face.

"What is it?" He asked.

"It's the 'Prophet', Jim! What an amazing book. This guy was a genius, I looked him on the internet, and I had no idea he's so famous internationally. People around the world bought millions of his book translated into dozens of languages. Wow! Thank you again. I read the first three chapters on love, marriage, and children twice already, and I had tears of appreciation reading them. If spirituality can produce such poetry and understanding of the human soul, I want that for me too!" Janet was rolling with excitement.

"I'm so happy you like him. He's my favorite poet. I'm reading his other material, too, and I find him unique and inspirational."

"I'll keep on reading the other small chapters until I fall asleep. This book makes me forget my body pain and lifts my soul."

"That's the whole idea! We had a good dinner, and Todd made us laugh with his mundane jokes. They love you, and Todd was curious, he wanted to know if we kissed or hugged already! They are such wonderful kids!" Jim stated.

"Todd asked a good question; don't you miss that? I do!" Janet teased.

"Okay, you two are from the same dough. Let us get healthy and strong first, and then we revisit the subject, okay?"

"Okay, boss! You can go home. I'll get back to my books, and I'll write down questions that cross my mind. When is our next session, professor?" Janet asked.

"I'll come back Thursday. Tomorrow I have my session with my teacher. Then, perhaps I can persuade the kids to wait a couple of hours before I take them to the city on Saturday; this way, you and I can spend productive time together. How does that sound?"

Janet agreed and kissed him on his cheek again. He went down, hugged the children, and told them he'd be back in two days.

Chapter 12
Overcoming Temptation

Jim entered his hotel room, his mind racing with poetic tunes that sent him straight to his desk to write,

Nestled in a womb of Love, Life's radiance returned, with fresh flowers to bloom in the garden of grace.

Darkness was conquered with the light of day, to observe clearly the magic of conscious awareness.

New melodies were played with the flute of hope, and new songs were sung from the threads of the heart.

Patience got rewarded with transcendent music of the soul from strings of Silence played harmoniously within.

Memories of a remorseful past buried under the ground, and seeds of the present moment are planted instead.

The spirit of joy arrived dancing to dismiss old sorrow from the basement floor with a proper farewell.

Curing vibes from the sea of love arose, and sent ripples to heal the pain of body, mind, and soul.

Rivers of affection and compassion flowing freely into the ocean of invisible presence and lasting peace.

Invitation offer to teach a hungry soul for love, resonate clearly inside the mind without fear or hesitation.

The road to salvation decorated with beauty and rewards got designed with flowered beds on both its sides.

Gratitude was prized for good efforts made, and support put in place for a future unknown.

Jim was pleased about the recent developments of the past days. He noticed the atmosphere at home brewing with warmth, accentuated by

Janet's willingness to explore the realm of a spiritual path. He corrected himself for having thought that she's doing this to lure him back. The dim remnants of their fire of love were still alive, and not to be feared. The week alone that Janet had when Jim, and the children were away must have stirred heavy emotions of regret and sorrow, only to end with an unfortunate accident that must have also shaken her to look for peace.

Jim thought of Brian's remark about Sylvia's intent and was happy to remind him of Janet's condition. Jim exercised self-control as he also sensed Sylvia's curious approach to know him better. He would have responded reciprocally, had Janet not opened up her heart again. Sylvia would have been the type he would be tempted to know, due to her spiritual interest and her outer beauty. Jim decided not to allow his thoughts to get caught by the ego that could quickly turn new acquaintances into dreams of desire.

◆

Brian came to meet with Jim the next day, and before they delved into new discussions about the books Jim was reading, he said,

"Jim, during the dinner, Charles and I had with Sylvia, this woman wouldn't stop talking about you!"

"What do you mean? What did she say, and how did you respond?" Jim asked, eagerly.

"How highly impressed with your personality, generosity, and aura, and so on," Brian said.

"What aura? Do I have an aura? Jim responded.

"You know you have an aura, Jim. Everyone in the office talks about that. You have a unique presence when you walk into any room or gathering. Sylvia sensed that right away, and she finds it to be a desirable characteristic in a man."

"So, are you telling me that she is in love already? She's a mature and responsible lady, and she knows I'm married. So, give me a break!"

"Not only that, she told us she would like to have you give a speech to her congregation when it suits you," Brian said.

"A speech about what, my aura?" Jim said, laughing.

"No, to share your life testimony, how you transformed into the realm of spirituality, and give them a piece of advice."

"Are you, or is she, joking? I can hardly advise my own life, and you guys want me to preach and tell people my life story?"

"She believes it will touch the lives of many and help them to transform like you did."

"Oh please, let her find somebody else! Why don't you do that? You are advanced and capable charmer!"

"I don't have your aura or social status. You are a role model; I'm not."

"Please, don't underestimate yourself now!" Jim said.

"Anyhow, you should expect a call from her. Don't say I told you!" "Fine, can we go back to our study now? It's more important."

Jim read several self-help books in the past four months, and now he was delving in the classical Chinese masterpiece, the Tao te Ching, by Lao Tzu. It is a spiritual philosophy written more than three centuries BC. Its teachings are in eighty-one short chapters used primarily as a guide on how to live a spiritual and ethical life.

"So, the essence of the Tao is the spirit of the Universe, and what exists in the Universe are the manifestations of that essence?" Jim asked.

"Scholars still don't fully say it this way, but basically, it is true, as long as the spirit and the manifestations are unified as one."

"What is this thing about desire? If we have desire, we cannot see the essence of the Tao?"

"As you know, the Tao is nameless and eternal, and to modern teachers is considered as God. Desire here refers to attachment. You cannot be spiritual if you are 'attached' to manifested objects, people, things, or situations."

"How about this 'Wu Wei' concept, or action without effort?" "Wu Wei is a major concept in Taoism. You learned about that already, because it is about living in the present moment, unattached to material things, and it represents the power of Silence, or relaxing meditation. Also, it explains wisely the concept of dualities and how they coexist together: beauty vs. ugliness, short vs. tall, good vs. evil, joy vs. sorrow, and so on. They cannot exist without another, also like success and failure. So, as long as you're not 'attached' to success, as an example, success stays and never goes away; you will always be successful." Brian explained.

"Good to know! One other question. What is meant by 'the Tao is empty?" Jim asked.

"Since the Tao is before the creation of the universe as we know it, it is the source of everything created. That source is 'emptiness'; it cannot be a thing or matter; it is invisible non-matter and eternal."

"It is interesting how all modern teachings are derived, or inspired by ancient teachings, the Tao, the Torah, the New Testament, and so on," Jim remarked.

"You hit it right on! All sages and modern-day teachers have an ultimate common message, though each interpreted it differently. That is why *you* can be a teacher who delivers the same message in your style, as long as you base it on the same essence." Brian elaborated.

"Wow! Brian, I should choose a Chinese name for you now! You've become an old sage!"

"Okay, call me 'Brao'; how does that sound?" Brain said, and they both laughed.

♦

Jim received a phone call from Sylvia at 10:00 am the next day, just as Brian warned him.

"Hello Jim, this Sylvia, do you remember me?' "How could I forget you? How are you?"

"I'm fine, I have something to discuss with you in person, can we meet for lunch, if you are free today?" Sylvia asked.

Jim paused for a couple of seconds pretending he's checking his schedule then said,

"Yes, it is okay, how about 12:30 at Amali, on 60th street, it is halfway between our two offices and serves good Mediterranean food?"

"Fine, I know where it is, and I'll see you there!" "Okay, good! I'll make the reservation. Bye."

Jim was a bit nervous when he hung up the phone. He hoped that it would strictly be a business meeting, not more. He certainly did not want to mess things up again, with Janet.

When he walked in, he saw Sylvia, who waved at him; she was seated at a quiet table. He walked over with a smile, dressed in a business suit and tie, looking handsome. He shook hands with Sylvia, who looked beautiful herself, dressed elegantly in a dark-blue pantsuit. After a few social exchanges of generalities, Sylvia said,

"I know you're busy, so I'll go straight to the point and tell you why I asked for this meeting. I want to invite you to speak to our congregation at a time of your choice, it is for our Sunday service at 10:00 am."

"You are relentless, aren't you? First, I'm a shy public speaker, and second, I'm not qualified to preach as I mentioned before." Jim replied, then asked if they can see the menus to order. They took two minutes to choose while Jim was immersed with thoughts about the subject.

"First, I don't think you are the shy type. You handle big business, and you must have appeared many times in front of big audiences. Second, I'm not asking you to preach, but to share your testimony, your story so to speak from the heart; how you went through a shift of consciousness that transformed you into the spiritual realm. We have many well-to-do businesspeople in our church, and they would be eager to hear you talk about your outer business success and how you turned your attention to your inner success. I hope this clarifies my intention!"

"I am flattered, and I need time to think about this challenge, Sylvia. Besides, my mind is somewhat preoccupied with the family situation. I have a wife who is bed-bound still and cannot move freely yet; from the accident she had. I go there to check on her and the children two-three times a week, and she still needs my attention and support."

"I hear you! No rush, and take your time, but I would appreciate this gesture from you. I know you will deliver a superb speech, promise?"

"I'll seriously consider it, I promise!"

"Do you still love your wife, Jim?" Sylvia asked curiously. Jim was expecting something like that from her asking him to meet. He said,

"We were in love when we got married almost sixteen years ago. We got the two children, and I was working hard seeing the love we had slowly fading with time. My success led to my frequent absence from home, which in turn distanced me from my wife, and the two children. I succumbed to the ego that convinced me to leave home and see what else the world had to offer.

"I did, and I hurt her feelings pretty bad. I asked for her forgiveness several months later, but she refused. She had the accident while my children and I were on vacation, and now two weeks later, she's still being treated for a serious bruise in her liver. I am a compassionate person, and I surfaced in her life again to help her and the children. Now she's open to exploring the spiritual realm, and even asked me to be her teacher. That's my story!"

"I appreciate the rundown, and I am glad I'm not the only one who thinks you'll make a great teacher. I understand, but you did not answer my question, do you still love her?"

"I don't know! My understanding of love nowadays, as you may appreciate, goes beyond its physical and emotional aspects. I am learning how to practice True Love, a spiritual love that gives without asking to receive. So, to answer your question, yes, I still love her in that sense. She now understands better my spiritual choice of life and ironically wants it for herself, though she rejected me earlier because of it. I ask myself, is it because she wants to lure me back into her life, and to reunite again? I don't know! It is something that only time will tell. It's not an easy process! We have a lot of past hurts to bury first."

"Wow! You are such a great and honest man, Jim! I love that in a man." Sylvia said with great admiration.

"Thank you, and this is humble me! Far from being perfect!" "Can we be friends, at least?" Sylvia asked.

"But, of course!"

"Then let us leave it at that for now, and I hope to hear from you soon regarding the favor I asked. I am honored to have met you!"

"Oh! Please, the honor is mine! See what you have accomplished already, a beautiful young woman like you with such a big responsibility?" Jim responded.

"Do you find me beautiful?"

"If you don't believe me, go in front of the mirror, and it will tell you how dazzling you look!"

"Thanks, I'm flattered, handsome man!" Sylvia was quick to say. "Okay, I need to go back to work, and I'm glad we had this meeting. We'll keep in touch!"

When they parted in different directions out on the street, Sylvia was comfortable to give Jim a friendly kiss on his cheek.

♦

Jim drove up to the house after work, and this time the children asked if they can order Chinese food to be delivered. He agreed and told them to order soon, he's hungry, and he'll be there around 6:30 pm.

Before he ate with the children, he went up to check on Janet, and the nurse, sitting outside the room, said she's resting. He told her he'd be back in forty minutes.

The food arrived on time, and Jim helped Laura setting the table. The order was enough to feed ten people.

"Todd wanted it this way, Dad. He said he likes Chinese leftovers." "The food is ready, come eat, Todd!" Laura hollered.

Todd ran at a fast speed and sat next to his father. Jim asked, "will you show me how to use the chopsticks, Todd."

"Come on, Dad, you know how to use them, I want to eat I'm hungry!"

"You're always hungry, son, and you're thin like a stick, what's your secret?" Jim asked, teasingly.

"I don't know; I think I got it from you! Look at your athletic body!" "What a compliment, thanks!"

"How was your day, Dad?" Laura asked.

"Pretty good thanks, I had lunch with a church minister who asked me to give a speech to her congregation, and I said I'd think about it."

"Is she the same minister you spoke about to Mom two days ago?" "Yes, she told you about her?"

"Yeh, and she sounded jealous, which is a good sign, I think!" "Jealousy is never a good sign, my dear. Mom need not be jealous; I have no interest in any new relationship at this stage."

"You see, Laura, I told you! Dad still loves Mom," Todd intervened. "Shush, Todd! Dad knows how to speak for himself."

"Hey, take it easy, the two of you! Of course, I Love Janet, and I told you from the beginning. The current situation doesn't guarantee a revised bilateral meeting of the mind. Can we focus on her getting well now? What's in that box there, a mile away?" Jim asked.

"It is Todd's favorite; he keeps it at the end of the table so no one else can touch it," Laura said sarcastically.

"Is that true, Todd? Did I teach you to be selfish? Pass it to me, please." Jim opened the box, and a strong smell came out. What is it, Todd?"

"It is a spicy octopus! Try some it's delicious." Jim took a bite and almost spat it out,

"It's so spicy, how can you eat that? Here, you can keep it!"

"It is delicious the next day. You mix it with some Greek yogurt to balance it out, and there you have it." Todd proudly stated.

Jim looked at Laura and asked, "do I have a normal son?" and they all laughed. "I love you too, Dad!"

They chatted for a few more minutes, and then Jim excused himself to check if Janet is awake. Todd whispered to Laura, "I told you he still loves her."

"I heard that!"

Jim didn't see the nurse outside the door, so he figured Janet is awake. He knocked and entered. Janet was eating her dinner. She said,

"What is that smell? Chinese food, I guess!"

"You guessed right, and Todd is at it again with his weird choices of dishes."

"I should have warned you! He orders the weirdest stuff, and Laura always argues with him. Anyhow, how are you?"

"I'm fine; tell me about you, better, I hope!"

The nurse who was helping her with the food said, she's getting better, sir!"

"You see! If I told you, you wouldn't believe me, thank you, Olga!" "Good I'll go down and make some coffee while you eat."

"I'm about to finish, can you get me some too?" "No, no! Not yet, Madam."

Jim went downstairs and entered the kitchen and saw the children putting the food in the fridge. Todd asked him, "what, you fought already?" Jim gave him a nasty look and said, "you don't know how to stop, do you?" "I'm only kidding, Dad, I'll have some coffee with you, though!" he told his father. "You are in a good mood today, son! That's good, stay like that." Todd laughed and said, "it's the Chinese food, Dad." "I think you should study the language and find a job in China for a couple of years when you graduate from college, how about that?" Jim said.

Todd thought for a while then said,

"I want to work for you, Dad, and I know you go to China a few times a year, you can take me with you then."

"Who says I will hire you?"

"I know you will, I'm your only son, and I will inherit the business once I learn to be as good as you are," Todd affirmed.

"We shall see, at this rate, I'll soon be working for you, my dear smart elk!" Jim said a went back up with his coffee. Todd uttered, "to be continued." "I heard that, too, Todd."

"What a son you have downstairs! He never stops. He said he wants to run my business when I retire. I told him to go and work in china for a couple of years after his college; he said no, he wants to work for me and learn the trade."

"Do you blame him! He has the best teacher in the world." Janet said, then continued, "I am loving the "Prophet," I am about to finish it. Luckily it is a small book. I read some parts again and again, what a genius? You saw his art; it's mystical."

"You said it; many consider him a mystic. His fame put his small country, Lebanon, on the map. What struck you the most?"

"What did not strike me? Let me see!

"When love beckons to you, follow him, though his ways are hard and steep" or *"as love crowns you, so shall he crucify' and 'for love is sufficient unto love."* I can go on and on with this guy! It is as if he wrote my love story eighty-five years ago!"

"What else do you remember," Jim asked, enjoying her excitement about the book.

"When he talked about marriage and giving each other space saying, *"Fill each other's cup but do not drink from the same cup."*

"I like the one where he said, *"let it rather be a moving sea between the shores of your souls."* Jim recited. His poetic prose shows you how spiritual he was too.

The thing is, I got scared when I first read, *"Your children are not your children, they are the sons and daughters of Life's longing for itself."* But then, when I read the rest of the chapter and re-read it again until I understood what he was trying to say. Gee, I loved the whole section, and I intend to memorize it. I tend to be a possessive mother, and that's not the best for them."

"I'm so glad you're learning lessons from this amazing book. I bet you didn't have a chance to read the other one I gave you?" Jim wondered.

"You're right, and it is your fault, you should not have given me 'The Prophet' either." Janet surmised.

"No, that's okay, Gibran gives you a smooth entry into the spiritual field. It is uplifting and consider it as a good appetizer."

"Well said, teacher! How about you, anything new?"

"I saw Brian yesterday. He said during the dinner he and Charles, the president of the Center, had with Sylvia, the guest speaker; she told them that she was going to call me and ask me to speak at her church. Indeed, she called this morning and asked if we could meet for lunch to discuss something important in person. I agreed, and we had a quick lunch; she asked me to please seriously consider. I said I'm quite busy with work and family, so I'll let her know if I ever can, I'm neither a speaker nor truly qualified."

"Why she chose you, and not Brian or Charles?

"I asked, and she said a large number of her congregation are successful businesspeople like me, and my story of transformation would be significant to them. They are the main donors to her church."

"What else, are you going to see her again?" Janet asked.

"I don't see the need to do that. I'm not interested. I even told her I'd be busy coaching you on the way to liberation. She understood, and then we each went our separate ways."

"Good, how was your session with Brian yesterday?"

"Very good. I am now studying the Tao Te Ching with him." "The what?" Janet asked. Jim smiled and said, "It is an ancient Chinese spiritual philosophy from three centuries BC. It is an essential guide to live a spiritual and ethical guide. Wayne Dyer studied it and wrote a book about it. It is not for you yet; I'll let you know when it's a good time to learn about it. For now, I suggest you write down the highlights of the 'prophet' in a notebook for future reference and start reading the other book. You may also want to have a journal to write down your thoughts and feelings of the day. No rush, whenever you are ready!"

"Yes, sir! I'm so excited to have this project together."

"Me too, it is not a project; it is a learning experience how to live a spiritual life. By the way, when is the appointment with the doctor?" Jim asked.

"Next Thursday at 5:30 in the afternoon."

"Good I'll come at five and take you."

"Thanks, Professor!

"I'll let you rest again. I'll go downstairs and spend some time with the children, and then head down to the city. I come back to see you tomorrow; Friday I go to the Center."

"Thank you for coming and have a good night." Janet said and gave him a peck on his cheek.

Chapter 13
Closing the Door to Ego

Jim profoundly enjoyed the privacy of his thoughts and the sincerity of his feelings when he sat down to write,

Janet showed concern about another beautiful lady contacting me. She didn't trust herself enough to hold back her suspicious opinions. Her prior experience ended poorly, and her attempts to reunite with me are threatening. She wonders if I could be trusted this time while observing my evident spiritual transformation. Janet's old wounds of rejection have yet to be healed in full, though it was she who turned down my honest appeal to reunite with her again.

The accident, perhaps, has awakened her to seek the truth about her life. She has yet to practice the experience of self-love; she showed useless threads of jealousy untimely penetrating her mind. She has yet to start the spiritual journey she chose to have with me as her teacher. Undoubtedly, the ego will develop a new conflict in her mind and play new games of fear and suspicion to destabilize her aspirations.

I, on the other hand, subtly sensing Janet's fears, am careful handling another woman's potential interest in me. The existence of a new relationship with another woman would devastate Janet's hopes for a reunion and hurt her

more deeply than ever before. I do not wish to fold her wings from entering the door to salvation; neither do I want to see her breath creating strong winds that may demolish the fragile walls that contain her heart.

Having said that, and regardless of the conflict Janet might face ahead, I ask vital questions to myself: do I want to return and live in the home I built with my wife and children with a new foundation of love and loyalty? Or, has the time come for us to stay apart as friends? Will we have a strong foundation of True Love to sustain a healthy desire to see a joint life of aligned spirituality together? Will, a new door to the morning mist, bless us with joyful songs during the day, and heavenly silence during the night?

I am also aware I'm not immune from the games of my ego, either. Though I succeeded to mute ego's powers lately, the devil never sleeps, and he watches diligently any vulnerable move on my part. When ego senses weakness, it immediately attacks. The ego is always alert, looking from the corner of its eyes, searching for opportunities to exercise its power. I learned my lessons from what I read and heard, to be strong and not fall into ego's traps. On one side, I notice the moves by a beautiful woman, alive with open desires; on the other side, my estranged wife, yet restricted by her dormant feelings of true love.

I'm sincerely keen to help and support Janet's request for her journey to awaken inwardly, and to reinforce her strength not to fall under the grip of ego either. I will put on hold decisions about our potential future together until I see bright glimpses of her transformation, along with a body healed from pain. The forthcoming teaching should reveal the level of her commitment to stay on the path of her awakening.

In brief, I surrender my mind to the Universe, whose power would surely signal me to the new steps to take. I do not need to give a speedy response to the 'minister' nor should I adopt, prematurely, assumptions that the road for a future with Janet is already clear.

I hold my heart in the palm of my hand to regularly examine its depth and reveal all its secrets.

♦

The next day Jim saw Janet again, and the first thing she said when he walked into her room was,

"Hey, gorgeous man, are you still being chased by beautiful women?"

"Good day to you, too, dear Janet! What? You were dreaming about me all night?" Jim responded sarcastically to her silly greeting.

"It's good to see you! I read the entire book by Gibran, and the first chapter of Dr. Dyer's book." Janet proudly said.

"Which one you want to discuss first?" Jim asked.

"In the chapter on teaching, Gibran wrote: " *If he is indeed wise, he does not bid you enter the house of his wisdom, but rather leads you to the threshold of your own mind.*" Does this mean you would not share your wisdom with me? Janet asked.

Jim took the book and looked at the chapter, and he noticed that Janet did not fully understand that to know God, is an individual task not dependent on what the teacher says. He read to her the part of the last paragraph that says, *"each one of you is alone in his knowledge of God..."* Jim explained that a teacher guides and teaches, but the relationship with God, or the Consciousness within, is a very individual experience."

"So, two spiritual people could experience God, or the Universe, in different ways," Janet remarked.

"That's correct!"

"Now, in the amazing chapter on Prayer, Gibran says prayer is like *"entering the temple invisible,"* what does he mean by that?"

"In the context of chapter, you will understand Gibran's interpretation of prayer. It is not just uttering words or asking for favors from an outside entity called God. But more to enter the invisible realm that dwells within you, your spirit, or your soul. And the mere entry, therefore, reveals all your needs and all the answers to what you need. That is prayer, a form of silent meditation, and connection with the eternal soul that resides within you." Jim expounded.

"Wow! Thanks. Will you teach me how to meditate?"

"I can show you how to do it, but I can't teach you what to do when you meditate other than try to silence your mind from useless thoughts," Jim explained.

"Can you show me now?" Janet asked.

"Okay, sit up straight, close your eyes, breathe deeply in and out, and notice how, with every breath, thinking diminishes. And that helps you to connect with your true self, always aware of your breathing. Try it for five or ten minutes in the beginning; then you can build it up to a longer period. That exercise should put you in a relaxed position and clear your mind from unwanted thoughts or fears. God hears you, and you hear God in silence, and that's when you sense your prayers are answered." Jim said and demonstrated.

"Can we try it out for five minutes together before you leave." "It's a great idea, will do! How about "Your Erroneous Zones?"

"I don't have any errors! I'm pure and perfect!" Janet said, laughing and added, "If only I knew! I read his introduction and the first chapter. I may reread it, but I got a drift of what he says, which is that I have to do the work myself to take charge and responsibility for my life."

"You hit is right on! We have to do the work ourselves to achieve the desired happiness in our life. Any questions in that regard?" Jim asked.

"As I said, I want to read it more carefully and note down the questions to ask you in our next session. "The Prophet" took all my energy. But is have another question, "How do you feel about us doing this work together, does it bring you any closer to me?" Janet asked nervously.

Jim paused and then said,

"Humm… We are close. I'm happy I can be of some help with your new interest in a spiritual journey. I am confident that as you continue to stay on this road, my compassionate heart could bloom with warmer feelings of the love I had for you, and I trust that we mutually find the Truth in due course!"

"Wow, another diplomatic and poetic reply. So, you're not ready yet to say you love me and want us back together, true?"

"Not true, because it also depends on you. I would like to see you advance in your spiritual growth for me to feel more confident that we are moving together into the direction of reconciliation, singing the same song, not two, if you know what I mean!"

"I understand! But this may take some time." Janet said. "You're right, it might, why? Are you in a rush? I am around several days a week. We study together, and I have a great time with the children, so all is well. Patience is a virtue!"

"I understand! I feel a bit insecure seeing other women chasing you! Honestly, I don't want to lose you. I love you very much." Janet said with teary eyes.

"Janet, Janet… Can you please relax! Have faith, and believe I am a different man now. Please demonstrate your love with evidence of your self-love first. Cleanse your soul with the Love of God. Have no fear; you're not alone, I am here, by your side, eager to see you bloom with fresh flowers of love, the scent of which to spread widely in the rooms of your life."

"I swear to God, Jim, you're a gifted poet and a genius at work. I hear you, my dear, and I promise to continue with patience and trust."

"Good! Let's meditate for five minutes then I leave you to rest. The nurse must have your food ready by now. I'll join the kids, and see what Todd is going to feed me tonight."

"Thank you so much, my darling, (I hope you don't mind me saying that), and I'll see you Saturday. We all love you around here! Have fun with the kids, and good night." Jim received his reward, his peck on the cheek, and went downstairs.

♦

Todd met him at the bottom of the staircase and said,

"we're waiting for you, Dad, I'm starving! We heated the leftovers, and you and I will finish them tonight."

"Why, you and me, how about Laura?"

"She's eating cheese and apples for dinner."

"A wise decision! Make sure you keep the octopus away from me." Jim said, and Todd laughed loud.

"Why, did you think I am going to share it with you? Forget about it; it's mine! By the way, my birthday is coming soon, will you buy me a car?"

"Again, since you are in a good mood, I'll buy you a bus instead, provided you get the license to drive it."

"It's so much fun to have you are around, Dad, not with women all the time!"

When they sat at the table to eat, Laura who was listening to Todd jabbering said,

"The only smart thing you said Todd is the fact that having Dad around in much more fun than having you only, silly bum. So, Dad, how is Mom doing as a student?"

"You know she's very smart and diligent. She finished one book and starting with another. It's a lovely productive hour we spend together."

"Are you warming up to her lately?" Laura asked.

"Teaching is always more meaningful in a warm atmosphere!"

"What a diplomatic answer! Just keep the heater on, please!" Laura said, smiling.

"Todd, are you riding your bicycle?" Jim asked.

"Of course, Dad. That's how I go to school. I am not like lazy Laura, who prefers the bus! She also has a bike, why can't she use it? The school is only two miles away." "I don't' like the uphill ride, Dad. Don't listen to him, Mr. show-off." Laura explained.

"Are you coming here on Saturday?"

"Yes, of course, I'll spend about an hour with Mom, then we drive down to the city, okay?"

"Yay, I'm getting bored here with no school!" Todd said

Jim spent an hour with them playing scrabble, wished them a good night without a fight, and left. Laura and Todd went upstairs to kiss their mother a good night too.

◆

Jim went to the Center on Friday after work. He got the attention of both Charles and Brian together in the office. He updated them on the progress with Janet. Charles was not privy to the details as Brian was, so Jim repeated and explained to Charles that he is teaching Janet a Couple of times a week, and he had lunch with Sylvia.

"Apart from the teaching task, which Janet is miraculously serious about, she's also wanted to know if I am considering going back home anytime soon.

I told her it is premature, as I would like to see greater progress on her spiritual path. She said she understood, though she sounded somewhat insecure."

"Why would she be insecure?" Charles asked.

"I mentioned to her that I had lunch with Sylvia, who asked me to speak to her congregation, and that started expressions of suspicion in her mind, especially when I truly answered her questions about Sylvia's age, beauty, and social status."

"I see! You have to expect that from a woman who still cares about you. Women don't like competition. Janet is still in a fragile state of mind, shoveling out her fears, regretting her earlier decision to live apart. Yet, as you said, the accident must have stirred some awakening desire to become more enlightened, like you did. You are her man and her idol. She wants you exclusively to her, and no one else." Charles explained.

"I understand, and I told her I'm not ready yet to go back home. I also find Sylvia an amazing candidate to befriend. The human part in me is vulnerable to new attacks from the ego creeping into my mind with unsettling ideas."

"Such as what?" Charles asked.

"Look, I haven't had sex for several months now, and it is tempting when you sense a lady like Sylvia with hints of a potentially passionate interest. She does not hide the fact that she finds me attractive; neither do I hide it about her. Though I'm technically free to pursue a relationship with her, I'm still emotionally loyal to Janet, despite all that happened between us. I don't want a conflict in my life; what do you advise?" Jim asked both gentlemen. Brian said, "don't look at me, I'm not your man to give you any advice in this regard. Jim smiled and waited to hear from Charles.

"As you said, we are human, too, which makes us vulnerable to situations like that. From the conversations we had with Sylvia during dinner, I sensed that she liked you, and finds you unique, so I understand the caution. Though spiritual, she's human too, and a single woman, so I can understand her motivation too. The thing is, Janet loves you, and you love her. Putting her on a leash, waiting to progress spiritually, is an excuse on your part, if you don't mind me saying. You might be leaving an open door to see how things develop with Sylvia at the same time. That is what the ego wants!

"That indecisive state of mind will create a conflict in your head, and frustration on Janet's part. That is also an ideal scenario for the ego to step in and destroy dreams of peace and tranquility. If I were you, I would follow the vibes in my heart and take the path of least resistance. If it is Janet, you want, then express your love to her and abide by it. You could continue to teach her even if you were to live together again. But if your heart is with Sylvia, then come forth and hope it will work out. Where are you better off, with a person you know well, or someone you hardly know? You decide and bear the consequences of your decision." Charles stated.

"So, what you're telling is to decide, "fish or, cut bait," right?

"Right!"

"Thanks, Charles. Let us see how the drama unfolds. I'm certainly not eager to have new headaches. I'll keep you advised."

Jim and Brian went back to the hotel to pursue a discussion about the Chinese Tao philosophy.

♦

They sat around the table in the suite, and before they started discussing the Tao Te Ching, Brian asked Jim is Charles's remarks regarding Janet vs. Sylvia were harsh.

"No, not at all! I like direct answers. He's right, at any rate."

"If I may add, and since I miss having my family around, I am biased in favor of keeping the family intact. If your attraction to Sylvia is primarily physical, then I advise you to be careful. The external appeal fades, and will not last, despite her spiritual request that you may find attractive as well.

"I know many children of dysfunctional families and divorced parents who have serious emotional and psychological issues. Think about your children, whom I know you love so much, also think about Janet, whom you love too, and how sad you felt when she did not take you back. She changed since the accident. And, she will come along well spiritually, you'll see!"

"Thanks, Brian. I take your advice to heart, and you know that. I waited so long without any physical pleasure; I can wait a little longer. I will be careful with Sylvia too. Now, if we can go back to the Tao, I have a question, and I refer to the chapter where water was used as a role model. Contrary to what we heard, the cup should not overflow with water, can you elaborate why?"

"Yes, overflow means 'excess'. The Tao does not encourage excess in anything, even in business success. Too much success can bring you down." Brian explained.

"Isn't that true? You know my success story. It brought me down indeed; no excess then, Humm, I understand now. Another question about 'Mystic Oneness,' what is that exactly."

"Excellent question, it fits what we were talking about now. The chapter is about not being lured by temptation. It also says not to be affected by other people's opinions, good or bad. Trust in yourself."

"Interesting, how these signs appear at the right time. The same applies to the 'Mystic Virtue' chapter, where I noted the advice to teach and learn wholeheartedly to find a deep sense of being without getting wrapped up with the old self. The Tao has no beginning and no end, just a formless and imageless Being," Jim remarked.

"True, I add the advice you find in chapter fifteen: *empty yourself to find peace and tranquility.* Here, the Tao emptiness means to silence your mind and meditate to connect with your higher self."

"How about the example of the grass blade that bends with the wind but gets back straight, meaning, we bend when we suffer, yet we stand straight when we awaken in spirit. That is a joyful experience." Jim attested.

"You may have noticed the Tao addresses social and governmental issues in several chapters. You may skip those; they're not relevant to our work here. What I appreciated was the advice on how to behave: don't talk too much, be like rain in short bursts. Don't be arrogant and walk with your tiptoes; it's idiotic. Be grounded but not with heavy thoughts; be like a baby, simple and open. Be honorable, like a simple and great leader; and above all know yourself, it gives you strength, contentment, and enlightenment."

"Also, Brian, don't forget what he said about stillness or meditation. The beauty of life comes from within where you find oneness in spiritual power, peace, and vital energy. What I found interesting, and then we stop, is the advice from Sages who say you don't need to travel far to find God. You remember early on when I asked if I should go to an ashram, and you said no need. It's true, God is in our soul, and we always have our soul within us, so we always have God within us."

"With this remark, we conclude the teachings of the Toa. What other teachings would you like to do next?" Brian asked.

"I'm eager to study the teachings of Christ!"

"Okay, we'll select relevant teachings from the New Testament to discuss."

"Great! May I order a salad?"

"So sorry, Brian, I forgot about that. It's still early, I'll order right now, and I know what salad you like."

They chatted for a while waiting, and Jim was curious to learn from Brian how he manages to remain celibate for so long. Brian said it's been too long, and now he's more open to finding the right person with whom he can start a family again.

"Wonderful, maybe you should get to know Sylvia better! I know you like her."

"She likes you, Jim, not a simple man like me!"

"Don't say that, Brian. You're tall and handsome, smart like a whip and spiritual like no other I've seen. Don't underestimate yourself. You deserve the best. Go for it, and I'll stay out of your way!"

"You, you little devil, you!" Brian responded with a peal of laughter.

Chapter 14

Over the Bump and Moving Forward

What a day! Janet tells me she loves me and doesn't want to lose me; I beat around the bush and say be patient till I see some progress.

Charles tells me to be true to myself and not play games with Janet hiding behind Sylvia's door, who is not well known to you.

Brian tells me not to fall into temptation with physical desires that might ruin the progress of my love for Janet.

The ego tells me, don't listen, follow your heart's desire, go check out the new lady. She's beautiful, young, single, and spiritual, after all.

The ego adds, why wait for your wife's slow advance, and she might even disappoint you with her lack of spiritual depth?

I tell myself be careful, recognize you're still quite vulnerable and not as strong as you thought you were.

I sought advice from my wise friends and tried to shut the door to the neurotic games the ego plays.

I yearned to be forthright in my love for Janet, why would I want to hurt her again?

I love our children, and they love me back. Why not go back home and embrace Janet, who confessed her wrong for turning me away?

I also ask myself, did I not learn that physical pleasure alone is not worth the demise of a long-invested relationship, for so many years?

Why should I consider an alternative when I am blessed with a beautiful wife, two great children, and a comfortable loving home?

I tried the outer pleasures before and succumbed to the tricks of the ego, and what did I gain? Nothing; why would I lose my soul again?

I turned the telescope around to look within, and I know with the help of my true self how to see beauty, and live in peace, and joy. Why would I even consider changing such a blessed view?

Jim drove up to see the family on Saturday morning. The children were ready to go to the city with him to see the musical "Grease," the famous high school romantic story. Jim had bought the tickets on Friday and told them about it over the phone. He showed them the tickets he was holding, and they were so thankful and happy. He said,

"Your Mom and I saw the movie many years ago. You will like it. Who knows, Todd might even start changing his hairstyle to mimic the main character, and wear black leather jeans too?"

"Yea, Dad, who knows? I might!"

"Okay, let me go see your Mom for an hour, then we drive back." "I made some fresh coffee for you, Dad," Laura said.

"Thanks, honey, I'll take a cup with me upstairs."

"Hello, how do you feel today?" Jim asked when he entered the room after greeting the nurse sitting outside.

"Better, thanks! I can't wait to see the doctor on Thursday and ask to remove the plaster around my rib cage. I itch like crazy," Janet said.

"I'm taking the kids to see the musical, 'Grease' this afternoon." "They told me, they're so excited. I told the children we saw it ages ago when we were deeply in love! Todd laughed, of course!" "How are you coming along with the book?" Jim asked.

"Woo! He's a tough guy this Dr. Dyer. He goes on and on with a long-winded stretch explaining his points. He is generous sharing from his own experience and from the patients he had as a practicing psychiatrist. He makes his points come across clearly. I wrote down a list of highlights for you to see," Janet said and gave Jim the sheet with the list.

He went through the remarks Janet noted down while sipping his coffee, and three minutes later, he looked at Janet and said,

"I'm quite impressed. Good job! Do you reread the highlights?"

"Of course, how else can I learn. I want my lessons to register. I also cheat sometimes, and flip through the 'Prophet' to devour its poetry."

"That's not a bad idea. Many fans keep the book at the side table in their bedroom for the same reason. Do you have any questions to discuss?"

"Yes, I have one, maybe two?" "Shoot!"

"Dyer concludes the first chapter challenging me to believe that my mind is my own, of course, it is, so why does he ask?"

"We grow up feeding our mind with all kinds of stuff, we hear from parents, friends, culture, and movies and so on. So, our minds get crowded with so much material that is not ours. We need to clean that up and focus on what we believe and who we are and not be affected by other people's opinions or by the games of the ego from past stories and events. The mind is not the physical brain, which is, of course, yours, the mind is the brain in action and the stuff in it has to be sorted out."

"I understand, thanks! He also says we should control our own feelings. That's is not easy sometimes."

"It is not easy most of the time, especially when you are not yet connected with the inner self. Negative thoughts lead to negative feelings, and negative feelings lead to emotional outbursts that are dictated by the ego, who always wants us to believe we are right, and others are wrong. So, that is what is meant by controlling your feelings. Later on, in the book, he explains methods to learn how to control. The key is to learn how to choose what is best for you, and to enjoy living in the present moment." Jim explained.

"Wow, I love being your student! I love to hear you speak, and I love the radiant expressions on your face; the more I see you like that, the more I desire to hug you and kiss you. Thank you!"

"Maybe you can start doing that after they remove the plaster around your chest. Any other questions?" Jim asked.

"No, not, for now, it was a long chapter, you know! How was your time at the Center yesterday?"

"Good, I saw Charles and Brian then I went to the hotel with Brian to discuss the rest of the 'Tao Te Ching' book. We were so immersed in it. I forgot to order food. Brian reminded me, he was hungry, and we ordered two salads. He's such a nice, humble guy!"

"You like Brian, don't you?"

"Of course, I do! He's like a brother to me, not my spiritual mentor only! He is so strong he hasn't gone out with a woman since he lost his wife and daughter, as you know. I encouraged to try again; it's been more than three and a half years already."

"Did he listen to you?"

"He said he is more open to trying now; I even suggested he asks the minister, Sylvia, out to lunch or dinner. She would be the perfect match for this highly spiritual and ethical man."

"And? What did he say?"

"First, he said he does not have the aura or the personality that people like Charles or me have. To which I said, it's not true, he has an aura, and all he needs to do is to unveil it and not be so shy. He's tall and handsome and has a great mind too. He was my chief accountant, as you know, and still handles my personal accounts. I trust him with blinders on."

"Do you think he'll do it? Will he call her? They met before, and that should not be so difficult?" Janet suggested.

"I'll keep reminding him, don't worry! I'm sure you will be more relaxed, when this lady's ghost stops haunting you."

"Honestly, it is true! I get jealous of the man I love." Janet said with a gentle diminished voice.

"You don't need to be jealous, whether she connects with Brian or not. She's not on my mind."

"Easier said than done! I know women, they're like snakes and men do not know it when they suddenly get exposed to their creepy games." Janet expressed.

"But she is a spiritual leader, not a snake, my dear!"

"Oh, you'll never know! She's human too. She has feelings and desires as well, like any other woman around."

"Okay, fine! So, you want to be jealous now?"

"Please, push Brian to act fast, please! I want her out of your mind, and I want to see you regain your interest in me. I am beautiful too, I lost weight, and I will be in good shape, once the remnants of the accident are gone. To say it simply, I want you to love me, and me only; that's all!" Janet stated clearly and confidently. Jim stood up and kissed her on the forehead and said,

"I hear you! The kids are waiting for me. We'll have lunch and then see the musical. You rest well and study hard, and all is okay! I will see you tomorrow afternoon. Bye!"

Janet was thrilled to hear that Jim had no intention to go after Sylvia, who became a haunting monster in her mind. She prayed that a relationship with Brian would soon get started, and to forget about Jim all together. Janet smiled and closed her eyes to create more positive dreams. She sensed that Jim was warming up toward her, and she decided to patiently wait until he's ready to make his move to return home.

◆

The musical was very entertaining. Laura imagined herself in the forth-coming high school years, and Todd was more interested in how the boys were dressed and some of the songs. He cared less about romance.

"So, where do we go to buy my leather outfit, Dad?" Todd said with a firm tone.

"Serious?'

"Yes, Dad, I want to start attracting beautiful girls. I'll be thirteen next month. Buy it for me as a birthday gift."

"Todd, you told me you have no interest in girls, what hit you all of a sudden?" Laura asked her brother.

"I don't know, hormones, I guess!"

Jim smiled and admired his son, who was quickly gaining height, almost as tall as Laura, who is fourteen, to be fifteen in three months.

"I'll tell you what, why don't we all go for some ice cream instead, and we wait for the leather outfit later?"

"Okay, Dad, provided we go to a Chinese restaurant for dinner." "No way!" both Jim and Laura shouted at the same time.

"Gee, what a considerate family! Then we go to Burger King." "Again, No!" Jim said. "I wait to have a good meal with you guys, give me a break. Eat your hamburger during the week."

At 7:00 pm Jim reserved a table at a French restaurant near the hotel and wanted to familiarize Todd with a more sophisticated cuisine. When they were seated at the table, Laura told Jim that she is noticing a continued positive change in her Mom's attitude at home.

"What makes you say that?" Jim asked.

"I talk to her privately sometimes, and she brags about the enjoyable lessons she's having with you and hints about how happy she gets to see you around so much… Stuff like that!"

"Come on, Laura; the writing is on the wall, can't you tell? Mom and Dad will be back together in no time! You want to bet?" Master Todd declared.

"Who authorized you to speak on my behalf, son?"

"No one did! I just read what's written on the wall; that's all!" They all giggled, and Jim then said,

"I agree that warm vibes of love are brewing between us, and we're both aware of these vibrations. We agreed not to rush, though, and focus on two things, for now, Mom's health, and her commitment to pursue a spiritual path."

"Isn't that conditional love? You talked to us about un-conditional love before why not apply it in this case?" Laura asked.

"A good question, my dear! We have an inherent understanding of our desire to reunite, but it is coupled with the fact that we don't need to rush until, as I just said, she's up and running again, and the foundation for our reunion is deeply cemented in our hearts. So, keep thinking positive, and watch the play unfold in the theatre of our lives."

The conversation shifted to their friends, neighborhood boys and girls they know, and Laura's coming first year in high school. The children enjoyed the French dessert, and they all walked back to the hotel to relax and watch a movie on TV.

◆

When they returned home, they found Janet walking around in the living room. Jim asked her how she came down the stairs and whether it was painful. Janet said she could tolerate the little pain and wanted to move around as she missed the rooms downstairs. She reminded them it'd been two weeks already, and it is time to become mobile.

They all sat down together and had an enjoyable conversation, about the musical, Todd's desire to buy leather pants to impress the girls in school and wanted to eat Chinese again.

"Did you really, Todd?" Janet asked.

"Yeah, Mom, they refused to eat Chinese, and Dad took us to a fancy French restaurant instead. Luckily the dessert was good!"

"You also want to impress the girls in school with a leather outfit?"
"Yeah, it looked good on the kids in Grease, and I also would like to dress my hair like them, with gel and stuff!"

"Boy! You're growing up fast. You're not my little boy anymore!"

"I hope Dad takes me shopping at a leather shop soon, before my birthday next month." Todd reminded his father. "Did you promise him that, Jim?" Janet asked.

"No, you know your son, he plants a seed in his mind and considers it done. He can buy his leather outfit when he graduates from high school." Jim responded.

"I thought you love me, Dad!" Todd complained. "That's why I said that because I do love you!"

"But how about the girls in school next year?" Todd asked

"What about them? If you want to impress girls, you impress them with your charm and gentle manner, with your school grades, and with your sports activity. Does that help, son?"

"Okay, whatever!" Todd said and excused himself to go to his room. Laura, who was enjoying the dialogue, also excused herself as well. She wanted to give some privacy to her parents.

"Todd is quite a character, isn't he?" Janet remarked.

"He reminds me of me when I was his age, though I was not privileged like him, spoiled and assumptive!"

"He is a good kid, anyhow!"

"Absolutely! I love him dearly, but I have to keep an eye on him." Jim said.

"Good, I hope destiny would bring us back together under the same roof as it will also facilitate our communication with the children."

"I agree!"

"Did you hear from Brian?"

"No, why? I'll be seeing him this evening; we have a session together."

"Who knows, maybe he called the lady, and they went out already!" Janet hoped.

"You're still obsessed with that woman? Can we leave her alone, and let them do what is best for them? I would ask him later if he dared to call her. On Friday, he said he'll consider it. We'll see, and I will keep you posted, my eager beaver."

Janet smiled and said she is into the second chapter about Love, and "I bet you it is triggering many questions in my mind. I am not finished with it yet, but I remember what he said early in the chapter about the definition of love. Let me paraphrase; he said, *"love is being able to allow the ones you care for to be what they choose to be for themselves, without insisting they satisfy you."* Boy, it is not easy to comply with giving the one you love so much freedom without expecting satisfaction in return. What do you think?"

"This requires a great deal of self-esteem to allow that in a love relationship. True Love is liberating. The Greeks call it Agape, meaning you love someone without expecting them to love you back. It is a 'giving' kind of love, without the promise of 'receiving' love in return. That requires inner strength on the part of the caring person, a deep spiritual understanding founded in self-love. Does this help you to understand it better?"

"Of course, my professor! It requires trust as well, something I need to work hard on. That's why I feel insecure when other women come in the picture. I should trust you and not be jealous. As you said, I should practice self-love, and I believe that will nourish me as I move further on this journey of awakening." Janet said.

"Bravo! Once we understand a certain concept, it becomes easier to apply it. You're on the right track, dear Janet, stay the course! I have to leave soon because Brian is coming at 6:00 this evening. Let me help you up the stairs, and I will also say good night to our beloved children."

It was almost 5:00 pm, and Jim helped Janet up with her arm around his shoulder, and he heard say, "it feels so good to be held by you." Jim remained silent and helped her to get in bed. He kissed her on the cheek and went out to say good night to Laura and Todd. The evening nurse shift was not required anymore, and Janet said Laura would get her food that was prepared to eat for dinner in an hour. Jim also suggested summer camp ideas for the children in August, as discussed with them already.

◆

Brian arrived on time, and before they started their discussion, Brian voluntarily said,

"I took your advice on Friday, and I called Sylvia to see if she's free for a meal together. She agreed, and we had lunch together on Saturday. Are you happy now?"

"You see! It's not that difficult; how did it go?" Jim asked.

"I am beyond words; it went very well. The woman is amazing, Jim. I think she liked me, and we agreed to keep in touch. I appreciate your advice, and I can easily fall in love with such a lady. I did not feel for one minute that I was with a church minister. She's so humble and sweet. I told her all she wanted to know about me and my life story. She was very sympathetic. Thank you again for encouraging me. You are a true friend."

"Brian, I'm sincerely very happy to hear that. Tread carefully and don't overburden her with many calls. Control yourself and leave the encounters to the weekends for now. Buy her some flowers on occasion or a small gift you think she likes; this is such good news! I will call Janet now and tell her because she asked me if you two connected. It will ease her concern that Sylvia is not after me, and no need to be jealous anymore."

Jim called Janet and told her the story as Brian, who is with him, narrated it. Janet was happy to hear that, and Jim wished her a good night's rest.

"Now, what do we have for today?" Jim asked.

"Teachings of Jesus Christ! We will immerse in a vast set of teachings, and I have selected the ones related to our situation without being too analytical or critical."

"Fine, do I have to do any reading before we start?"

"In case you don't have the New Testament, I have one to give you here. Read the gospels the next couple of weeks, then the epistles of Paul that talk about Christ. These two sections should be sufficient to enrich our knowledge and learn from his teachings. Later, you can read the rest if you wish." Brian said.

"Did you read these parts of the New Testament before?" Jim asked. "Yes, a few times, indeed! There are three main themes to know about Christ, 1) He suffered as the agent and servant of God; 2) He died to atone or forgive our mistakes (sins) and make it right with God, and 3) He was a man of obedience, and he corrected the disobedience Adam made.

"We will focus on his parables, and who he was as a spiritual teacher. Another thing to note is the fact that not all scholars agree that the written word and the historical dates are literarily true. What is important is the relevance of His teachings to our everyday spiritual life." Brian explained.

"Did His teachings advance you in your spiritual journey?"

"I am a big fan of Christ, as a Master Teacher, and as a personality that perfectly divine and human at the same time. He had universal appeal and delivered a great message to humanity. You will find his teaching unique when compared to other great teachers and Masters, especially in the areas of Love and Forgiveness."

"Interesting! I'll get started right away and note down any questions for us to discuss," Jim said.

"What else would you like to know?"

"It can wait, it's about Paul and whether he was the one who started Christianity as I heard before?"

"I can tell you for sure that Jesus Christ did not start the religion of Christianity. It is not mentioned anywhere in the Bible that he had anything to do with it. He said once, according to Mathew, "I will build my church," He didn't say churches, and he did not mean an institution, but a fellowship. He even said, "Many shall come in my name and deceive many." Whether Paul or Peter started the religion does not matter, the church as we know it today is man-made, not Christ created."

"Thanks, Brian, this all sounds fascinating. Let's order some food and relax a bit." Jim announced.

"So, how are things between you and Janet?" Brian asked. "Much better, thanks! Not only she's coming along well in her spiritual pursuit; we're both warming up nicely toward one another. The children are so happy to see me around o briefly, and Todd is becoming a young man who needs closer care by me. Todd asked to go to a soccer summer camp for two weeks, and Laura would like to work on her tennis game too. Both camps are not far, in Upstate New York. By then, three weeks from now, Janet will be able to move around easily, and I can take her out and spend some special time together."

"That sounds great, Jim. I am glad you are moving in this direction. Perhaps soon, we can out one evening together, with Sylvia?"

"That would be interesting. I intended to call and tell Sylvia that I would be willing to share my testimony with her congregation on a Sunday, early September. I will ask Janet and the children to be there, perhaps some friends from the Center as well. You're my friend, and it would be nice if the four of us can become friends as well."

"This is music to my ears! I'm also sure you'll do a wonderful job with your speech!" Brian affirmed happily.

◆

Jim called Sylvia the next day from the office.

"I thought you'll never call, how are you, stranger?"

"I'm fine, Sylvia. I'm sorry I didn't get back to you earlier. I thought about your proposal, and I am ready to do it early September if your invitation is still open."

"Absolutely! Thanks a lot. I'm sure you will do a great job."

"Good! By the way, I saw Brian on Friday, and he told me you had lunch together. He enjoyed your company, and I tell you, Sylvia, he's one of the greatest men I met in my life. I hope you two can enjoy a long and happy friendship. "

"Thank you, Jim, I like him too! How's your wife's health?" Sylvia replied coldly, realizing he had no interest in pursuing a personal relationship with her.

"She's getting better, and on Thursday, we go check her liver with the doctor and see if they would remove the plaster around her rib cage. I told her about you and how great you are. She looks forward to meeting you. Perhaps she would join me when I deliver my speech. So, the first Sunday in September then, okay?" Jim said.

"Well noted! And thank you for accepting; that means a lot to me, and bye for now!"

Jim felt good getting it out of his chest, sensing Sylvia's disappointment. He spent the rest of the day working hard; then he drove up to the house.

◆

Again, he saw Janet downstairs when he walked into the house; she was pacing back and forth in the living room while chatting with the kids.

"Hey, how are you guys? Janet, you're restless, huh?"

"You said it, I am, and I feel better walking around. How was your day?"

"Good! Since we're all together, are we all set about the summer camps for two weeks, each?"

"Yeah, Dad, it would be wonderful for me to improve my tennis game, meet new people, and change environment," Laura said.

"Me too, I hope they let me play goalkeeper in the soccer team," Todd added. "Of course, they'll let you! We'll talk to the coach when we go there," Jim said. "We're all going to eat together tonight. Laura and I will make pasta, the one you like, and have a salad to start. I miss having a meal together, and I hope it's okay with you too!" Janet asked Jim.

"Are you kidding, it's an honor! Sorry, Todd, no Chinese food tonight," Jim said then Janet added, "good, we'll eat first, and then you and I will continue with our session, okay? Laura, let's boil the pasta, my dear, everything else is ready."

Jim stayed with Todd in the living room. He asked his son,

"So, I'm glad to hear that you are willing to make friends with girls now. Remember how you resisted that before?"

"It's part of growing up, Dad!"

Chapter 15

Revived Family Reunion

Jim and Brian continued with the sessions about the teachings of Christ. Jim was deeply immersed in reading the gospels, always wondering how Christianity has developed as a religion, different from what Christ had taught. Jesus had no intention to structure his teachings to be restricted to a select number of believers. His message was for all humankind, and not to create a religion in His name.

The gospels of Mathew, Mark, Luke, and John were the main accounts covering the life of Jesus Christ on earth. There are varied opinions whether they were the authors of the gospels or embellished later by others in the second century. Paul also wrote many letters describing how Christ would have like us to live.

"What makes the New Testament unique from other religious books or teachings?" Jim asked Brian.

"Perhaps the concepts of Love and Righteousness make it unique. *"Seek ye first the kingdom of God and His Righteousness,"* Mathew 6:33 and *"God so loved the world that he gave His only son and whoever believes in Him should not perish but inherit eternal life,"* John 3:16. These are two powerful statements that make the New Statement unique."

"Why there are four different gospels, not just one, and how are they different?" Jim asked again.

"This is a good question, and I don't know the full answer, especially that some scholars question the authorship of the gospels. However, the written gospels do emphasize different themes form one another. Mathew wanted to prove that Christ is the Messiah, the anointed one, the savior. Mark focused on the human side of Christ. Luke wanted followers to strengthen their faith that Jesus came to fulfill God's will, and John focused on the Love of Jesus, and He is the light of the world, and the best way to salvation."

"I notice that several times Jesus was identified as the way, the light, the gate to salvation, the good shepherd, the bread of life, the true vine of God's vineyard, and the resurrection. He also considered himself and the Father as one. Was that a voice of confidence or pride on his part?"

"Scholars refer to his declaration as one with God as the *"I Am-ness."* He was sure of his connection with 'the Father,' God. He did not do anything wrong or commit any sin, plus he wanted his disciples and followers to know they can also connect with God, *"who lives within."* Even now, when people pray or meditate, try to connect as he taught. More than two thousand years ago. Luke, in chapter 17:21, clearly confirms that God is within us, which modern teachers also refer to, as the Universe, the Creator, or the Source."

"I see! another question, what is the difference between the soul and the holy spirit?" Jim wanted to know.

"Again, many scholars believe the soul is human, and the holy-mind-spirit is divine. Words can be deceptive and may not represent the true meaning. What matters is to search for the divine power within, where we sense the presence of God or the Universe. Christ was very aware of his meditation and connection with God when he withdrew from the crowd to connect quietly with the "father'. This practice encourages us to do the same as he did daily." Brian explained.

"I wrote down here the main practical lessons I learned from the sermons and parables of Christ. Let me know if I missed out on any, please!" Jim showed Brian the list:

- Love others (God, neighbor, and enemy) as you love yourself.

- Don't worry about your food, clothing, or finances- see the birds.

- Serve others it elevates you to greatness

- Don't treat others in a way different than how they treat you.

- Ask, and you will receive.

- Don't judge other people. It's not your business.

- Don't mix words, be honest and direct.

- When you give to others, be discrete, not flashy.

- Forgive and say you're sorry; it frees you from your chains.

- Have faith; you can move mountains with little faith.

- You are gifted with unique talents- use them

- Control your mouth and don't use foul language

"Good work, Jim! You covered a lot of Christ's teachings. You notice how all the lessons are universal for all humankind, not meant for Christian followers only. Do you know why Jesus used parables?"

"To help people see and understand his message better, I guess!" "You guessed, right. Next, we move to lessons from Paul's letters." "Okay, fine. I will do my homework and will discuss a week from this Friday. Tomorrow I take Janet to see the doctor and hope she will receive a clean bill of health."

"How are you two coming along, if I may ask?" Brian asked. "Pretty well, Brian. I feel I'm getting close to burst the bubble of silence and declare my willingness to return home."

"This is great news! Stay the course, and I will see you on Friday."

♦

Jim arrived in time to take Janet to see the doctor in the hospital. The doctor instructed the nurse to remove the plaster and asked for a CT scan of Janet's abdomen. He reduced the use of pain killers considerably and asked her to take only if necessary. He advised her to take long walks and get fresh air. The CT scan showed some inflammation around Janet's liver, and he prescribed anti-inflammation pills and to check with him again in two weeks.

Jim and Janet were satisfied with the definite progress, and she felt so much better and mobile without being wrapped around her ribcage. They hugged and smiled on the way back home. The children were anxiously waiting, and they knew everything went well merely by the look of their parents' happy faces. Congratulations were in order, and Jim said they would all go out for dinner to celebrate Janet's recovery.

"How about our session? I'm ready!" Janet asked.

"We'll find time to do it when we return from dinner. It's almost 7:00 already."

After a happy meal at their favorite Italian restaurant in town, they were back home by 8:30. The children went to their rooms, and Jim went with Janet to her room for the lesson. She pulled out her notes about the chapter she had finished, 'breaking free from the past.'

"This is so relevant to our situation, Jim. We both erred big time because we toiled with the past and allowed it to hurt our relationship. This repeated thing we say easily, "sorry, that's the way I am," clouded our thinking and made us stubborn unnecessarily. In my case, the past made me self-centered and narcissistic." Janet stated.

"How do you plan to put the past behind you then?" Jim asked.

"It's not going to be easy to get rid of past habits overnight. I will set goals to act differently, but I also need your help to point out the behavior you see out of line; to establish a trusted relationship to help each other out. I will also keep a journal to jot down every time I notice I'm being self-centered. Also, Dr. Dyer suggested that I do something different than what I used to do in the past." Janet explained.

"Different, such as what?"

"Not to jump to conclusions prematurely or be suspicious of you anymore."

"Good work, Janet, I will help you, and I also count on you to help me in the weak areas related to my past. I am not perfect, either."

"So, we move on, I guess! Let us celebrate this progress privately, you and me, why don't you come here and sit next to me and let me kiss you for a change, something different, you know?"

Jim moved to sit next to her in bed. He hugged her and kissed her neck first, then their lips connected, and together they shared a passionate kiss that had been forgotten for more than a year now. Janet sobbed with tears of joy and kept hugging Jim tightly despite her freshly removed plaster. Jim was lovingly responding with sweet words assuring of his readiness to rejoin the family. Janet looked at him with teary eyes and said,

"I love you so much, please forgive me!"

"I love you too, sweetheart. We are meant to be together. I am so grateful, and I feel so free from the burdens of the past. I will take the necessary action to come home as soon as possible. Let us go out and call the children and tell them the good news."

Jim and Janet walked out and knocked on the children's doors, asking them to come down; they have something important to say. Within three minutes, they were all gathered in the living room, eager to hear what Dad had to say. Jim reached out and held Janet's hand and said,

"Your Mom and I talked, and I am coming back home soon!" Both children jumped from their seats to hug both parents with joyous expressions they had done in a long time. "This is the best news ever!" Todd shouted.

"When do you plan to be with us, Dad?" Laura asked.

"I don't think I need more than a week to put my things together and check out from the hotel."

"Great! It'd be before we go camping, so you and Mom can have another honeymoon together." Todd said lovingly.

"Good thinking, son! What else do you suggest we do?"

"Go somewhere, and enjoy the sun, or the beach, I don't know?"

It felt good to be together again as one happy family, gazing at one another with smiles of joy and relief. Jim overwhelmed with love, and Janet still shedding her tears of happiness. Laura sat by her side cherishing the special moments of true love. Jim then excused himself to go back, it was getting late. He kissed and hugged them all and then said he'll be back Saturday.

Before Jim went to sleep, he sat down at his desk to write about the pleasant events of the day,

I woke up still bound by the chains of my heart, harnessed to seek unchained freedom in the citadel of my life!

In the evening tide, I broke the chains and set myself free. I glued together the fragmented parts of my soul to declare love as my new hero!

The lost sheep was found and reunited with his flock, not wandering in the wilderness of loneliness and separation!

I cast off the garment of fear from my heart, and I now wear the chosen garment of love from my soul!

I implore all the past shadows of fear to fade, and I invite the light of love to show me the blessed way.

Emotions of guilt and worry muted with no concern about feelings of rejections and revenge but smiles of welcome to prevail.

The present moment is the real power of life, not the pains of the past and not the fears of the future.

◆

Jim told Brian and Charles about his decision to move back to rejoin the family when they met with him on Friday at the Center. They were thrilled to hear the good news, particularly Brian, who always hoped Jim would go back to his family.

Brian briefed Jim on the progress of the new Center in Philadelphia, with fifty reliable members, and told him about the plans for another Center in Miami, starting next week.

Jim spent one hour at the Center, including listening to a lecture given by a Muslim Sheikh, that Charles knew. The speech was about the validity of the Quranic teachings in modern times. Jim noted five main points:

- Be kind and mindful of others.

- Speak well and don't use foul language.

- Do good deeds, be creative, and forgive (pardon) others that hurt.

- Don't be lazy, use your mind, and reflect on helping others.

- The Quran is full of wisdom, enjoyable to read, and apply in life.

Jim found it interesting how similar the Quranic teachings are to other lessons, like the Bible, or the Tao.

◆

Brian walked with Jim to the hotel after the lecture. On the way over, Brian told him that he and Sylvia talk on the phone every other day, and they will go out to dinner tomorrow, Saturday. Brian also knew that Jim decided to give a speech early Saturday and hoped to introduce Janet to Sylvia soon.

"So, everything is cool between you two!" Jim remarked.

"That's true, and I tell you, Jim, I feel a good chemistry between us. I don't know what she found in me to like?"

"Here we go again, Brian, stop underestimating yourself. You want me to repeat what I told you earlier?"

"I know! What can I say? I'm flattered. It's been a long time since someone gave me a warm compliment. I hope this continues to be a smooth relationship because I like Sylvia."

You are a smooth operator, don't even think twice about it. She's lucky to know you!"

"When do you plan to move out of the hotel?" Brian asked. "Within a week! I may need your help to pack some stuff!" "Just let me know, and I'll be there."

As soon as they arrived at the suite, Jim ordered the salads with freshly baked bread and some cheese. He even ordered half a bottle of red wine to celebrate the new developments in both their lives.

"Okay, now the great Paul, where do we start?" Jim asked.

"You read about his strong personality and his story as a previous torturer of Christ's followers before he converted on his way to Damascus! Anyhow, the main theme of Paul's message is that 'Christ Is God' born in the flesh. Christ died to atone the sins of humankind and was resurrected to ensure the believers they will inherit eternal life."

"Yes! And allegedly, Paul is the one that started the Christian church, is that correct?"

"Well, certainly not Jesus, and maybe not Peter, the disciple! It does not matter. Let us talk about his teachings. Did you note anything down or should we flip through the pages of his epistles?" Brian suggested.

"I save you the energy; I did my homework! Here is a sheet with my notes, as they relate to our living mission nowadays, I'll read it first,

- To be a messenger of God is not restricted to a select group of people; anyone can be a messenger of God.

- God's grace saves us, so we have nothing to fear.

- We should all have priorities in our life and put God first.

- If we make mistakes in life, it is okay, and God forgives us.

- Our past does not define us. I love that; it jives with what we studied before.

- We should have a quiet time and meditate as Jesus did.

- We should be compassionate and care for others.

- Remain humble, and know you still have room to grow.

- Do not be greedy with big hopes for the future, be content, and live in the present moment. (Again, like Tolle teaches.)

- Be consistent in your faith and live a Christ-like life.

"You are a good learner. Very well done! You read and reflect on how the material can affect our daily life now. So far, we covered a good range of studies, and I believe you deserve a graduation certificate with honors. You're going to be spending more time with the family, and I'll be doing some traveling, plus some attention to Sylvia. So, no need to follow a strict schedule twice a week. We meet when we can, and I'm only a phone call away. You should expect Charles and me with some other members from the Center, to be there listening to your speech, we're sure you'll do a good job!" Brian said with a gracious smile.

Brian considers me a graduate of the first school of the spiritual realm, which was very rewarding.

Jim reflected on the tree that he planted seven months ago, now bearing fruit to share.

The winter ice of life melted its shadows, by the warmth of the sun that gave light to his days.

The garden flowers bloomed with sweet fragrance to inhale and lighten his heart with freedom from the chains of past emotions.

His mind now enriched with precious teachings of Sages, Masters, and Teachers of Love and Peace.

His soul hummed with new songs of love, inviting him to dance on his new floor of joy.

The circle of outer experiences brought him back to where he belonged, grateful to the wisdom of heavenly angels.

Jim cherished the above revelations that he wrote before he went to sleep. He dreamt he was flying with strong wings high above the clouds, greeting them with a massive smile on his face.

◆

He woke up Saturday morning fresh and rested. He had his coffee and an hour later, he drove up to the house to see Janet, and the children to spend the last weekend in the city.

The children were waiting for him in the living room. He went upstairs to see Janet. He knocked and entered her room. He found her dressed elegantly and she looked beautiful, with make-up welcoming him with a big smile.

"Are you going somewhere? You look great!" Jim asked.

"No, this is for you, I'm trying to seduce you! Can't you tell?" Janet teased.

"How am I going to teach you now, I can't concentrate with you looking like this!"

" I can sit in your lap, or you sit with your back to me, you decide!" "You're being a naughty girl!"

"Don't you like that? I'm celebrating my clean bill of health and my new spiritual path. These were your two conditions, remember? I am your obedient student and wife."

Listen, Janet we don't have too much time to be romantic now! The children are waiting and this will be their last weekend in the city, be patient please."

"Fine! Then try to teach me for thirty minutes and I'll try to behave myself." Janet pretended with a soft complaint.

"Okay! Did you take any notes on the chapter you studied?" "Yes, Sir! Here you can read my remarks!"

"I see! You worked on the 'declare your independence' chapter. A good choice, I would say!"

"Gibran inspired me when he wrote about marriage, that we are two independent souls. I spent my life being dependent, as you very well know, so I wanted to learn how to be independent yet in love, loyal, and all the other good stuff." Janet said.

"I can see you wrote two full pages on the subject. You basically wrote your own Declaration of Independence. We should frame it and feature it in the Congress Hall." Jim remarked with a smile.

"Don't make fun of me, Mr., I declare I will no more be submissive to others. I will be respected for my independence, and I will treat others exactly the way I expect them to treat me. What do you think?"

"Bravo, just be yourself, and the rest is easy! I commend on the good notes you wrote and I take it you don't have any questions to ask."

"I told you I'm a fast learner and thank you for your guidance."

"I wanted to tell you that I should start writing my speech I'm supposed to give early September. I would like you and the children to be there with me. I may ask you to stand up for identification during my speech. I want to show you guys off to the congregation." Jim said.

"Okay! Let me know if I can help."

"It is going to be poetic prose, are you good with poetry?"

"Wow! That must be amazing. A Poetic speech! I can't wait. May I kiss you now?" Janet asked and didn't wait for Jim's answer, she reached straight to him with her lips at his mouth for a deep delicious kiss. Jim liked it!

"Listen, don't get me too excited, I have to drive the children to the city and you can come with us if you like. You can share the room with Laura and Todd can sleep on the sofa bed. What do you say? You've never seen my hotel suite and it's good to say goodbye like that."

"What do you think the children will say if I come?"

"They will love it, they know I'm back already, it'll be a lot of fun! I'll go down and tell them while you pack what you need for a one-night stay. Tonight, we all go out and have a great dinner at one of your favorite restaurants."

"What a delight! That sounds wonderful. Go tell them and give me ten minutes to be ready."

Jim went downstairs and told the children about the plan. They were excited and giggled saying "Yay, Mom will be with us this weekend."

They all were joking and laughing on the way back to the city, and for Janet that was a real treat!

The family had an amazing time together in the city. Janet received a lot of love from Jim and the children. The activity was based on what Janet liked and wanted. They ate at her favorite restaurant, saw a movie of her choice, played her favorite card game and went to the museum of modern arts to make her happy.

Furthermore, they all helped Jim to pack his personal belongings on Sunday morning and he notified the front desk that he was checking out at 2:00 in the afternoon. Janet was thrilled that Jim was returning home with them to stay.

♦

The camps started the following Saturday, and the parents drove each of the two children to the designated camps. On the way back home

Jim asked Janet if she would like to go somewhere to celebrate their reunion,

"How about one week in a health spa? We have cleansed our hearts so why not cleanse our bodies with special treatments, massages and facials… we go to a place where we can walk, talk, and relax." Janet suggested.

"That's a brilliant idea. Do you a place in mind?" Jim asked.

"I always wanted to go the Canyon Ranch Spa in Lenox, Massachusetts. It is a five-star spa with all the amenities you want., and only two and half hours away by car. It is a perfect place to detox and clean my body from all the painkiller pills I had to take. We can both rejuvenate and get spoiled for a change. It is a palace with beautiful grounds, great for walks as well. How about that?" Janet said.

"Sounds great, let's do it for a week starting next Thursday. Can you please take care of the reservation, or I can ask Mary if you prefer?"

"No, I'll do it! I'll get the brochure online and reserve the daily activities of our choice. Yay, I'm so excited. I love you!"

This new project gave Janet and Jim the time to study the brochure together and select what each one wanted for their daily program. Jim thought it would also be an ideal to set aside some time to write his speech, while Janet continued with her spiritual studies as well.

Jim needed to finalize some pending items at work and with the Center before going on vacation with Janet. He notified Brian and Charles about his journey to Lenox, MA and as expected, they were pleased and wished him a good time. Brian was comfortable telling Jim about the progress in his relationship with Sylvia, giving Jim the credit for encouraging him. He told his team at work not to bother him for that week, unless it is urgent.

Janet sent letters to the children (phone calls not allowed) informing them that they will be away for one week and gave them the numbers to pass on to the administration of the camp if it were necessary to be reached. Janet also scheduled her meeting with her doctor on Friday, the day after they return.

◆

The resort was off the beaten path in the Berkshires region of western Massachusetts. The grounds were beautiful and the old palatial building impressive. The quiet surroundings and the fresh air atmosphere were what the reunited couple needed to rekindle the fire of their love with a higher level of understanding. Their program was in place as ordered online, and they chose a light schedule, a long walk and massages on Thursday, the day of their arrival.

They started their walk in the mid-afternoon, holding hands and strolling on a path near the green hilly meadows that takes them to the lake below. After twenty-five minutes walking, they found a bench shaded by an old oak tree. They sat close holding hands still admiring the gorgeous view down to the lake.

"How do you feel, my love?" Janet looked at Jim and asked him . Jim paused for a few seconds and said,

"I am sincerely blessed to be with you in this beautiful spot. With such an environment, all thoughts of the past and the future disappear, and the power of the present moment prevails. I am grateful to the divine powers that awakened us to overcome our fears and revived our sacred love." Jim took a deep breath, then continued,

"To see us together on this journey of spiritual awakening is a dream come true to me. I swear in the presence of the hills and the prairies, the forest and the lake, to soothe your heart in your days and invite heavenly peace to permeate your dreams. I vow to nurture our rekindled love with care and complicity, to inhale the fragrance of its scented flowers that will decorate the gardens of your life."

Janet could not control her tears from cascading down her cheeks. She held both his hand tightly with both her hands and said,

"I don't know what to say! Now I know your poetry originates from within, your pure well of inner being. I love your words that come from your heart, they are sound like the music of angels. I pledge to do whatever it takes to safeguard this new awakening. I love you deeply!"

They stood up and walked in silence enjoying the stillness of nature, enhanced by the warm feelings of their sweet togetherness. Half an hour later they returned to their room, rested for a while and then put their robes on to go for their respective massages before dinner.

The rest of the week was spent as scheduled, and the remaining days passed joyfully. Jim managed to write his speech and Janet finished the book "Your Erroneous Zones" with many notes to reread. They drove back home fully satisfied with revived energy and rekindled love.

◆

The visit to the doctor the next day went well and Janet had a final clean bill of health. Before picking up the children from the camp on Saturday, Jim took Janet with him to the Center on Friday evening, to visit with Charles, Brian and the other members. The gathering was vibrant with smiling faces, and happy conversations. The speech was about 'Forgiveness Rewards' by a visiting minister from Seattle, WA.

Janet felt comfortable in the company of everybody at the Center and was quick to understand the influence it had on Jim's process of transformation. She was very welcome as Jim's wife, and Charles introduced her to the audience and welcomed her, before the speaker took the podium.

After the speech, Brian spoke with Jim, while Janet was chatting with some of the ladies roaming around.

"I spent four days in Miami and met with potential candidates. I inclined to recommend a lady minister I met in one of the Centers for Spiritual Living, and she seems excited about the opportunity. I invited her to come visit us next week and we'll see how it goes. The relationship with Sylvia is developing nicely and she is eager to her your speech in a couple of weeks. How about you?" Brian briefed Jim.

"Janet and I had a wonderful week together at a spa in Mass., while the kids went to a two-week summer camp upstate; we'll pick them up tomorrow. I prepared my speech, and Janet finished the book; she's coming along amazingly well. I'm happy to be back home, Brian. I thank you for all your help and support."

"Listen since you're here in town with Janet, I was going to have dinner with Sylvia later at 7:30 perhaps we can all ear together; you're my guests, what do you say?" Brian asked.

"Humm… I need to ask Janet. She might be interested to meet Sylvia. You don't think it is too early?" Jim wondered.

"Come on Jim, they will meet sooner or later. They might as well see for themselves the women their men chose to be with?"

"Okay, I'll ask her." Jim said and signaled to Janet to come over. Janet walked over and Jim asked,

"Brian is inviting us to dinner with him and Sylvia this evening, do you feel up to it?"

"That'll be great, I'd love to meet Sylvia." Janet responded.

Brian was happy and he went to the side to call Sylvia. She agreed and they left the Center at 7:15 to go to the restaurant four blocks away.

Jim was more nervous than Janet in meeting Sylvia. After a few minutes of intense observation, the two ladies relaxed with genuine smiles. Brian broke the ice, looked at Sylvia and said,

"Jim and Janet went to a spa to revitalize their energy and Janet wanted to detox after the pills she had to take since the accident. Jim also confirmed that the setting of the area induced him to write the speech."

"Where was this spa, Janet?" Sylvia asked.

"It is called Canyon Ranch in Lenox, Mass. The treatments were excellent, relaxing atmosphere, beautiful grounds and great walks. The food was good and we each lost three pounds. We returned home feeling truly rejuvenated."

"Will you again?"

"Jim and I did not discuss this, but I would, how about you Jim?"

"Yeah, once a year, at least, would be great. It's also a great place to meditate and reflect on our spiritual path. I would recommend it! Tell me Sylvia, are we still on for the following Sunday?"

"But of course, I already added it to the schedule and advertised it in the written program that we distribute two weeks in advance. We're looking forward to having you, and I hope you, Janet will be there as well."

"Yes, I also plan to bring the two children too."

"I am so happy to hear that, and I hope the family would consider becoming members of our church also." Sylvia said.

"You know perhaps, Brian told you that Jim has been teaching me to be on a spiritual path like him and Brian. Would you say your mission is somewhat similar?"

"I think so, because our church, is open to people from all religions and without being religious, but spiritual in our teachings. Our doctrine was initially based on the church of Religious Science but has evolved to a wider horizon of spirituality that allows its members to be less rigid in rituals and spiritually free in their daily life." Sylvia explained.

"So, Brian, are you going to be a member too?" Jim asked.

"You bet, I am. I was there last Sunday, and I am very impressed with the work Sylvia has done so far. I want to support her and help out in every way I can. She knows I am dedicated to my mission with the Center, and the job I now have, thanks to you. Sylvia and I have complimentary missions in the realm of spirituality, which I find as a big blessing."

"What job do you have at the Center, Brian? I thought you're the chief accountant at Jim's firm." Janet asked.

"You have a very humble husband, Janet, he does not go around and brag about funding projects like the one I'm doing now. Jim is financially supporting the first phase of our expansion in Philadelphia, Miami and Chicago. This required my fulltime attention. So, he fired me from his company and made sure I am hired for this new role."

"Why did you not tell me Jim?" Janet asked.

"We were too busy working on our reconciliation, my dear. Also, I wanted you to familiarize you with the Center, and to meet Sylvia, our spiritual leader in this community. You are welcome , now that you have chosen a similar path, to help us in any way you can!" Jim proudly said.

"Janet, I also told Jim that he has a unique talent as a teacher. Do you agree now that he is also tutoring you?"

"Absolutely, Sylvia, you hit it right on. He has an amazing style of explaining thing, and he does it poetically. I am honored to be his student."

"Yes, but what Sylvia suggested, by virtue of her psychic powers, is that I should quit my work and become a fulltime spiritual teacher, Right, Sylvia?" Jim asked.

"Right! I still believe that. I felt it when I first met you at the Center. And Janet, I bet you will also agree with me when you hear him speak. Brian, you know him well in this regard, what is your opinion?"

"First, let me say that I have yet to meet someone who learns as fast and explains as clearly as he does. I also admired him as my boss, but I truly love him as my brother now. I certainly agree with Sylvia that he'd make a great teacher." Brian remarked.

"So, are you going to quit your job and become a spiritual guru, Jim?" Janet asked.

"We're just talking, my dear. I'm still a novice in this field. I never thought of myself as a spiritual teacher. I would support the missions these two have, but I doubt I can become a fulltime teacher! Perhaps, my mission is to work hard and support financially."

There was silence around the table while the food was being served. Janet and Sylvia were eyeing one another with smiles on their faces. Brian then interrupted the silence and asked about the children.

"We're picking them up tomorrow! They've been away for two weeks and we miss them a lot. Laura is becoming more and more the sweet lady we love, and Todd, who will be thirteen in a week, is growing fast and wants me to buy him a leather outfit for his birthday." Jim said with a peel of a laughter.

They enjoyed the rest of the evening and Janet and Sylvia hit it off well, looking forward to seeing each other the following Sunday. Jim thanked Brian for the dinner and they agreed to see each other during the week in the office.

Chapter 16

A Journey into Light

Sunday arrived, and it was a beautiful day. Jim and the family drove to Sylvia's church in the city. They arrived ten minutes before the service and Jim saw several members from the Center who came with Charles and Brian. Dr. Goodwin saw them, too, and began to shake their hands and happy to meet the children.

When it was time for the speech, Sylvia introduced Jim to a full house of no less than two hundred people, highlighting his business success. Jim walked to the podium to start his speech.

Good morning! I met Dr. Goodwin a few weeks ago at our spiritual Center, here in the city, she was our guest speaker that evening. Her speech was about achieving a balance between work and home. I remember telling her, after the speech, I wish I had heard her message when I needed it the most, a year ago.

Dr. Goodwin later asked me to reciprocate and share with you my story. I said I'm not a good public speaker, and I'm shy. She insisted that I could do it. So, here I am, and I thank you for agreeing to listen.

When I was young, I was driven to succeed. I chose blinders to narrow my vision from distraction; I trained myself as a horse, to focus and look ahead only.

I worked hard as a student, and when I later threw away my blinders, I found that I had replaced them with a thicker veil that further restricted my sight from a normal life of a young man. Nothing else mattered, at that time, the focus was to succeed in whatever I do. I thought this obsession would eventually redeem me from the past shadows of my impoverished upbringing.

I refused to pursue the usual pleasures chased by the young, and I hid behind shyness for my good behavior. I closed the door to partying with boys or going out with girls. I saw that as a waste of my time that would detour me from the road to achieve my goal.

Then I met a beautiful young lady during my graduate years. Her striking beauty prompted me to lift the veil from my eyes to see her clearly and admire her smile. I was naïve and shy, yet she accepted me for the person I was, and eventually we fell in love.

That lady whom I adored, later became my wife. We were blessed in love to have two beautiful children. My beloved family came with me this morning and allowed me to ask them to stand, my wife Janet, my daughter Laura, and my son Todd. Having them in my life hastened my dedication to work harder to achieve greater success.

I gradually realized my early dreams of financial independence; I cherished the fact that I was able to support my family and provide them with comfortable living.

In hindsight, I wish I knew better how to understand the value of success at that time. Instead, I listened to the tricks and games of ego, that kept reminding of my less fortunate past thus encouraging me to see the world outside my home. I succumbed to the ego which induced me to employ my outer success toward experimenting with the pleasures of the external world. My boosted false self, the ego, made me believe I was invincible, hence entitled to do what I want, and free to explore a different life away from home.

I tried to ignore the blind invitation to shift to the darker side, but the demons in my mind, masterminded by the ego, were more powerful and won the battle of the world, at the expense of losing my soul.

I foolishly turned my back on the beautiful family I was blessed with, and I indulged myself in the dungeons of the dark. It took a few months for me to realize the mistake I made, and I found that kind of life was not cut for me.

I suffered from guilt and master ego, who never gives up, took advantage of my despair, and played the new game of guilt to break my heart. I spent several sleepless nights, and I became quite restless.

Then I had dreams about the home life I missed, and the love of my family. I realized how deeply I hurt my wife and my children for no fault of their own. I quickly lost all interest in the pleasures of the night and prayed for inner guidance in my lonely hours. I shed tears beseeching the Universe to show me the light of the day.

I invited love to permeate my soul and plant a tree of peace in the cobwebs of my mind. I trusted the Universe to guide me, and that's when Brian, my ex-colleague, unexpectedly appeared to show me the way to a better life – Brian, please stand.

I slowly came out of the dark, and I saw the light of hope on the road to spiritual awakening. I wanted to correct my wrong, and I confessed to my lovely wife, asking for her forgiveness. Though I hurt her deeply, it did not take her long to have the courage to accept an open dialogue together. It was a good practice of patience and understanding.

Unfortunate events occurred in Janet's life, shortly after her indecision to take me back. That was when the power of the Universe led her to end her suffering, and I was shown a window of hope for my potential return. I shared with Janet the spiritual path I chose, and though she had resisted my approach before, a miracle happened, which lifted the veil of darkness off her eyes, and awakened her to seek a spiritual journey on her own.

Her shift to conscious awareness brightened my day and brought peace to our children's hearts. We all began to breathe the fragrance of fresh love emanating sweetly from our inner space. We became grateful seeing our home being transformed into a garden of grace, empowered by peace and nourished with abundant love.

You may wonder why am I sharing my private story with you?

Buddha said, 'Suffering is not holding you. You are holding suffering,' and he also said, 'Pain is certain; suffering is optional.' The actress, Angelina Jolie, a couple of thousand years later, admitted, and I paraphrase, 'pain and suffering is the key to open all windows; without suffering, there is no way to a better life.'

What I am saying is, we all suffer at some point in our life, and suffering is not only that which causes physical pain. Body pain can be temporary and treatable with medication. But emotional or psychological pain is more severe and may last much longer if it's not treated with awareness and inner search for peace. Most people suffer from non-physical pain. I know I did.

I succeeded in creating material possessions, but I used this double-edged sword, called success, to bring me down too. I surrendered my prosperity to the monster in my mind, the ego, which in turn led me to think I'm gaining the world, when, in fact, it was at the expense of losing my soul. Such a loss can be vast and devastating.

A wise man once said, 'Success and Failure drive on the same two-way road and wave at each other as they pass one another.' To say it differently, the tree-roots of success and failure are intertwined beneath the soil, and their branches grow in each other's shadow above the ground. There is a very thin line between success and failure.

I learned the hard way that to realize meaningful and worthwhile success; I ought to be humbly aware of the power of Presence, or God that resides within me. I also learned that success could be better enjoyed with joyful melodies of satisfaction and gratitude. Otherwise, success can quickly turn into failure, the kind that sends ripples over the surface that drown me in an ocean of ego and false identity.

To succeed is to be grateful and generously giving to others in need. To succeed, is to be aligned with my true self and get on a path of spiritual awakening. We all cannot avoid events in life that make us suffer, but we have the option, as Buddha said, to use suffering as a launching pad for our enlightenment. The choice to live an enlightened life is a pleasant journey of awareness that brings us pure joy and peace.

Now, I try to wake up every morning, with a promise to myself, to be grateful to the present moment, and not to dwell on the past or worry about the future. Awareness leads me to live in the Now, because life IS Now, the Eternal Truth that generates joy to living. I now try to connect with my inner self before I start my day, if only for a few minutes in silence, just to bathe in the realm of pure consciousness, and experience the power of Presence.

Finally, if I may add, my choice to walk on the path of spiritual awakening did not negatively impact my work or business success; on the contrary, it made it positively and noticeably higher. My mind is clearer, my stress is disappearing fast, and I'm more efficient and productive than before. I hope I'm setting a good example for my colleagues and friends, as well.

Regardless of what job you have, try to do it with an aware, conscious mind and with a generous heart of love; I promise you; you will find that success never leaves you.

Thank you!

The entire church stood up and applauded Jim for his testimony. He bowed with thanks and walked back to sit on his chair. After the service, Dr. Goodwin invited her congregation to have tea or coffee in the basement hall. Jim and his family also went down to join. Within a minute, a crowd of people surrounded Jim and his family to introduce themselves, some of them saying how touched they were by his message. The social gathering lasted about an hour before everyone had to leave.

♦

On the way back home, Janet asked the children,

"What did you guys think of your father's public speech? "Dad is the best speaker ever!" Todd quickly replied.

"My father is a courageous man who did not mind sharing his private life for the sake of teaching others. I am so proud of you, Dad. I said it before, and I repeat it, I wish I will be with a man like you one day. I, your daughter, was touched deeply, hearing your story written from the heart. Mom, I truly understand why you could not resist falling in love with this man." Laura said, passionately. Janet looked at Jim and said,

"I thank God for waking me up from my deep slumber and opening my eyes to see you with me again, my love. I watched you speaking to a group of spiritual seekers like me, and you made it hard to hide my tears. I am so grateful for your love and patience, your wisdom and understanding, and your tolerance of my ignorance. And on behalf of our children, we are honored to have you as the head of our family." Janet expressed her deep love and admiration.

"Wow! You guys are so sweet and loving. Thank you! I pledge to be a great husband and a great father, and again I ask for your forgiveness for my short absence from home, when I hurt you so foolishly. Since we are in the city, and we have many choices for a good brunch somewhere, what and where do you prefer to eat? Other than Chinese or hamburgers, of course." No one had any suggestions, then he thought,

"How about The Roof, on west 57Th street, I heard it is great for brunch, it also has beautiful views of the city?"

"Yeah, Dad, a friend of mine in school said she went there with her parents once for brunch on a Sunday, and they had a good time," Laura said.

"Okay, let us go there if Todd is on board!"

"I love my sister, Dad, and she has good taste, let's go!" "Thank you, dear Todd, what a first compliment from you!"

They all went to the restaurant and had a delightful meal, during which they talked about the camp activities and contact with the friends they made. They asked if they could do it again next summer. Both parents agreed and said they could even consider going for one month. Todd right away said,

"You guys want to have a longer honeymoon now; one week was not enough, Huh?" They all laughed, ate their dessert, and Jim drove them back home to relax and prepare for school the next day.

◆

Brian called Jim on Monday at work and told him how happy he was to see him on stage, sharing his story. He added that Sylvia, with whom he had dinner Sunday night, was very grateful you agreed to deliver such a meaningful speech, and many members of her church said your advice touched them.

"Sylvia and I believe you should write a self-help book, embedding your poetic gift in its text," Brian said.

"I see! How are you two coming along?"

"Very well! It is a smooth and graceful relationship." "Are you discussing any future plans?"

"Not yet, but we're almost there!"

"Do it, Brian! Have faith and courage. She's a wonderful woman, and the two of you together make a great couple."

"Thanks, Jim! Coming from you means a lot to me."

"I only have one condition! Choose me as your best man!" "That is a given; you are my mentor, my brother, and my best friend, no one else can come close to you. Consider it done!" Brian confirmed.

"Good! How about your mission?"

"I am about to recommend a good candidate for you and the board. She' a middle-aged minister of a small spiritual living center just outside Miami. I had several meetings with her already. She's visiting us this Wednesday, and I hope you can meet her too."

"Let me know what time and I'll be there! How about the Philly center?"

"Doing quite well, and we have close to seventy members now."
"I'm so happy to hear that! Are you comfortable with the balance in the fund?" Jim asked.

"Absolutely! You know me, I'm cautious of what I spend. We have enough for three more centers, if you ask me."

"Good, I have to go now. I'll see you on Wednesday."

♦

Jim told Janet and the children during dinner at home that Brian suggested he writes a book. They all said it's a great idea, and Todd asked if he'll be in it.

"Of course, son! If I decide to write you will be in it, how else can the readers find the book amusing? Your jokes will make it worth reading." Jim responded.

"It is evident you have this unique talent of communicating a message so clearly and poetically. I believe you should seriously consider writing a book, don't you agree, Laura?" Janet

"Absolutely! Your gift and your message, Dad, should be heard by millions of readers, not just a few. Your story is from the heart and will help many to transform into the spiritual path you convey."

"You guys believe in me more than I believe in myself. When am I going to find the time to write? Perhaps I should wait until I retire!"

"No, Jim, your message is needed today, not tomorrow. There is a new global wave of spirituality roaming around attracting millions of people to listen and transform their way of living. You are needed now, and you'll find the time. We will support you and give you the space you need to create your masterpiece. Please think about it seriously." Janet said.

"Wow! What a blessing you all are! I appreciate your support, and I will think about it, I promise! Laura, how about a game of tennis this weekend. I'm rusty, but I still have a good serve!"

"That's exciting! Don't be a sour loser, though? I'm sure I can beat you!" Laura said.

"I bet you five dollars Dad will beat you, right, Dad?" Todd said "We all go to watch, and the one who loses will wash the dishes tonight. How about that? You warm up ten minutes, and you only play one set," Janet suggested.

"Deal!" They all agreed. Todd asked his sister, "why are you trembling already? The writing is on the wall!"

"Shush, you wall-writing genius! Stick to your soccer game!" That was precisely the family atmosphere that Jim had loved and missed before. His heart was tickled with joy, and his smile expressed fresh waves of lasting happiness.

◆

Jim went to the Center on Wednesday, as promised. Brian introduced him to Ms. Debra Jensen, the candidate to head the new Center in Miami. Debra had an impressive resume, including several self-help books she wrote, and two of them were bestsellers on the NYT list. Brian had also invited Sylvia to be with him that evening, and he seized the opportunity to inform Debra that Jim is contemplating writing a self-help book.

"Is that so? Perhaps I can help you, Jim. What do you have in mind for the title?" Debra asked.

"I don't have any idea yet? Brian and Sylvia threw this at me unexpectedly. I've never written a book before, and I don't understand why they think I should start now?" Sylvia jumped in and said,

"Let me tell you, Debra, I knew it the day I met Jim, that he has this unique gift of communicating and teaching the masses. He gave a speech last Sunday in our church, and you should have been there to hear it. I recorded it, and I'll be happy to give you a copy. The congregation was mesmerized by his message and his style of delivery. He is unique, and he has to start believing it. Please guide this great man, and he'll excel, that I am sure!"

"Wow! Thank you, Sylvia." Then Brian continued, "Also, Debra, he is the man I told you about, without his support we wouldn't be having this meeting this evening, and we wouldn't have launched the Philadelphia center. As Sylvia said, he is unique!"

"Enough said, you two! Let us focus on Debra now!" Jim said. "Before we talk about me, may I send you a couple of my books,

Jim, to familiarize you with my style and contents?" Debra suggested. "Please do! I'll be happy even to study them, thank you!" Jim replied.

Charles then joined the circle and the first thing he said,

"So good to see you with us, Jim, our hero, what a great speaker!" "Here we go again, thank you, Charles. Debra here seems to be a wonderful candidate to run the Miami center." Jim said.

"Brian, the board, and now you all agree, and I hope Debra would agree to our offer before she leaves tomorrow," Charles stated.

"Debra, please agree! We are a good bunch of people here. We are all one big family, and I would love for you to join!" Jim requested.

"As I told Charles and Brian earlier, I would like to meditate and sleep on it tonight. Yes, you all are a great spiritual family."

Sylvia then took Jim on the side and asked him if he and his family would consider becoming members of her church. The Sunday service is not conflicting with the Center's activities. Jim promised to look into it with Janet and the children, and he'll revert. Sylvia then thanked Jim for encouraging Brian to befriend her, as he turned out to be a wonderful person indeed. Jim assured her that Brian is one of the best men he met in his life, and he had met quite a few. They both rejoined the circle and talked with Debra, who was quickly being admired by all those who met her.

Charles asked Jim and Brian if they could join him for a few minutes in the office, and they excused themselves from the two ladies who continued to talk about their respective ministries.

"Jim, what do you think of Debra, will she agree? I sense, though she is a spiritual being, she may not be happy with the salary and budget we gave her." Charles began. Jim looked at Brian, Mr. Careful-with-the -money, and asked,

"Why? What did you offer her, Brian, I know you!" Jim responded. "Not enough, I'm afraid!"

"Did she mention a figure that she would be satisfied with?" Jim asked.

"Not precisely, but she hinted something like that," Brian said cautiously.

"Do me a favor, both of you, please! Use that figure and add 10% and make sure you don't lose such a personality for some measly money. Okay?" Jim demanded.

"Okay, Boss! Will do! And thank you for your generosity!" Charles confirmed.

They rejoined the ladies who were still talking cheerfully, and Charles asked Debra if he could speak to her for a minute. They walked back to his office, and he told her about the conversation with Jim, who is the benefactor and honorary chairman of our group. He said,

"Before you go to sleep tonight, please note that we really would love to have you in our family, and as Jim requested, we should not lose you, please. So, we accept the amount you had in mind, for your salary and budget, plus 10%."

"Oh, that is very generous of you, thank you!"

"We all thank Jim, Debra, he is God-sent, and we are very grateful." They both walked back to join the others with happy smiles on their faces. Debra then spoke,

"I would like to tell you that I do not need to sleep on the offer tonight. I accept to be part of this great family of friends and spiritual collaborators!"

Jim reached out and kissed Debra on her cheek and said,

"Congratulations, Debra! You made a wise decision. This place and these people saved my life and my marriage, particularly these two, Charles and Brian. Why do I say that? Because they practice what true love is all about! So, welcome on board." Jim said happily.

Brian and Sylvia expressed their congratulations as well, and Charles announced the agreement to the members present, and introduced Debra officially as the head of the Miami Center, and asked her to give a short speech about her plans. Jim stayed to listen, and then excused himself to go home for dinner.

♦

At home, Jim sat down with Janet at the dinner table. She waited for him while the children had their dinner, and now upstairs doing their homework.

"I met with Debra, our candidate, to run our Miami Center. She's an elegant lady in her early fifties and she's highly educated. She wrote several self-help books, and Brian who came with Sylvia, told Debra that I might be writing a self-help book. Debra said she's willing to help in editing my book and encouraged me to write it. She's sending me a couple of her books that hit the NYT bestseller list."

"So, was she hired?"

"I initially sensed that she was reluctant, thanks to my frugal brother Brian who did not offer her the figure she would have liked. So, I took both Charles and Brian to the office, and they admitted that she might not agree, and would let them know in the morning before she leaves. I asked them to immediately talk to her and accept her figure plus 10%. They agreed and notified her accordingly. Debra then said she does not need to sleep on the offer, and she's on board. We were all happy, and Charles shared the news officially to the members." Jim explained.

"Wow, they listened to you, didn't they? It's your donation that made it easy for them to agree. You're such a giving person, and it coincides with what I was studying today, 'the principle of giving and receiving.' One sage said, *"only by giving you are able to receive more than you have."* You will be rewarded manifold. I also liked what Deepak Chopra wrote, *"The law of giving is very simple: if you want Joy, give joy; if love is what you seek, offer love; and if you crave for material affluence, help others become prosperous."*. God bless you, my dear!"

"Well said, Janet! I love to share my blessings with others who need it. Another request asked by Sylvia, who also says hello, and who thanked me for encouraging Brian to befriend her, she requested me also to ask you and the children to become members of her church. So, what do you think?"

"I liked the energy of that place, and we do not have a spiritual place for the whole family like that close by. So, I wouldn't mind, and I also would like to introduce the children to the realm of today's spirituality as an alternative to traditional teachings. I think it is a good idea for a Sunday service!" Janet agreed.

"Fine, I will let her know when I see Brian again." "So, these two are happy together, aren't they?"

"I've never seen Brian so happy! She also admitted he's a wonderful man."

"Great news this evening, how about we meditate together before we go to sleep tonight?" Janet asked.

"That'll be my honor, my love! You can't imagine how impressed I am with your natural desire to grow and advance on your spiritual journey. I truly enjoy hanging out with you and the children too, we do things together, we learn and meditate together and we have fun doing it. This is the life of peace and joy that I wanted!"

"How right you are, and I feel you are becoming more amenable to write your book now," Janet said,

"We shall see! I'm seeking heavenly guidance in this regard!"

Chapter 17

All is Well

Four weeks had gone by since the Sunday speech, and the recommendation Jim was given to write a book. In the interim, the family joined Sylvia's church on Sundays and were happy with the service, the sermons, and the social gatherings. Janet became a good friend of Sylvia, who asked her to dedicate one day a week, to help women who suffer from separation, divorce, or other family issues. Jim encouraged her to do it, and Sylvia offered her the use of her conference room for that purpose.

Jim wanted to give writing his book a chance. He dedicated one hour before going to work, and one hour after dinner to this task. He read the two self-help books Debra sent him, together with other books written by spiritual teachers. He wanted to write a unique book, not repeating what is already known out there. He struggled, knowing that he was not a qualified spiritual teacher, like many of the well-accomplished writers, who taught millions of people globally.

He consulted with Janet, Sylvia, Debra, Brian, and Charles, and they all said no one could advise him more than what he can learn himself by searching within. They all advised him not to panic, and it will come to him; leave it to the Universe and be aware.

Jim and Janet invited Brian and Sylvia to dinner at home, one Saturday evening. The two couples had become good friends aware of Jim's search for a title, or even a theme for his book. The children met the guests for about ten minutes before they excused themselves to finish their homework. They sat around the table, gazing at the delicious pot-roast that Janet cooked. Before they started eating, Jim expressed how he is struggling with the book project, and said,

"You people encouraged me to do something I've never done before, and I don't even know where to start. I am a novice in my writing skills, and still a debutant in the spiritual realm. Don't you think I should wait until I become well-versed on the subject first?"

After a few seconds of silence, Janet was the first to respond,

"Sweetheart, you are struggling with technicalities, a novice here, and a novice there. You forget how strong you are within. Not all successful writers were skilled before they started writing. They expressed what they were inspired to teach from the pool of power of the inner self. You know, we all know how solid you are in your beliefs, and how fluently you can express these beliefs to the world once you get started. So, go within!"

Brian then added,

"Jim! Don't get intimidated by the works of the great teachers, some of whom you studied yourself. You do not need to be educated in the field, as many of them did. You don't have to have a doctorate in Divinity to qualify, (sorry Sylvia). If a thought or an idea inspires you, jot it down. If you come across a sentence from what you read that resonates with your story, write it down. Collect as many loose pieces as possible, and eventually, something will click, and you go with it. When it flows, it flows, and no one can stop you. I know that."

"Thank you, Janet, and Brain for your advice, what do you say, silent Sylvia, I mean Dr. Goodwin?" Jim asked.

"You want to hear my opinion? I think you are complicating and crowding your mind with the materials of other teachers. You struggle because you want to create something new, not yet available publicly. Inspiration is not a race but an experience! I think you should write your own life story, albeit from a spiritual angle."

"What do you mean? My autobiography?"

"In a way, yes! Reread your speech and turn it into a book embellished with more details about your childhood, your naïve youth, your love story with Janet, your business growth, your worldly temptations, your children, and so on, expressing the struggles you went through on every turn. And then, 'Boom' here comes your process of transformation and the shift to a higher level of your consciousness. This is what people want to hear or read. The book would be a new story, a big hit that shines as a spiritual autobiography!"

"Darling, you are a genius, thank you!" Brian immediately responded.

Jim and Janet looked at one another, dumbfounded by Sylvia's wisdom. Jim then spoke,

"You have just given me a great idea, Sylvia. Thank you for your observation and insight. Yes, I believe I can turn a five-page speech into a two-hundred-page book. You realize that I have to mention the names of people in my life, including you; it is not a fiction story; it has to be real. Is that okay?"

"Absolutely!" they all said almost at the same time.

"This calls for a celebration! I will open a bottle of red wine. I am thrilled and thankful for your good advice to embellish the speech, Sylvia. Brian, you will be my spiritual editor, and Janet, you will continue to be my inspiring source of love and joy. The three of you are now appointed my official advisors."

They happily clinked their glasses and wished Jim an incredible writing journey.

◆

The two couples moved to the big living room for dessert and coffee. The men sat in one corner, while the two ladies sat at the other end. Sylvia wanted to talk to Janet about three ladies scheduled to meet with her on Wednesday, starting at 10:00 am.

"Out of the three, one may require your utmost attention because her husband is an alcoholic, and he harms her physically. She's in her mid-thirties, and they have two young children under ten years old. She says she cannot break the marriage, despite her suffering, for the sake of the kids, and she still loves her husband. It's a complicated situation, but I'm sure you can help out. Her name is Suzan, and she saw you when Jim gave his speech."

"You know, Sylvia, I have no prior experience in this regard, but I will listen to her and my inner voice for guidance. How about the other two ladies?"

"Joan and Emily are both in their early forties, and they suspect their husbands are sleeping around, and who deny such claims. The women do not want their marriage to end and prefer to suffer and live with low self- esteem."

"I hear you! I think I can help them in this case." Janet said with a vicious smile on her face, which was easily understood by Sylvia.

Meanwhile, Brian and Jim were talking with lower voices and bent closer to one another.

"I heard you calling Sylvia, darling, that sounded new to me. Is there some progress you might share with me?" Jim asked.

"Yes, there is! We've been in this relationship for about two months now, and we both see it as a God-sent one. We decided to get engaged soon, and you are the first to know."

"Now, you're talking! I'm beyond words, and congratulations in advance."

"Sometimes, I feel this is not real, but a dream to be with such a beautiful person who is with me on the same spiritual level. Again, thank you for shifting my attention to her. I didn't believe she would accept me at that time. You are my hero!"

"Dreams of angels always come true!"

"I will keep you posted with dates and such, Jim. Wow! I'm in love again," Brian confirmed.

"Good to hear, lover-boy. How is Debra coming along?"

"She's great, and she found the right space for her ministry. She was promised support by many from her congregation, and she sounds confident about our future growth. Again, thank you for your support."

"Good news, how about Chicago?" Jim asked.

"That's my new challenge! My online research showed me twenty-six spiritual centers in the state of Illinois, and bout ten of them in Chicago alone. They are predominately members of the Spiritual Living Centers network, off-springs of the Religious Science Church. These centers have a robust presence in the state. On one side, it is a big pool of spirituality to choose from, though on the other side, it's going to be an arduous task, which I'm preparing myself to fulfill."

"You're up to it, Jim, and take your time, don't rush! Chicago is a big city, and you are the right man for the job!"

"You can't imagine how excited I am about the expansion program. What I love about the most, is to see it develop effortlessly, without the burden of an institutional organization or red tape behind it."

"I hope it stays that way! Soon, you will start moving west with your program. You're still young and visualize the growth twenty years from now! You're going to need more staff and hierarchy as you grow and that by itself calls for an organization in place. Anyhow keep going and no worries of this sort for now!" Jim explained.

"Yup! I can see that down the road. Thank you and Janet for your great hospitality, and we'll see each other at the service tomorrow. We will leave now!"

"You're most welcome, and the news tonight was also great, lover-boy!" Brian signaled Sylvia it's time to leave, she stood up hugged Janet and walked over to hug Jim and they all were grateful to the sound and productive time they had.

◆

Jim and Janet sat on the sofa for a short while, holding hands and sharing the news. Jim told her about Brian and Sylvia's plan to get engaged, and Janet told him about the ladies she's going to meet on Wednesday.

"Aren't you excited about the book now?" Janet asked.

"You bet I am! All of you gave me such good advice, and I'm so lucky to have you in my life."

"You should mostly thank Sylvia for her brilliant idea that makes the task much simpler and natural for you to accomplish."

"That's true too! Have you noticed how the Universe operates? Brian and Sylvia falling in love, you and me back solidly together? I love this spiritual journey of ours!"

"Also, I am learning how interconnected we all are, with friends and the rest of the world. This new task that Sylvia gave me is a great challenge for me to be sharp, loving, and helpful. Did you and I ever think that we would be involved with such tasks two years ago? I certainly didn't. I can't be grateful enough to God for turning things around in such a wonderful way, not only between us, but with our family life, our new friends, and our mission to help others. Thank you, my love, for your patience with me. You set a good example for me to follow."

"Your words are music to my ears and bring tears of joy to my eyes. We are blessed, my dear, and we should be grateful every minute of every day of our life." They hugged and kissed before going to bed.

◆

The family attended the Sunday service, and Sylvia was the speaker that day. The title of her sermon was 'From Tears to Laughter.' Some of the highlights Jim noted were:

- Our lives are like Quilts, bits and pieces, joy and sorrow, stitched together with love.

- without tears, there is no laughter.

- Both Joy and sorrow are interconnected. We also shed tears of joy when we are happy.

- Share your joy with your beloved, then you get a double portion, whereas when you share your sorrow, you get only half.

- Wipe your tears of sorrow and rise above to experience a new awakening of joy.

- Joseph Campbell once said: *"participate joyfully in the sorrows of the world. We cannot cure the world of its sorrows, but we can choose to live in Joy."*

- Joy is a choice in life, whereas sorrow requires awareness to accept it and move on."

Sylvia then held the book 'The Prophet' by Khalil Gibran in her hand and read:

"Joy and sorrow are inseparable… together they come and when one sits alone with you… remember that the other is asleep upon your bed."

Make sure you find joy in your heart when you go to sleep.

Sylvia finished her sermon by another quotation from Gibran,

"Love -which is God- will consider our sighs and tears as incense burned at His altar, and He will reward us with fortitude (joy)."

The sermon touched many hearts, and the minister received a standing ovation.

◆

On the drive back home, Laura told her parents,

"I met a new guy I'd like you to meet. He's a year ahead of me in school, a sophomore, and he's a point guard on the basketball varsity team. I watched him play, he dribbles well, passes the ball well, and has a high percentage of free throws. I invited Todd to watch him play too, you can ask him."

"Yeah, he's good, and not very tall, about six feet only. He's a bit the show-off type, though not intimidating!"

"He doesn't show off, Todd, he's a very nice guy, and I like him," Laura said.

"Do you like him because he's a good player, handsome, or because he's a nice guy?" Janet asked.

"All the above, Mom. I want you to meet him, can you come to school and see him play? I'll introduce you!" Laura said, passionately.

"Are you in love with him?" Jim asked.

"Not yet, Dad. I need to know him better first! We don't go out, or anything, I want you to meet him first, you guys can figure him out better than me, or Todd, for that matter!"

"Hey, I didn't say I don't like him, but he does not play soccer as I do. Which reminds me, Dad and Mom, in two weeks there will be a qualification prize to be given to the best player on the team, please come. I have an excellent chance to win."

"Wonderful son, we will go, I promise! Back to you Laura, when are you going to introduce this guy to us, I'm sure he has a name?" Jim asked.

"His name is Albert, I'll ask Mom to meet him first and to see him play, and if she likes him, then we can invite him to have dinner with us one night for you to meet him too."

"Will I have a say in this?" Todd wanted to know his role.

"Of course, you do! Majority rules, okay?" Janet confirmed.

Laura was nervously excited and said she'd let them know when and how to proceed.

"How about you Todd, did you find a sweetheart yet?" Jim asked.

"Not yet, Dad, school started not long ago. Besides, I will attract more beautiful girls when I win the MVP prize, soon!"

"And you say Albert shows off, how about you, slick monkey?" Laura reacted.

"I'm very selective, that's all! Exactly the way Dad chose Mom, you'll see!"

They all laughed, and Todd cleverly complimented his parents, to get a lot of their attention.

♦

Jim started writing his book, and within two months, he had already covered his story from childhood up to the time when he married Janet and had the first child, Laura. Two years after Laura was born, Janet got pregnant with Todd. Her second pregnancy coincided with Jim's rise in the trade as a brilliant trader, and the big competition was watching him closely. His company was growing fast, and in the tenth year of his operations, he became known worldwide.

He wrote how commodity producers and other traders enjoyed dealing with him, and how he honored all his contracts and commitments, regardless of the market fluctuations in prices and terms. Jim gave examples detailing the nature of his business and the reason for his rising success. By the time Laura turned fourteen and Todd turned twelve, Jim wrote how the devil played in his head and boosted his ego. Here is an excerpt of what he wrote during his period of temptations:

"I started chasing false dreams and thought I was invincible. My egoistic mind took me on journeys of grandeur and dreams of worldly pleasures. I naively thought, 'the grass is greener on the other side.' I wore the veil of darkness and blinded myself from seeing the truth, and I chose the road to hell. I obliterated the marriage vows from my mind and abandoned my responsibility towards my children.

"I distorted my true identity with memories of my inadequate upbringing and yearned for recognition and fame to take me on a detour far from reality. I became friends with the demons of the dark and gave them residence in my mind. The demons had no shape and could not be seen; they were invisible pawns following the baton of maestro-ego, the orchestra conductor that played my music of escape.

"I danced in the halls of pleasure, not aware of its narrow roads that led me to the valley of despair. I had sleepless nights that brought me fear, and I allowed the indulgence of nights to push me away from the light of days. I was in a place of no rest, pained by the scars in my heart, and missing the presence of my soul. I was hiding the hurt I caused to my wife and children, with a mask that I placed to cover my face. I, however, pretended that all is well, and I did no wrong.

"I then suffered from inner pain that burned me within and on my skin. The anxiety created fears that would not end. My soul ached from forgotten songs of love, and my tears would start to fall like nature's rain.

"How long would that last, I yearned to know! I tossed and turned beseeching dreams of hope to return. I cursed my success that led me blind and hated the meaningless pleasures of the world. I missed my home, my warm shelter from the coldness of the world. I prayed for Grace to permeate my soul anew, and suddenly I heard a voice within, alive and loud, saying, be aware! Be aware! Be aware!

"That night, I dreamt the chains around my feet, and my hands were broken, and I was free. I saw myself walking in a beautiful garden with birds

Janet and friends were eager to read what Jim had written so far, but he refused. He had about one hundred twenty-five pages written over five months and figured he had at least another ninety more pages to finish, before he shows it to Debra to edit, and to Brian to check the spiritual sections.

♦

In the interim, Todd was elected the MVP of the soccer team, having saved the highest number of goals in the season. That made him more accessible to attract girls in his class giving him the attention he liked.

Janet and Jim met Albert, Laura's friend, and they found him to be a true gentleman who treated beautiful Laura with respect. At fifteen, Laura turned out to be a gorgeous-looking young lady, very much like her mother, charming and considerate.

As planned, Brian and Sylvia got engaged. They set a wedding date in September, about two months away. Brian was busy monitoring the three new chapters, Chicago included. It took him two full months to find the right person for the Chicago chapter. He finally landed on the right candidate, a young associate pastor from a 'Unity church', in Chicago city, that emphasized New Thought teachings.

The young man, David, was enthusiastic about the job, as described to him by Brian. He also visited the team in New York to finalize his work engagement. David was single, about thirty-four, a charming personality, bright, and well-educated in spiritual teachings. He also visited New York to finalize his work engagement.

Brian told Jim that the first two branches in Philly and Miami became financially self-sufficient with the donations from the member. He added that he still had enough money in the fund for future growth in other cities.

In a meeting with Charles and other board members, Jim also suggested since the membership was outgrowing the space in New York, they need to find a larger one. They agreed to search, and Jim advised them to target at least twice the size.

◆

Jim aimed at finishing the book before the wedding of Brian and Sylvia. He enjoyed the second part that dealt with his spiritual awakening and how it started with Brian, and the Center. Jim mentioned the host of books he read and the multitude of lessons he learned. He wrote the sections with poetic prose with several reviews and rereads before he approved the final draft.

Jim ended his closing chapter with a poem called the Song of Life:

Life is,

A poem to recite, and a wonder to invite

A dream to remember from a Being unmasked A moment of Joy,
after a moment of sorrow

A Journey of light steered away from dark

A story from the heart, alive with laughter

A connection bridge, to all innocent souls A melody of hymns, written with love

A walk in the woods, embracing stillness

A song of nature, with silent harmony

A breath of fresh air, to lighten our load

A greeting to the sun, as it rises and as it sets A welcome to the morning, with a radiant face

A moment of Grace, abundant with blessings A feeling of Bliss, crowned with Love

A step to move forward, to never look back

A journey to the unknown wondrous days ahead

A grateful life with no fear of death

A joy of oneness with the source of all A thank you for being alive, and well A thank you for the people I truly love.

When Jim finished writing, he emailed a copy of the manuscript to Debra to edit, and to Brian for his comments. He also shared his work with Janet, Sylvia, and the Children, who had just returned from their summer camps. He asked that they respond with comments within a week, if possible. He had ten days left before the wedding date and wanted to be prepared as the best man.

The wedding ceremony was performed at Sylvia's church, adding fifty more seats to accommodate more guests. Jim gifted the reception, which was held in the ballroom at the hotel where he lived for about a year.

It was time for toasts to be shared. Jim and Janet were seated at the head table next to the bride and the groom. When it was time, Jim stood up to give his toast to the newly-weds. He said he prepared a small poem to share, instead of a speech. Silence prevailed, and they heard him recite:

Two Love Birds

Up in the sky, Brian and Sylvia meet, Sensing awareness with their heartbeat Two souls smile for love to greet, Together joined to celebrate their feast

Oneness shared their quest to co-exist,

With forward moves confirming their gist Love and peace drove them to Bliss, Together they prayed never to miss

A joyful time to cherish for good,

A life always shared with gratitude A beautiful song to dance with flow, A union of love ever graced to glow

May these two birds teach us too,

How to love and make one of two.

Brian was the first to jump and hug Jim, while everyone else applauded him cheerfully. Brian then stood up to thank all the guests for coming this special day, and to thank Jim that made this reception possible. He admitted he is not a poet like Jim, and even if he were, no words are enough to thank him for his support, and his encouragement to get to know lovely Sylvia, his wife now!

The newly-weds left the next day to a honeymoon at the Caribbean Selerno hotel, as a wedding gift from Jim and Janet.

Debra edited the book titled "Looking Within" and gave it to her publisher, who agreed to print and market it. Within nine months, hundreds of thousands of copies sold, the book hit the best sellers list. Jim became an accomplished spiritual storyteller, and received many requests for more books to write. As he had only one life story to tell, he decided to wait until he was further enriched with his spiritual knowledge, before he could write with the intention to teach.

Jim celebrated his forty-sixth birthday with his family feeling content, enjoying his walk on his path of wholeness and fulfillment. Janet advanced noticeably in her spiritual pursuits and continued her responsible work to help a host of women shift to a higher level of consciousness. The children were happy to live in an atmosphere of love and peace at home and became role models to other children their age.

Brian and Sylvia became best friends of Jim and Janet, sharing a similar goal to serve others and to guide people to enjoy a spiritual path of their choice.

Jim always adhered to the analogy of turning the telescope around to look within, and *All Was Well!f*

www.ingramcontent.com/pod-product-compliance
Lightning Source LLC
Chambersburg PA
CBHW070746160726
48004CB00001B/79